Berkley Sensation titles by Thea Harrison

Novels of the Elder Races

DRAGON BOUND
STORM'S HEART
SERPENT'S KISS
ORACLE'S MOON
LORD'S FALL
KINKED
NIGHT'S HONOR

Game of Shadows Novels

RISING DARKNESS
FALLING LIGHT

PRAISE FOR
THE NOVELS OF THE ELDER RACES

Withdrawn

Kinked

"Sexy and romantic and refreshingly different." —*Dear Author*

"Harrison really brings the heat and the spice in this one."
—*Vampire Book Club*

"If you enjoy an action-packed, suspenseful, humorous and sizzling paranormal romance about addictive couples who literally argue their way into love, then look no further than Thea Harrison's Elder Races series and prepare for the ride of your life." —*Smexy Books*

"One of my favorites in the Elder Races series. The plot was fantastic, so imaginative and heartbreaking and wonderful. Harrison continues to impress me more and more with every book. I can't wait until the next one!" —*BookPushers*

Lord's Fall

"Harrison proves that chemistry can get even hotter in life after Happily Ever After. The Elder Races series is so much more than your average paranormal romance . . . *Lord's Fall* is another example of interwoven mythology, relationship challenges and friendships that create a wonderfully rich and satisfying story."
—*All Things Urban Fantasy*

"Overall I was very pleased with my return to the Pia and Dragos story line. They will forever be my favorite couple in the Elder Races. This series offers its readers magic, awesome action scenes [and] wonderfully fleshed-out characters while still focusing [on] a beautifully told ongoing love story." —*Fiction Vixen*

"Truly, this is one of Harrison's most delicious and addictive books to date. The Elder Races series just keeps getting better and better." —*Dark Faerie Tales*

continued . . .

"*Lord's Fall* is what happens after the happily ever after, and what Pia and Dragos experience only makes their characters come to life. Thea Harrison delivers an epic story of myth, mayhem and love that is sure to keep readers satisfied and breathing fire!"
—*Fresh Fiction*

"Let the rejoicing begin! Pia and Dragos are back . . . In no time at all Harrison has vaulted to the top of the paranormal romance genre by showcasing her stunning storytelling ability."
—*RT Book Reviews* (Top Pick)

Oracle's Moon

"Grace's human limitations are pushed to the edge as she learns to wield her new powers. Series fans and new readers alike will cheer her on."
—*Publishers Weekly*

"Harrison's flair for developing rich and well-rounded characters anchors the thrilling action and intense emotions found within her books. Harrison provides proof positive she is fast becoming a major star of paranormal romance!"
—*RT Book Reviews* (Top Pick)

"A delightful romantic urban fantasy . . . The key to this excellent entry and the fabulous predecessors is [that] the Harrison mythos of humans living alongside seven otherworldly species comes across as real."
—*Alternative Worlds*

Serpent's Kiss

"It's a huge boon to readers that Harrison's first three Elder Races novels are being released in quick succession, ensuring the action and world-building never slow down . . . With a perfect blend of romance, action and drama, Harrison continues to prove she is fast becoming a name synonymous with excellence!"
—*RT Book Reviews* (Top Pick)

"A story charged with deep emotion and anchored by characters I do not want to forget . . . I am hooked on the amazing world of the Elder Races."
—*Romance Novel News*

"Thea Harrison's Elder Races novels are my current addiction . . . *Serpent's Kiss* is a bright spot in an already wonderful series . . . I am continually impressed with the attention Harrison lavishes on her characters' relationships, going beyond destiny or chemistry to write pairings that complement and strengthen one another."

—*All Things Urban Fantasy*

"The author deftly weaves a fantastical romance that spans generations . . . A delightful read with intriguing potential for many more highly anticipated tales."

—*Night Owl Reviews*

Storm's Heart

"Vividly sensual love scenes and fast-moving action sequences are the main reason I love this paranormal series. Each and every character brings *Storm's Heart* to life . . . Ms. Harrison takes us once again into an intriguing tale of love and suspense."   —*Fresh Fiction*

"[Harrison's] world-building has simply grown, become richer, more dynamic, more unique and altogether fantastic."

—*Romance Books Forum*

"Thea Harrison is a masterful new voice in paranormal romance. Her world-building skills are phenomenal. And *Storm's Heart* is proof . . . It is a very sexy tale with a hint of action and adventure and highly memorable characters."   —*Romance Novel News*

Dragon Bound

"Black Dagger Brotherhood readers will love [this]! *Dragon Bound* has it all: a smart heroine, a sexy alpha hero and a dark, compelling world. I'm hooked!"

—J. R. Ward, #1 *New York Times* bestselling author

"I absolutely loved *Dragon Bound*! Once I started reading, I was mesmerized to the very last page. Thea Harrison is a master storyteller, and she transported me to a fascinating world I want to visit again and again. It's a fabulous, exciting read that paranormal romance readers will love."

—Christine Feehan, #1 *New York Times* bestselling author

continued . . .

NIGHT'S HONOR

=⬥=

Thea Harrison

BERKLEY SENSATION, NEW YORK

THE BERKLEY PUBLISHING GROUP
Published by the Penguin Group
Penguin Group (USA) LLC
375 Hudson Street, New York, New York 10014

Ⓟ

USA • Canada • UK • Ireland • Australia • New Zealand • India • South Africa • China

penguin.com

A Penguin Random House Company

NIGHT'S HONOR

A Berkley Sensation Book / published by arrangement with the author

Berkley Sensation Books are published by The Berkley Publishing Group.
BERKLEY SENSATION® is a registered trademark of Penguin Group (USA) LLC.
The "B" design is a trademark of Penguin Group (USA) LLC.

For information, address: The Berkley Publishing Group,
a division of Penguin Group (USA) LLC,
375 Hudson Street, New York, New York 10014.

ISBN: 978-0-425-27436-1

PUBLISHING HISTORY
Berkley Sensation mass-market edition / September 2014

PRINTED IN THE UNITED STATES OF AMERICA

10 9 8 7 6 5 4 3 2 1

Cover art by Tony Mauro.
Cover design by George Long.
Interior text design by Tiffany Estreicher.

NIGHT'S HONOR

*"Hell is empty
And all the devils are here."*

—WILLIAM SHAKESPEARE,
THE TEMPEST

⸺ ONE ⸺

Vampyre's Ball, New Year's Eve

Cautiously, Tess peered at the crowd through a side stage door. She might be able to control her behavior, but her body told a different story. Her mouth had dried out, her heart pounded and her palms had turned clammy.

All the monsters were beautiful. Vampyres loved beauty, and they were some of the most celebrated in all of the Elder Races.

Charismatic and elegantly dressed in black tie and couture gowns, Vampyres filled the banquet-style great hall. Some sat at large round tables in the middle of the floor, but many stood and mingled. Human attendants wove through the clusters of glittering creatures, doing the bidding of their patrons.

Most of the attendants were dressed in subdued, discreet clothing, but there were a few standouts, such as the dark haired woman wearing a diamond collar that flashed with brilliant fire. Barefoot, she wore a silk, champagne-colored sheath dress. The paper-thin material of the dress was short, barely covering the woman's ass. Sapphires studded her leash, the end of which hung negligently on the slim wrist of her Vampyre patroness.

The redheaded Vampyre wore a black velvet evening gown and a haughty expression. She never glanced at her collared attendant, who shifted and turned to keep flawless pace with her patroness, rather like a well-trained dog. As the pair faced Tess, she saw that the collared woman wore a small, private smile. She didn't look abused, and her creamy skin appeared flawless. If anything, she looked like she enjoyed being on display.

To the sides of the great hall and up on a mezzanine level were more private areas where the most powerful of the elite could lounge in comfort. Any Vampyre who was anybody of note in the Nightkind demesne attended the annual Vampyre's Ball, even the Nightkind King himself, Julian Regillus.

Tess checked the number on her ticket. When she had joined the candidates, the line had gone out the back of the building and down the alley, but she'd finally made it inside. Now there were only three people ahead of her.

A new candidate took the stage. She had a California-girl style of beauty, tall and leggy with long, blonde tresses— yes, tresses—that had been styled to fall in thick waves around her perfect heart-shaped face and slender shoulders. Green eyes sparkled with a coquettish vivacity as she slipped off a short, red dressing gown. Totally naked, she spun in a circle on five-inch, nude-colored stiletto heels. Taking the microphone from the human, middle-aged emcee, she began a catwalk strut across the stage while she talked.

"Hi everybody, I hope you're all having a wonderful evening! My name is Haley, and I'm so excited to be here with you tonight! I'm twenty-one years old, and I'm working on my bachelor's in sociology at Berkeley. . . ."

This was like an X-rated version of *America's Got Talent*, except with Vampyres.

A tension headache began to throb behind Tess's right eye. She hadn't thought she was a prude, but the other woman had just disrobed as casually as if she were about to step into a bathtub in her own home. Haley was the same smooth honey tan all over. Nothing jiggled or dimpled anywhere. Her breasts looked like perfect, gravity-defying circles glued to her slender torso.

Now, those couldn't be natural.

Tess glanced down at herself. Not that she was going to strip down for anybody when it was her turn to take the stage, but even with her clothes on, it was perfectly clear that everything about her was horrendously average.

The best thing anybody could say about her body was that she was fit, and even then, she did jiggle in a few places. Her straight, dark hair was cut into a sensible bob, but she was two weeks overdue for a trim. She wore faded jeans, black shoes with flat heels and a black sweater, mainly because it was the only outfit she had left with her that was still clean.

The Vampyres continued with their conversations. Not a single one in the crowded hall looked at Haley. No one lifted a bidding paddle.

Tess turned her attention to the mezzanine level. She could just see the Nightkind King's strong, rough profile as he talked with the monster sitting opposite him. The Vampyre with him appeared to be a young man, with nut brown hair pulled back in a simple ponytail and a pleasantly nondescript, mild-mannered face.

His appearance couldn't be more of a lie. Xavier del Torro was one of the most notorious of all the Vampyres, a feared hunter famous in all of the Elder Races—and famous among humans as well—and Julian's right-hand man. Neither del Torro nor the King glanced at the stage.

Haley worked hard for her allotted two minutes. Her routine was polished, professional and raunchy, and it left the onlookers in no doubt. Clearly she was ready and willing to do anything to become a Vampyre's attendant. When the buzzer sounded, she swept up her discarded robe and exited stage left with a bright smile and a cheerful, Miss Universe pageant-style wave.

The next candidate walked onto the stage with quick, jerky

movements. This one was a man in his forties dressed in a department store suit. He looked tense and so uncomfortable, Tess's muscles clenched with empathy. She could relate.

When the emcee handed the candidate the microphone, he cleared his throat, pulled out a photo and held it in the air. It wavered visibly in his unsteady hand. In the photo, a girl grinned at the camera, her head tilted to one side.

"My name is Roberto Sanchez, and I am here on behalf of my beautiful daughter Cara. Cara is fourteen years old, and she is in the hospital. She has childhood leukemia. She was in remission for three years, but now the cancer has returned. Please, I am begging you—someone have mercy on her. If you would only agree to be her patron, you could help to heal her. She's a good girl. She can work hard for you, if only she felt better. . . ."

Tess winced. Sanchez was breaking several of the rules that had been handed out on cards to those candidates who had been lucky enough to get a ticket and now stood in line, waiting for their turn on the stage. All medically based petitions must go through the visa application process at the Bureau of Nightkind Immigration.

The annual Vampyre's Ball on New Year's Eve was an occasion to make a different kind of petition altogether, a kind of massive job screening process where Vampyres of standing might choose to take on human attendants to add to their households.

Supposedly the relationship between a Vampyre patron and his human attendants was a mutually beneficial arrangement. The attendants assured the Vampyre a steady blood supply in addition to working to support the household as a whole. In return the Vampyre offered his protection and assured that the attendant would have a safe, secure place in which to live, and a long, healthy life. There was even an outside chance that a candidate might become a Vampyre himself one day.

Both opportunities were rare. According to the website FAQs that Tess had read, the Nightkind demesne in the United States received over ten million visa applications a year from humans hoping to be turned, while the number of newly created Vampyres each year was the tiniest fraction of that and strictly controlled by the Nightkind demesne working in coordination with the CDC headquarters in Atlanta, Georgia.

Probably Sanchez had already applied for a visa for his daughter and had been turned down. Clearly desperation had pushed him onto the stage.

Just as it would push Tess, when it was her turn.

The next few moments were excruciating, and not just because of the rawness of Sanchez's pleading, although that was bad enough.

The worst was that the Vampyres did nothing.

Nothing.

Nobody moved to interrupt Sanchez. The emcee did not order security to remove him. Nobody turned to look at the pleading man or raised a bidding paddle. They all acted as if he did not exist.

A sickened anger tied her stomach in knots. This was horrendous, degrading, and it didn't matter that cold logic said there could be no good way to handle candidates like Sanchez, or that his petition had been doomed from the start. The number of visa applicants was overwhelming to begin with. If the Vampyres gave into one Sanchez who broke the rules, they would never be able to stop the flood of others.

She didn't know what was worse—their show of indifference or the humans who chose to abase themselves onstage.

And I'm one of them, she thought. She wiped her face with a shaking hand. How in God's name could I have ever thought this might be a good idea?

Scratch that, I never thought it was a good idea. It was my only idea.

The reason was simple. When you pissed off the devil, you ran out of options real fast.

The buzzer sounded. With agonizing politeness, the emcee escorted Sanchez off the stage, and the next candidate came on.

The person behind Tess elbowed her with a hiss, and she eased the stage door closed to step into the wings. Her blood pounded in her ears, and her shaking breath caught in her throat. This was far worse than any kind of normal stage fright, magnified as it was by anger, revulsion and fear.

As if from a long distance away, she heard the buzzer sound. And again.

When it was her turn, she stepped forward and waited just behind the curtain for her cue. If she held herself any more rigidly, she felt like she might break into pieces.

The emcee walked toward her with a practiced smile and a sharp, disinterested gaze. Holding out a hand, he beckoned to her. She walked forward into a flood of hot lights, stopped at the X taped on the floor and faced the crowded hall. Her cold fingers curled automatically around the microphone when it was shoved into her hand.

The lights on the stage had turned the Vampyres into shadowy figures that made them seem even more menacing. She wanted to scream at them, or laugh at the absurdity of the whole scenario.

Instead, the intolerable tension fractured and she iced over with a clear, clean anger. None of them would listen to anything she might say anyway.

Not bothering to raise the microphone, she said in a calm, flat voice, "My looks are entirely forgettable, and I'm smarter than almost anyone here."

Screw them, if they weren't able to see what advantages there could be in any of that. Screw all of them.

On the mezzanine floor, one of the Vampyres turned from his conversation to look down at her.

He raised his paddle.

Blinded by the bright lights shining in her face, Tess couldn't see if her words had caused any reaction. She only knew she wasn't going to stay on the stage for one more moment. She had to go somewhere quiet to try to figure out her next move. Pivoting, she strode to the emcee "Where's the exit?"

Giving her a strange look, he walked with her to the opposite edge of the stage, where another young woman in an aide's uniform waited in the wings. Plucking the microphone out of Tess's hand, the emcee moved on to the next candidate.

Despair weighed down her limbs until she felt as if she were moving through water. She asked the aide tightly, "How do I get out of here?"

Like the emcee, all of the servers and aides at the Ball were human. The woman gave her the same strange look as the emcee had, incredulity mingled with envy, and darkened with the faintest tinge of resentment. "I know candidates can't see it when they're on the stage, but you've been selected for an interview."

Tess blinked. She couldn't have heard that right. The words didn't make any sense. "Excuse me?"

"Someone wants to interview you." The aide checked the screen of her iPad then rapidly input something with a stylus. "Go down the hall to the back staircase, then up to the second floor. Remember, one flight up is the mezzanine level. The second floor is two flights up. Your interview will be in room 219. He'll be with you shortly."

He.

She was almost getting used to the slightly nauseous tension that clenched her stomach. "Who is it?"

Even as she asked, the aide turned away to beckon the next candidate offstage. As the woman stepped into the wings, she clutched at the aide's hands. "This is my sixth year auditioning. How did I do? Did someone ask for me?"

Tess turned away. The only way she would find out who wanted to talk to her was by going up to the room. Feeling dazed, she went down the utilitarian hall and walked up two flights of stairs.

The building was old. During the California gold rush, it had been one of San Francisco's premiere hotels, but it had been partially gutted and renovated in the 1920s to be used for the Vampyre's Ball.

Away from the glittering elegance of the main ballroom, the building showed its age. Still, the upstairs was a little better than the hallway backstage. There were a few touches of faded glory, in the scratched and peeling gilding on the stairway railings, in the worn carpet, and in the crown molding at the edges of the ceiling.

The upstairs rooms had once been hotel rooms. As the thought occurred to her, she clenched both hands into fists.

Relatively few Vampyres reached enough prominence to support a household of attendants, but when they did, they set their own rules for what happened in their domain. She had heard rumors that in some households, attendants provided more than just blood and assigned work. They also traded sexual favors in return for the kind of lifestyle that a wealthy Vampyre patron could offer.

Even if an attendant never gained the opportunity to be turned, regular bites from a patron boosted a human's natural immune system, and they could live as long as a hundred and thirty years. There were reasons why Haley had gone naked onto the stage, not least of which was the opportunity to live more than half again one's own natural life span and to die in one's sleep of old age.

Room 219 was tucked between others in the middle of the hall. As soon as she gripped the door handle, her muscles locked up and she stood frozen, unable to make herself step into the room and yet not able to walk away, while rapid-fire thoughts snapped at her heels like feral dogs.

This "interview" could be another version of the casting couch scenario.

If there's a bed in the room, that's it, she thought. I'm out of here.

I think.

Stop being histrionic. Sex is merely a biological function. People have been trading sex for survival for thousands of years. You're not a fourteen-year-old virgin. You've had sex before, and guess what? While none of your partners had been memorable enough to stick around, it wasn't the end of the world. Death is the end of the world.

Think of the devil you left behind. If you leave now without exploring all your options, you've got to find another way to protect yourself from him. And the whole reason why you're here in the first place is because you haven't found another way.

Just remember—if you're going to choose to trade sex for protection, make sure you get an agreement in place beforehand.

Suddenly angry at her own dithering, she yanked the door open and stalked inside. It wasn't likely that sex would become part of any discussion anyway. Not with the Vampyres' love of beauty, the glut of gorgeous people readily available to slake any appetite, and her own average, forgettable looks.

The unoccupied room was entirely bare, except for a utilitarian, conference-style folding table, four chairs, and two unopened bottles of Evian set at one end of the table.

No bed, and no monsters. Yet.

She exhaled a shaky breath and stepped inside. The same worn carpeting from the hallway covered the floor, and the crown molding in the ceiling's corners looked cracked and in need of repair. The closet was empty, and the bathroom appeared as if it hadn't been used in a long time.

With the hallway door closed, the air felt too stifling as the demons in her head crowded the room. She had too many phantoms populating her imagination, and too many nightmares in her memory. Dragging over one of the folding chairs, she propped open the door to the hallway. Then she took a seat at the table facing the open doorway.

Traditionally, the position was the seat of power in the room. It was a small thing to take, although she didn't fool herself for one minute. She had very little power in the upcoming exchange. She had very little power at all, which was one of the reasons why she found herself in such a god-awful mess.

Opening one of the bottles of water, she sucked down half the contents in a few gulps. As she screwed the cap back on the bottle, a slim, elegantly dressed man walked silently into the room.

Xavier del Torro.

The bottle slipped from Tess's nerveless fingers and fell to the floor.

The killer that stood in front of her wasn't especially tall, perhaps five foot ten or so. His long, lean body, along with an erect posture and an immense poise, served to make him seem taller. Seen up close, he looked as if he had been turned in his midtwenties. He could still embody the illusion of youthfulness, with eyes that were somewhere between gray and green, a clear-complected skin and refined features that somehow missed being either conventionally handsome or delicate.

His turning had been a famous event in history. A younger son of Spanish nobility, he had been a priest until the Tribunal of the Holy Office of the Inquisition tortured and destroyed a community of peaceful Vampyres near his home in Valencia. The Vampyre community had included del Torro's only sister and her husband.

After the massacre, or so the legend went, del Torro walked away from the Catholic Church and approached Julian, who turned him into a Vampyre and set him to cut a swath through the officers of the Inquisition. The ten years that followed were some of the bloodiest in Spanish history.

"Good evening," said the Vampyre. He was quiet spoken, yet his beautifully modulated voice penetrating the silence in the room was shocking. "You are Tess Graham, correct?"

As he spoke, he turned to move the chair from propping open the door.

She said, "If you don't mind, I would like to leave the door open."

He straightened immediately, left the chair in place and approached the table. Everything he did was utterly flawless in execution, no gesture wasted. He moved like an animal, with complete fluidity that showed just how useless the open door was as a precaution, and how silly and fragile an illusion of safety she gleaned from it.

Open door or not, nothing would stop him from doing anything he wanted. He could rape and torture her, and drain her of all of her blood, and there wasn't a single Vampyre who would lift a finger to stop him. Or very many who could stop him, even if they wanted to try.

Cold sweat broke out over her skin. Heat from a nearby vent blew along the back of her damp neck. The small sensation felt almost violent.

Del Torro pulled out the second chair on his side of the table and sat. When he settled into place, he went immobile— truly immobile, not the mere human equivalent. He didn't breathe, didn't blink. His formal black suit seemed to absorb the light, and his shirt was so white, it almost looked blue.

He was perfectly immaculate in every way. Somehow it should have made him look lifeless, like a mannequin, but it didn't. His presence was so intense the air itself seemed to bend around him. She grew hyperaware, not only of him, but of herself too—the tiny shift of her torso as her lungs pulled in air, the muscles in her throat as she swallowed, the hand she clenched into a fist and hid underneath one arm, in case it provoked the relaxed predator in front of her.

She remembered the water bottle and bent to retrieve it from the floor. Even that small, prosaic movement seemed fraught with excess compared to the silent, composed figure sitting in front of her.

How old was he? She was no history scholar and knew almost nothing of the Spanish Inquisition, but she was fairly sure it had gone on for a few hundred years before it was finally abolished, so he had to be at least four centuries old and was probably older. How many people had he killed in his lifetime?

She had no idea what she was going to say, until it came tumbling out of her mouth. "What happened earlier with Mr. Sanchez was unspeakable."

Del Torro's gray-green gaze regarded her gravely. "You refer to the candidate with the sick child, yes? Unfortunately, she was much too young to become an attendant and she was never a viable recipient for a visa—it's against the law to take blood from children or to turn them into Vampyres. Those situations are always difficult, and there is no good way to handle them."

"But nobody did anything."

The Vampyre inclined his head in acknowledgment. "In the past he would have been taken from the stage, yet that policy caused its own outcry. In the end, it was deemed best to allow those like Sanchez the same dignity as any other candidate, although of course we can't ignore regulations and choose any of them, no matter how sad their story."

"Dignity?" The word shot out of her with quite a bit more force than she had intended. "Do you think there's any dignity in that auditioning process?"

One of his slim eyebrows lifted. Amidst his stillness, that slight gesture seemed like a shout, but when he spoke he sounded as calm and unflappable as ever. "An individual has as much dignity on that stage as she chooses to have, Ms. Graham. Take yourself, for example. You went out there and did exactly what you intended to do. Those who cared to pay attention did so. Nothing more, nothing less. Nobody promised you anything more than that."

He was right, of course, although she did not like him for saying so. They were Vampyres, not a social service agency.

With effort she tried to rein in her careening emotions, while more truth spilled out of her mouth. "I'm sorry, I don't know why I'm so angry." She tried to smile but her facial muscles felt so stiff, she gave it up almost immediately. "Believe me, I'm quite aware that this is an odd and counterproductive way to start an interview."

"You're frightened," he said. "For some people, fear quite naturally turns into anger."

His voice had gentled, and that might have been the

most shocking thing that had happened all evening. Embarrassment burned in her cheeks. Nothing was going like she imagined it might. She thought about denying what he had said, but of course that would be stupid. He could hear her accelerated heartbeat and no doubt smell her fear. Sitting here fully clothed, she still felt as naked as if she had stripped just as Haley had.

"I'm curious." Del Torro cocked his head, his all too discerning gaze dissecting her. "Why are you here tonight, when it clearly distresses you so? You do not carry the scent of illness, nor do you appear to have any interest in Vampyre kink. What do you hope to gain from an attendant-patron liaison?"

Vampyre kink.

She hadn't expected him to be so blunt, and her cheeks burned hotter.

"I need a job. The Ball was this weekend, so I got in line along with all the other candidates." She paused. Technically, all of that was true. She was running low on cash, and she didn't dare access the money in her bank accounts. But if he pressed her for any more details, she was going to run into some rocky ground very quickly. She had to turn the question away from herself, perhaps back onto him. "If you don't mind me asking, what about you? Why did you request an interview with me?"

Any other person she had ever met would have gestured or shown some flicker of response. Del Torro didn't. He just looked into her gaze steadily. His eyes were clear, intelligent and revealed absolutely nothing.

"Your defiance intrigued me, as did your claims. What skills would you bring to a liaison—that is, assuming you would agree to one?"

Was he actually considering her for a position, or merely satisfying his curiosity? He had no tells. He was utterly impossible to read, and his restraint of manner all but unendurable. She felt completely at sea and caught on a hook, and while she twisted at the end of a line, he slowly reeled her in.

As she tried to let go of some of the tension in her aching muscles, she found herself studying him, looking for any kind of flaw. When she discovered a thin, white scar at the corner of his mouth, she stared at it. Whatever had caused the scar had to have happened before he had been turned. It should have made him seem more human, but it didn't.

"I can speak Japanese, French and Italian," she said. "I can also read French and Italian, along with a bit of Elvish, although I can't speak that with any fluency yet. I like languages, so I'm working on that. And I have degrees in accounting and computer science. I have experience with managing money, and I can build a firewall like nobody's business. My skills may not be flashy or sexy, but I'm very good at what I do."

The skin at the corners of his eyes crinkled slightly. If she hadn't already been staring at him so intently, she would have missed the subtle expression. "I disagree. Competence is quite sexy."

She blinked. He had brought up sex twice in the last five minutes, but the utter dispassion with which he spoke left her with no room for misunderstanding. He wasn't flirting, simply asking questions and stating facts as he saw them.

Still, she had no idea how to respond. Before she could decide, he asked, "How are you at breaking through firewalls?"

Of everything they had discussed so far, this was the one question that didn't surprise her. Still, she hesitated as she decided how to answer. Most people didn't really understand firewall security, or the fact that you didn't actually break through a wall.

In the end, she chose to keep her answer simple. "I'm good at that too."

"How good is good?"

"Very." She had done more than her fair share of hacking in her teenage years, and she let the certainty fill her voice. "I also don't promise anything I can't deliver."

His eyelids lowered. "Are you willing to do other things, besides accounting and computing?"

Involuntarily, she flashed to an image of them naked in a bed, with him bending over her, his normally composed, self-contained expression filled with fire and white, sharp fangs descended.

Something powerful welled up inside, although she had no idea what it was. Her emotions were already in a chaotic uproar, while he still wore the same, dispassionate expression.

Was he needling her to see how she would respond, or was he trying to find out how far she would go to get the position? She felt like she stood at the edge of a cliff, and her next step would send her hurtling into air.

Would she trade sex for safety, if he asked her to?

"That depends on what you ask me to do." Her voice turned taut. "Some things are off-limits. I won't be complicit in hurting innocents, and I won't stand by and watch it happen. Among other things."

If anything, his voice grew gentler. "I should have been more specific in my question. Your skills in accounting and computer programming are intriguing, but I maintain a small household by most standards. My attendants serve in different capacities and do a variety of different things."

"What kind of things do you have them do?" Everything inside of her stilled as she waited to hear his answer.

"Think of it, if you will, as an intentional community," he told her. "Each person is required to give blood, of course, but there are other duties that must be done for the good of the community. While I have no need for food, everyone else must eat; therefore Jordan, one of my attendants, is the cook. Another one, Angelica, looks after the house. When I have guests, I require that their needs be looked after. Raoul is in charge of security, and so forth. Most of these are not professional duties, but still they must be done."

Was that all?

Dragging air into her constricted lungs, she said, "I see. Yes, of course, I would be willing to take on duties like that."

His eyes narrowed. His expression turned severe, and suddenly she could see the age hidden underneath his apparent youthfulness. "No doubt, you will have heard some Vampyres require sex from their attendants. While that is true, I am not one of them. I might require difficult things from my attendants from time to time, but I do not put people who are under my care in such a position."

It took her a moment to absorb what he said. Then the rigidity left her body as her muscles slowly unlocked. "Thank you for telling me."

Moving two fingers, he brushed the subject aside in one beautifully economical gesture. "Do you have experience with firearms or other weapons?"

This time she didn't hesitate. "No, but I'm strong, I have good hand-eye coordination and I'm willing to learn."

He nodded. "Have you ever taken or wanted to take drugs?"

"Yes," she said. "And no. Once I tried pot in college, but I didn't like it. All it did was make me paranoid and hungry, and I don't like to eat when I'm scared." Again, she tried to read his expression and failed utterly. "Is that a problem?"

The severity vanished from his expression, and one corner of his mouth quirked. "No. If you were a habitual drug user, that would be a different story. Drinking from a source that has been polluted with heroin, meth, or other hard drugs can have a debilitating effect on a Vampyre."

She shook her head. "I have no desire to repeat the experience with marijuana or to try any other drugs."

"Very good. Do you have any dependents?"

She shook her head again. "No."

"Magical ability?"

"Sadly, no," she said. "I can telepathize, but that's it."

She had no idea if her answers were gaining her any ground, or if they counted as marks against her, but a Vampyre of his Power and age would definitely have truth-sense, and she didn't dare do anything but tell the truth.

Finally he fell silent for a few moments as he studied

her. "There's only so much information one can gain from these interviews. The truth is, becoming an attendant can be a surprisingly complex and delicate process, while it calls for a tremendous commitment on both sides. Some people cannot make the transition to that kind of lifestyle even when they want to, or for one reason or another, they are a poor fit for a Vampyre's household. There is no shame in any of this. It's merely a process of discovery."

"I'm sure you're right," she managed to reply, while her chest grew tight again. Was he getting ready to turn her down? As horrible as this whole experience had been, she couldn't blame him if he did. While the opportunity to become an attendant might be rare, she hadn't exactly shown any enthusiasm for it.

Oh God, she thought. If I don't get this job, what will I do?

Then he said, "I can see some ways in which you might be of some use to me. I'm willing to offer you a trial period of one year. If, within that time period, we have not worked out a tolerable arrangement that suits us both, we will each be free to sever the relationship."

Her mouth dropped open, and she almost blurted out, "Why?" But she managed to catch herself before it escaped her lips.

He raised his eyebrows. "Do you find this acceptable?"

⇒ TWO ⇐

Xavier watched with patient interest as Tess's mouth opened and closed several times.

She said, her voice strangled, "You're offering me a chance, just like that? You don't want a second interview, or—or references?"

Some kind of interesting, complicated emotion lay behind her question. Maybe she had a checkered employment history, or she had gotten fired from her previous job. Briefly, he considered asking for her resume and references, just to see how she handled the request, but the fact was, he didn't care if she had been fired. People got fired for a wide variety of reasons, and something that a previous employer might have seen as a weakness could be the very trait he was looking for.

Besides, nobody gave a prospective employer bad references. They only gave references for people who would say flattering things about them. Through the years, he had seen people game the interviewing system in every way imaginable, while the truest test of a person's mettle could only come over time.

Also, this young woman could have no references for the kind of things he wanted from her. He would need to find out for himself what she would be capable of doing, or what she would even want to do. For now, it would have to be enough to avoid frightening her any further.

He told her, "As I said, there's only so much that can be learned from the interview process. By the end of a year, we will both know whether or not we're able to create a successful liaison."

Her expression turned thoughtful. "I suppose a year for someone like you is not very long."

"Quite true. A trial year is a standard offer. Most Vampyres offer it to prospective attendants."

His truthsense was well developed. He knew she had been telling the truth about her skills and attributes. She was smart, good with finances and clever with a keyboard, although she had hesitated just long enough to intrigue him. What had she refrained from saying? He filed that away to pursue another time.

And she did have some kind of moral code. It had been a long, long time since he had considered anything sexual as an issue of morality, unless the sex involved coercion, outright force or some other kind of imbalance of power.

She, however, had clearly been uncomfortable with the thought of engaging in sex as part of the position, and she had been quite serious when she'd said she would not be a party to harming innocents.

She had also been telling the truth when she'd been onstage. She believed her looks were entirely forgettable, and in some ways they were. She had none of the glossy good looks that so many Vampyre attendants had, or that most Vampyres themselves had, for that matter.

But she did have her own quiet kind of beauty. Her brown hair shone with healthy chestnut highlights, and there was real intelligence in those large, dark eyes. Her narrow face had a precise, strong bone structure with a wonderfully aquiline nose, and her mouth was delicately shaped and sensitive.

Many modern eyes would pass over her in search of more flamboyance and color. Hair dyes had grown complex, and eye color could be intensified or changed altogether. Even Vampyres could sport golden, sprayed-on tans if they so chose, and muscles and breasts could be surgically augmented. People had grown used to the fact that virtually everything could be enhanced or altered.

An intelligent person with quiet looks could be very useful to him.

He considered the negative side of the scale. Her poise was abysmal. Intense emotions played across her face, and her rapid heartbeat sounded like thunder in his ears. That would have to change, of course. She would need a lot of work to realize any of the raw potential he saw in her, but the only way to shape a fine tool was with patience, attention and care.

He waited while she thought things over. "Thank you," she said. "Yes, I would like to try."

"Excellent." He straightened the cuff of one sleeve. "I will expect you at my estate tomorrow evening at sundown. You will be very busy for the next few months, so arrange your affairs accordingly and bring what you will need for an extended stay."

"I—yes, of course," she said. "Where's your estate?"

"On Pirate's Cove, across the Golden Gate in Marin Headlands. The number you gave on your candidacy application—is that a cell phone?"

"Yes." Her dark eyes watched him with equal parts wariness and fascination.

"My secretary Foster will text you directions. When you turn off the main highway, the road is narrow and winding, so the drive takes longer than you might think. Be sure to allow plenty of time in daylight."

"That won't be a problem—"

Julian strode into the room. Xavier watched the blood drain from Tess's face before he turned to face his old friend.

The Nightkind King was the kind of man that took over

a room the moment he entered it. He had rough, weather-beaten features, with lines at the eyes and the corners of a stern mouth, and a dark, penetrating gaze that could cut like a laser. Flecks of silver sprinkled his short, dark hair.

When Julian had been human, he had been a general during the Emperor Hadrian's rule, at the height of the Roman Empire. He was broad across the chest and shoulders, flat through the abdomen, and he carried the heavy, powerful muscles of a man who had spent his life as a soldier. Life had been brutal in the Roman army, and when he had been mortal, he had not aged particularly well. He had been in his late thirties when his sire, Carling, had turned him, but he looked ten years older.

The formality of his black evening suit highlighted his rugged looks, and despite the sophisticated, hand sewn suit and the five-hundred-dollar razor haircut, he gave the impression of a wild, shaggy wolf, watchful of everything around him.

With one keen, lightning-quick glance at Tess, he assessed and dismissed her, then turned to Xavier.

I see you're still playing with your new pet. Julian's telepathic voice was like his physical voice, deep and rough, like a shot of raw whiskey. *When are you going to be done?*

Xavier regarded him, perfectly relaxed. *In just a few moments. We're almost finished now.*

Good. We need to head back to Evenfall. The Light Fae delegation is already waiting, and gods help me, Tatiana sent Melisande. Plus, all twelve council members have confirmed they'll be in attendance for the meetings over the next couple of days. Julian glowered at him. *I'd rather be trapped in a pit of snakes.*

Xavier closed his eyes briefly. Having all the Nightkind council members under one roof was going to be bad enough, but Melisande and Julian had had an explosive affair in the late 1990s that had ended famously. Badly. If the Light Fae Queen had sent her eldest daughter to conduct treaty negotiations, she was either punishing Melisande for something or she was seriously annoyed with Julian. Or both.

Understood, he said.

Unexpectedly, Julian turned his attention back to Tess. He rested his broad, scarred hands on his hips, which pulled his black jacket away from his torso. *That reaction of hers isn't all for me. You do realize she's scared to death of you.*

Yes, I know. Xavier would not add to Tess's distress by looking at her.

I don't get what you see in this one. Are you really going to take her on?

He gave an infinitesimal shrug that only Julian would catch. *It says something interesting about a person when they don't let their fear dictate their actions. That's what she's doing. We'll see what else she has to her. Over time.*

Julian spoke aloud. "Better you than me. I got ninety-nine problems, but finally, a bitch ain't one. I'll wait for you outside."

As the Nightkind King strode out of the room, Xavier looked at Tess. Her gaze had gone wide and shocked.

He was unsurprised. Julian tended to have that effect on most people. He had always been rough and a bit antisocial, and over the last two hundred years, as his sire turned more and more unstable, he had grown even more so.

She said, "Did he just reference that song by Jay Z—?"

Xavier gave her a level look. "That will be all for now, Ms. Graham. Thank you for your time. Good night."

Having been politely and yet thoroughly dismissed, Tess left the building and walked down the street to the parking lot where she had left her blue Ford Focus.

Her hands and feet felt numb, and a disbelieving part of her was convinced none of it had actually happened, until her phone beeped five minutes later. She pulled it out of her pocket and checked the display. As promised, it was a text message from Xavier's secretary, with directions to the estate.

That was fast.

Pocketing the phone, she tucked her hands under her armpits and picked up her pace. She had left her jacket in the car, and while it had been sunny and warm all day, the temperature had turned considerably chillier. The Bay Area enjoyed mild weather throughout the year, but it could get very cold at night, especially in the winter.

While she had been inside, thick clouds had rolled over the city and now lowered overhead, promising rain. Shivering, she unlocked her car, climbed in and shrugged her jacket on.

The night was already half over. She didn't know when sunset was this time of year, but she couldn't have more than eighteen hours to get through before sundown tomorrow.

Everything in San Francisco had been more expensive than she had bargained for, including parking for the Vampyre's Ball. While she had over a hundred thousand dollars in her checking and savings accounts, she didn't dare access those funds. All she had in cash was twenty-six dollars and eighty-five cents, and she was low on fuel.

She needed gas to get across the Golden Gate Bridge to her destination in Marin County. Thank God there weren't any tolls driving away from San Francisco.

After she put fuel into her tank, she should have enough left over to buy a cheap sandwich. It wasn't enough food, especially after a sleepless night, but dealing with hunger for one day was the least of her worries. Presumably, she should be able to eat well soon enough.

Now she needed to find somewhere safe and well lit, where she could wait out the rest of the night.

Even as she tried to think of somewhere to go, a couple walking toward her caught her eye. One was a ghoul, with gray skin, gaunt features and overlong fingers. The other was a female Vampyre, who angled her head and looked at Tess with intent interest as they walked toward another car.

Tess's skin prickled, and she glanced around. There was no one else within sight.

While it was illegal to feed on humans without their consent, who would know if the Vampyre chose to satisfy her hunger? The Vampyre was fast enough to attack and be sated before anyone could catch her. If she was old enough, she could even obscure her victim's memory, and keep her description out of the hands of the police.

And even if this Vampyre chose to be law-abiding, San Francisco was the heart of the Nightkind demesne, and home to many different creatures. There were other predators here that roamed the night, and some would not choose to be so law-abiding. This was an elegant, expensive and dangerous city.

Chewing her lip, Tess started the car and pulled out of the lot. She couldn't afford a hotel, so she needed to leave the city. Once she reached Marin County, she could find an all-night restaurant and drink coffee instead of buying food. When daylight came, she could find somewhere unobtrusive to park and take a nap.

She made her way by trial and error through the city to the Golden Gate Highway. The traffic was as intense as rush hour in daylight. Lights shone everywhere and in some places it looked as bright as day, a deadly illusion that could lull the unwary into thinking that the lights indicated safety.

Reaction set in as she pulled into the line of traffic to cross the bridge. This whole thing was as insane a gamble as anything she had ever taken, and she wasn't a gambler by nature. Only time would tell if it would pay off.

She didn't have to show up at Xavier's estate. She had a day to think of other alternatives, other places she could hide. Right now, she was exhausted from stress, her mind frozen, but she still might find a way out of this.

Xavier surprised her. He hadn't seemed so bad for a monster. Then she remembered everything she had ever heard about him and shuddered. Still, he seemed like her best bet for protection.

In terms of raw Power, nothing and no one, not even Xavier, could stop the creature she was running from. Malphas was a first-generation Djinn and quite literally one of the world's most Powerful creatures.

He was also a pariah, an outcast who lived outside the laws of his own kind. As far as she knew, the Djinn didn't police or monitor his behavior. A being of pure spirit, he could travel almost anywhere and breach any containment she'd ever heard of, and given enough incentive, he would have no qualms in doing so.

The only thing that might possibly stop him would be potential fallout from his actions, which meant political power, not magical Power. It had to become more uncomfortable for Malphas to pursue her than it would be to let her go, and that was what a position with Xavier might offer.

She was under no illusion about herself. As a lowly attendant, she wouldn't have much value to anyone, but if Malphas attacked her while she was under Xavier's roof, it would become a transgression of territory.

And that would matter. That might matter so much it could become an act of war.

Xavier was so highly placed in the Nightkind demesne that even a first-generation, outlaw Djinn would have to think twice about making him an enemy. The Djinn might turn a blind eye to Malphas now, but an official complaint from the Nightkind demesne could change their attitude.

Beyond the safety railings of the Golden Gate Bridge, the black waters of the bay glittered with reflected illumination. When she finished crossing the bridge, she looked for a late-night restaurant and a gas station.

Very soon, she found a 1950s-style diner located across from a gas station. After pumping twenty dollars of fuel into her tank, she crossed the street and entered the restaurant.

The place gleamed with chrome and bright colors. She took a seat, ordered coffee and watched out the window until pale streaks of color broke through the black cloudy night.

She felt hollow and light, her nerves jumping from too much caffeine and not enough choices.

Even after spending hours trying to think of another alternative, she knew she couldn't afford to turn down this opportunity. Just the fact that she had landed the position—or at least the possibility of a permanent position—was like winning some kind of infernal lottery.

What would it be like to give blood to a Vampyre?

A Vampyre's bite was supposed to induce euphoria for the human, but the very thought repelled her. That sense of euphoria was nature's way of lulling the victim into compliance, even to the point of death.

Vampyres were predators that fed on humans and viewed humankind as prey. Only the sheer numbers of humankind, along with all the other Elder Races, served to keep Vampyres in check and forced them to create laws that governed their own kind. There was nothing sexy or enticing at the thought of being considered food. She shuddered at the thought.

Finally she paid for her cup of coffee, thanked her patient waitress and left all of her change on the table for an inadequate tip. Her eyes were dry and scratchy, and her body ached. Stretching, she climbed into her car and headed for Rodeo Beach, just a few miles away.

Along with the money she couldn't access in her bank accounts, she had left behind comfortable, good quality furniture and what few mementos she owned in a spacious, stylish apartment. Now, for any practical purposes, everything she owned was in her car, a jumble of hastily packed clothes, and odds and ends.

One thing she had grabbed as she left home was a thick, soft throw blanket, since she knew she would be sleeping in her car. After pulling into the parking lot near the beach, she retrieved the throw and headed down the path to look for a likely spot to relax.

By the water, the world was wild and windswept. She could just see the tip of Evenfall, the palace of the Nightkind King, which was one of California's great architectural oddities. The massive Normandy-style castle sprawled prominently along the southwestern coast of the peninsula. The blues of the ocean stretched into infinity, while the green shoreline curved up to gently rolling hills that had been molded over time.

The threat of imminent rain had fled along with the night, leaving behind an uncertain, moody morning. A fresh, piercing wind blew away the cobwebs that had gathered in her head. After living in the desert for two years, the view seemed impossibly lush. If it weren't for the persistent fear that dogged her footsteps, she could have been very happy in that moment.

Wrapping the blanket around her torso tightly, she walked until she found a spot where the beach had eroded a niche into a higher point of land, and she settled with her back against the bluff, looking out over the water. The spot afforded some protection from the wind along with some privacy, and gradually, she relaxed.

Maybe being an attendant wouldn't be so bad. Normally, humans could only donate blood every eight weeks. Because a Vampyre's bite stimulated more than just the immune system, their attendants could donate more often, every four to five weeks, or even more frequently.

Still, it wouldn't happen every day, or even every week. If Xavier was as principled about not having sex with those under his authority, he must be adept at controlling himself, despite the euphoria his attendants must experience.

Unless he had lied.

She sagged, feeling stupid that the possibility hadn't occurred to her sooner.

Either he had lied, or he had told the truth. She would find out soon enough. All she knew was, despite everything, if she had to do the last two weeks over again, she would still do the same thing.

I guess that says something, she thought. Even if it costs me my life.

Tired of dealing with the constant fear, she wrapped the blanket tighter around her torso and pulled a corner over her head to block out the sun and wind. Her heavy eyelids drifted closed, and a veil of darkness descended as she fell into an uneasy doze.

In her apartment, the spring night was so warm, she had propped open all her windows and her front door. As she turned away from setting her dining table for supper, a creature slit open the screen at the front door and crawled inside. Neither a cat nor a dog but a demonic combination of both, its slanted eyes glowed with evil intent.

Terror pulsed. She grabbed her carving knife even as the creature slinked toward her, its sleek body menacing and boneless. It leaped, daggerlike claws spread—she grabbed it by the throat and fought to stab it. . . .

And it melted away into nothing.

Dread tasted acrid and repulsive, like somebody's ashes. She backed in a circle, knife out, her frightened gaze darted everywhere. Invisible hands settled at her waist. She screamed and whirled, and Malphas stood in front of her.

The Djinn's presence was so Powerful a corona of energy surrounded him. She had no magic other than a spark of telepathy, but even she could sense his Power burning in her mind's eye.

Djinn were creatures of pure spirit, so Malphas had no fixed form, but the physical shape he chose to take was angelic. He looked like a slimly built man wearing an elegant suit, with golden hair, seraphic blue eyes and a beautiful, deadly face.

He gave her a light smile that showed too many teeth. "Of course I'm looking for you, Tess. It's only a matter of time before I find you."

"Get out!" she hissed. Horror tightened an invisible hold around her neck, restricting her breathing. She brandished the useless knife. "Get out of my head!"

"You shouldn't have done it, Tess." Malphas's voice held a caressing tone. He strode toward her, moving at a leisurely pace. "Eathan was mine, and you stole him from me. And I never forgive someone who steals from me."

"He wasn't yours to take," she said between her teeth. "He didn't know any better. He was just a stupid kid."

"You know, most people don't really understand the definition of agony," said Malphas as he circled her. "Nor can they grasp the concept of eternity, yet both of those things together are a powerful combination."

At his words, wind blew over her and grew hot, until every inch of her skin burned. The pain was truly unendurable. She screamed again and, desperate to stop it any way she could, she turned the knife on herself.

The noise she made, half grunt, half whimper, woke her up. As she bolted into an upright position, her breath sawed in her throat and her gaze darted everywhere.

Her tired back muscles protested the sudden movement, sharp pain shooting down her spine. The day had progressed significantly, the sun was high overhead, and the temperature had warmed so much that she was burning up, wrapped as she was in the blanket. She pulled it off then tore out of her jacket to let the balmy air cool her overheated skin.

She could sense no presence other than the ocean, no other sound but the wind and the waves.

"It's just a dream," she whispered, drawing her knees up and wrapping her arms around them. "It's not real."

She had been telling herself that for a week, ever since she had run away from Las Vegas and Malphas's employment. No matter how many nightmares she had, they were all just dreams. Not even the most ancient and Powerful of the Djinn could enter a person's dreams.

She didn't think.

But her words were a cold comfort. While her dreams might not be real, they were still, in the end, quite true. She used to believe she had a bright future, and now, suddenly, her life was reduced to choosing the lesser of two evils in an effort just to survive.

Compared to endless torture by a vengeful pariah Djinn, life with a Vampyre might not be so bad after all.

≈ THREE ≈

Most of Marin Headlands on the Northern Peninsula was federally protected land, given over to the Golden Gate National Recreation Area, but for two major exceptions.

The first was Evenfall, the Nightkind Palace that lay just north of Rodeo Beach, along with a small city of shops and services that clustered around the castle's stone walls.

The second exception was Xavier del Torro's estate. According to the directions, the property lay roughly twenty minutes' drive north of the Nightkind Palace.

After such a sullen start to the day, the sunset turned the sky and ocean into a fiery blaze of color, a canopy of gold, orange and rose arching over water that was almost purple. The last strong strands of sunlight pierced through tall red-wood trees that bordered the narrow, winding road, causing blinding patches of dark and light that strobed through her windshield and made driving a challenge.

Light-headed from hunger and the lack of proper rest, she drove carefully, tense from wrists to shoulders. Xavier had not been exaggerating. Once she left the highway, the road had no safety railings and almost no shoulder.

After an intensely uncomfortable trip through the dense forest, the road broke out of the tree line and followed the curving, rocky edge of the coast. The last part of the drive was startlingly beautiful, with the ocean to her left and the forest on her right.

Due to the position of the road as it followed the coast-line she saw the estate a few minutes before she came to it. A large, Spanish-style mansion graced the shoreline, with a pigmented stucco facade that was a warm yellow-gold color that seemed to glow in the blaze of the sunset.

The house lay behind a matching wall that barricaded the property from the road for several acres, but even from a distance, she could see glimpses of gracious arches, tile roofing, and large, black-metal framed windows, along with the rooftops of other buildings.

Finally she pulled off the road and onto the short drive, and almost immediately came to a halt by an intercom box in front of huge arched metal gates. As she rolled down her window, a pleasant male voice came over the intercom.

"Good evening. How may I help you?"

"My name is Tess Graham," she told the unseen man. "Mr. del Torro asked me to come this evening."

"Of course. We are expecting you. Please follow the drive around the main house and park in the small lot at the side. I will come out to meet you." With a well-oiled hum, the gates opened.

"Here goes nuthin', kid," she muttered. She drove in, and the gates swung smoothly shut behind her, blocking out the world.

That could almost be a comfort, except, well, it wasn't.

Inside the walls, she got her first real sense of the size of the estate. Several acres of well-tended, emerald green lawn stretched around the main house, which despite its size was gracious rather than ostentatious. Well-placed trees dotted the expanse, along with a variety of bushes and flowers.

She didn't know the names of the various kinds of foliage, but she could see how everything had been designed to keep the eye flowing from one area to another, like the composition in a painting. Other, smaller buildings were tucked discreetly off to the sides. In her tired mind, details melted into a whirl of jumbled impressions as she followed instructions and drove carefully along the immaculate asphalt drive to the parking lot at the side.

Even as her car rolled to a stop, a man walked out of the house toward her. He was dressed casually in a polo shirt, jeans and dark shoes. While a sprinkle of gray lightened the temples of his short blond hair and his lean, tanned face bore lines at the corners of eyes and mouth, he moved with athletic grace, power and assurance.

She climbed out of the car and turned to face him as he drew closer. As he offered a large, broad hand, she took it, and strong, careful fingers closed briefly over hers.

"Good evening, Ms. Graham. I'm Raoul."

Xavier had said that Raoul was head of his security. While he wore no visible sign of weaponry, she realized that she looked into the smiling gaze of another dangerous man. "Call me Tess."

"Sounds good, Tess." He gestured to her car. "Now, please put your hands on the roof of your car and spread your legs."

"What?" Her tired mind ground to a halt, and she gaped at him.

He looked polite and entirely relentless. "I'll need to pat you down. It's nothing personal, of course. It's just routine."

"No problem," she muttered. "I think."

Was this okay? What kind of person needed to conduct body searches and car searches, just because you drove onto their property? It wasn't like Xavier was the president, or even the Nightkind King. But then, what kind of person needed to have a head of security in the first place?

Reluctantly, she turned, put her hands on the roof of the car and widened her stance. While she scowled at him, Raoul patted her down. Despite her discomfort, she couldn't find fault with anything he did. While the search was thorough, his touch was quite impersonal, and he never crossed the boundary into anything inappropriate.

When he was finished, he stepped back. "Thank you."

Relieved that it was over, she straightened away from the car. "Sure."

"May I have your car keys?"

Caught off guard again, she stared, and her hands clenched into fists. Why on earth would he want her keys? She said between her teeth, "This doesn't feel good. I don't know any of you, and that car is my freedom."

"I understand this might cause you some initial discomfort," he said calmly. "But I don't know you either. Chances are, you're exactly who you say you are, and you don't have bombs, drugs or weapons hidden anywhere inside your vehicle. But I'm not in the business of taking chances, Tess. Think of it like airport security. You have to go through the process to get on the plane. Here, you have two choices. We can search your car and verify that you're safe to have in close proximity to Xavier and ten other people who live here, or you can leave."

While he said it with an easygoing smile, she had no doubt he meant it. Her jaw clenched, but she couldn't find fault with anything he had said, and she didn't have the money to go anywhere else. Slowly she pulled out her keys and held them out to him, watching his expression closely. "And this is all still routine, is it?"

He didn't appear discomfited by her scrutiny, as he tilted his head in acknowledgment, took the keys and placed them on the hood of her car. "After Diego has had a look, your keys will be returned to you, and we can get you unpacked. For now, please follow me. How was your drive?"

If he wanted small talk, she would oblige. Looking at her car one last time, she fell into step beside him and tried to get her muscles to unclench. "It was good, thanks. The last part, especially along the coast, was gorgeous."

"That stretch of road is one of my favorites in all of the world," Raoul said.

She gave him a quick glance. His accent was indefinable, but something in the way he spoke lent weight to his words, as if he had seen many beautiful sites from all over, which, if he had been working for Xavier del Torro for any length of time, he probably had.

As they entered the main house through the side door, he asked, "Have you eaten dinner yet?"

Hunger had turned into a sharp, unrelenting spike that drove through her abdomen, but her stomach was also tied into knots. She said cautiously, "No, I haven't."

Raoul gave her a smile. While their initial encounter had turned her into a mass of nerves, he appeared entirely at ease. "I am to give you a quick tour, and we'll take your things to your room. Then you will be speaking with Xavier again. When he's done with you, you can take the rest of the evening to get settled. Jordan will make up a supper tray that can be brought to your room later. We had roast chicken for supper, and there were plenty of leftovers, unless you're a vegetarian?"

So the tour was their chance to search her car. At least they would get it over with quickly enough and feed her supper. She told him, "Roast chicken sounds great, thanks."

"Good. I'll let Jordan know." He led the way through the house with a purposeful stride. "The main house here has almost twelve thousand square feet. There are also four other buildings—including a garage, a guesthouse, a gym with a pool, a steam room and a dry sauna, and the house where most of Xavier's attendants live."

Now that she had truly committed to this course of action, she focused on what he was saying as she looked around. The kind of wealth needed to support such a property, especially a beachfront estate in California, was mind-boggling.

She tried not to gawk too much, but the house had a restrained elegance that was utterly beautiful, with an understated use of simple, high quality furniture in lots of space. "How many attendants does he have?"

"Counting you, right now he has twenty," he said. "Eight stay in his house in the city, including Russell, who manages both properties. Eventually you'll get the chance to meet them. Here, several attendants keep the grounds and pool, or they work with me. Jordan is the cook. Angelica is in charge of maintaining the main house, along with the guesthouse. Both Jordan and Angelica have assistants. In the attendants' house, we divvy up the chores to keep the house clean. You'll be expected to pitch in."

She rubbed the back of her neck and nodded. "Makes sense."

Xavier had said that he kept a small household by most standards—if that was so, she could only imagine what an extravagant Vampyre household might look like.

The setup was almost like a modern American version of Downton Abbey. Except with Vampyres.

There was so much to take in, many of the details blurred on her again. Even then, Raoul didn't take her through the entire house, although he did tell her facts just as though she were a guest—the main house had six bedrooms, seven bathrooms, formal reception rooms, a study with an extensive library filled with original editions, a gourmet kitchen that was mostly used when they had guests, a terrace off the master suite, and an extensive wine cellar. It even had a small ballroom.

They paused at the arched doorway of the ballroom, which was an extension off the main floor. Forgetting the last of her discomfort, she gave up trying not to gawk, for it was simply exquisite, with a vaulted ceiling and three walls comprised of floor-to-ceiling Palladian-style windows that were framed with the same elegant black iron as the rest of the house.

Immaculate parquet floors glowed a warm golden brown in the dying light, and the ballroom offered an unobstructed view of the lawn that fell away to a rocky beach and the ocean. Aside from a black baby grand piano strategically positioned in one corner, the gleaming room was empty.

Raoul waited while she took in the scene. When she turned to look at him with wide eyes, he gave her a small smile. "Others might say differently, but I think this is the jewel of the place."

"It's breathtaking."

"Yes." He turned and led the way back to her car. "The house has metal shutters with an automatic electronic sensor system. As soon as the sensors detect direct sunlight, the shutters close. The system is very well built and almost soundless, but I did want to let you know in case you're around when it happens."

"It doesn't close up the entire house when the sun rises?"

"No, some Vampyres prefer complete enclosure and have systems that instigate a total house shutdown, but Xavier likes the views and the fresh air, and it's safe enough as long as the direct sunlight is blocked. As the sun moves from east to west, the appropriate shutters close while others open. It's quite efficient, and as elegant as the rest of the house."

And as elegant as its master.

Whatever else might be said about del Torro, she thought reluctantly, he had superb taste and a certain self-assurance.

As they stepped outside again, the last of the daylight was fading from the sky and well-positioned lights had turned on, dotting the outside grounds with bright illumination.

When they reached her car again, her keys lay on the roof. She gave Raoul a quick look. At his nod, she scooped them up and tucked them into her pocket. The doors were unlocked, which was the only sign that her car had been searched. Everything else looked the way she had left it.

She had two suitcases in the trunk and pulled out one, while he took the second. They walked together along the path to the attendants' house, which was an attractive building in the same style of architecture as the main house and lay tucked into one corner near the protective wall that surrounded most of the property.

"You'll have your own room for privacy, but everything else—kitchen, living room, dining room, TV room, etc.—is communal," Raoul told her. "You'll share a bathroom with a few others. I'll show you the gym tomorrow, and you'll get the chance to meet everyone."

"Having my own room is great," she said faintly.

Over the last several minutes, a sense of unreality had begun to coat everything in a thick, cloudy film, distancing her even further from her surroundings. On the one hand, she couldn't believe her luck, but on the other, sometime soon Xavier was going to want to take blood from her for the first time.

He might even want to drink from her that evening. The thought of forcing herself to let him sink his fangs into her made her stomach clench all over again.

Stepping inside, Raoul led her through the attendants' house, up to the second floor and down one hall. They didn't meet anyone else along the way, although she heard a TV going in another room downstairs, and voices sounded from the direction of the kitchen.

Opening the last door down the hall, Raoul stood back to let her enter. As the room was located at the corner of the house, the windows at two walls gave it an airy feeling, and during the day it would be flooded with natural light. The dimensions were on the smaller side, but still, with a hardwood floor, a double bed covered with a bright, thick duvet and an armchair positioned close to one window, the room looked attractive and quite comfortable.

She glanced into the empty closet as she set her suitcase on the bed, and Raoul put the other one at the foot of the bed. While not spacious, the closet space was entirely adequate. There was even a small sink in one corner, so she could do simple things like wash her face and brush her teeth without ever leaving the room.

The walls were bare of any decoration, and they appeared to be freshly painted. "You can decorate it however you like," Raoul said. "The nearest bathroom is across the hall and two doors back toward the stairs."

One window faced the main house. She looked out the other window at a cluster of sheltering pines. To the right, she could just see the edge of the property wall as it ended at the top of the bluff, and beyond the pines, she caught a silvery glimmer of water.

She had been living with such a sense of desperation for the last week, but here, she caught a glimpse of the possibility of another life, one where she might be able to find a sense of peace in this quiet place.

That had to be as much of an illusion as the impression of safety in the false daylight created by the lights in the city.

But if it was an illusion, she was too tired to resist it. For a moment, simple wonder overcame all other concerns. The setup was so idyllic she almost expected fat, happy bunnies to hop across the rich, thick carpet of lawn.

Touching the corner of the bright, soft duvet, she muttered, "This is amazing."

Raoul regarded her for a moment, his expression inscrutable. "I'm glad you approve," he said. "Now it's time for your meeting with Xavier. Do you need a moment before we head back to the main house?"

It took her a few heartbeats to realize he was asking, in the politest way possible, if she needed to use the bathroom. She shook her head. "No, thanks."

"Very well, come with me."

They fell silent as they walked back to the main house. Full night had fallen, soft as a black feather, and the temperature had plummeted again. A breeze blew steadily off the ocean, feeling wet and icy. Raoul didn't appear to be uncomfortable in his shirtsleeves, but she shivered and wrapped her arms around her middle, and tried not to think about what might happen in the next fifteen minutes.

A muscle in her jaw was tired from being clenched so much over the last couple of days.

This is my choice, she thought. Nobody is going to be taking anything away from me that I haven't willingly bargained for, and it's even an excellent bargain. After all, what's a little bloodletting between friends?

As Raoul opened the back door, she asked, "How long have you been with Xavier?"

"Forty-eight years."

Her head snapped up, and she stared at him. He looked like he was approaching fifty, but that couldn't be accurate.

He gave her a faint smile. "In case you were wondering, I'm seventy-five."

"So, you must like it. Working for him, I mean." Arms clamped tighter around her middle, she stepped inside, and he followed.

"I wouldn't be anywhere else. Xavier is not just my patron, he's my friend."

She took a moment to mull that over. "But you're still human."

"Yes. He's offered to turn me several times, but I like being human. I enjoy food, and the warmth of the sun, and I'm not afraid of dying. That's going to be hard on him."

Raoul said the words so simply, even with compassion, and the picture they painted threw Xavier into an entirely new light. He might be one of the deadliest monsters she had ever met, but the property and his house showed that he had exquisite taste, and apparently he also had feelings.

Her back stiffened. She didn't want to know that about him, nor did she want for it to affect how she thought or felt.

They walked to the study, where a crack of light shone underneath the door. Raoul raised his hand to knock.

Stop, wait, Tess wanted to say. Don't let him know we're here.

But it was a foolish impulse, and she swallowed the words. Xavier already knew they were there. He had probably tracked them from the moment they had stepped outside the attendants' house.

Raoul's fist fell. He rapped lightly on the door panel.

The last two weeks had been filled with a series of decisions and choices. She had betrayed Malphas to save a spoiled, ungrateful boy, and then she had run away, as hard and fast as she could go.

Even though she knew everything had happened as a continuous stream of events, somehow, as she watched Raoul knock on Xavier's door, she felt that this was the defining moment.

The door would open, and her life would become categorized by everything that either came before this moment, or after it.

From within the room, the Vampyre said quietly, "Come in."

Just the sound of his voice caused her heart rate to accelerate, and her hands to shake. Raoul opened the door, pushed it wide and beckoned her forward.

She made her trembling legs move, and she stepped over the threshold and into her future.

There were so many books. Feeling dazed, her gaze swept around the large space. The room was located on the opposite side of the house from the ballroom, and the outside three walls were covered with floor to ceiling bookcases interspersed with tall windows, except for an elegant fireplace that dominated one end.

Aside from two doors, one of which she had just walked through, the interior wall was completely covered in bookcases that were filled with leather-bound books that looked old. They looked like they could be first editions.

Opposite that, between the windows, the bookcase was filled with modern paperbacks, both fiction and nonfiction. At one end of the room near the fireplace, aged leather couches and chairs had been grouped together to make a sitting area, while a large antique desk with a top-of-the-line computer took pride of place at the other end.

The study was on the north side of the house, she realized, and as such, it wouldn't get any direct sunlight throughout the year.

Nearest the fireplace where a bright fire blazed, Xavier sat in one of the leather armchairs, reading. Dressed simply in black slacks and a white shirt, he wore the cuffs of his sleeves rolled to midway up his forearms. His chestnut hair was neatly combed back and tied at the nape of his neck.

As she stepped into the room, he set his book aside on a polished end table and rose to his feet, his erect, slim form as elegant as his surroundings.

At his simple, lithe movement, her mouth dried out and her heart started pounding.

He cocked his head as he regarded her, looking much as he had the night before, with his face expressionless and gray-green eyes intent. "You can't do this in half measures, Ms. Graham. Come all the way in and shut the door behind you."

⩵ FOUR ⩵

"You might as well call me Tess," she muttered. What was it about him that made her feel so graceless and awkward? With a glance over her shoulder, she saw that Raoul was already easing the door shut, so she forced herself to move forward.

She drew closer, and his eyelids lowered as he watched her. It was the only movement he made that she could discern. Once again, she grew intensely aware of her own human failings—the tiny rasp of breath catching in her throat, the slight sound of her jeans rubbing at her inner thighs, and the damp palms hidden at the heart of her unsteady hands.

Like the night before, his intelligent, youthful face showed nothing of what he was thinking. As she came close to the sitting area, he gestured to the armchair opposite his. "Please, have a seat."

If nothing else, both he and Raoul had beautiful manners, much better than hers. She complied with his invitation and sat.

Once she had taken her place, Xavier sat as well, crossed

his legs, rested his elbows on the arms of his chair and laced his fingers together. He looked utterly relaxed and at ease, and his poise made her even more uncomfortable and envious. While they sat mere feet away from each other, the distance between them was immeasurable.

"I trust that Raoul has seen to your needs." His quiet voice caressed the silence in the room. "Is your room adequate?"

She nodded. "Yes, thanks. It's great."

"Very good." He met her gaze, and his was steady and shrewd. "Now tell me, Tess. Why are you here?"

She bit her lip. "Like I told you, I needed the job."

"I remember very well everything you said to me last night." He tapped his lips with his forefingers. "But I do find it curious that someone with your marketable qualifications would be so desperate for employment."

She lifted her shoulders in a jerky shrug. "Things happen. Accidents, unemployment, sickness. We aren't always in control of what occurs in our lives."

"True, but surely you could have found employment again, quickly enough. Just now when you walked into the room, I could taste your fear in the air. It is—disquieting. Why are you so afraid?"

Somehow saying, "Because you could tear my head off my shoulders before I could draw in enough breath to scream" didn't seem the most politic of replies. She shifted in her seat, listening to the leather cushion creak underneath her weight.

"Are you afraid of all Vampyres, or is it me?" He didn't look as if he would be terribly bothered by her answer, either way.

Oh, to hell with it. It wasn't like she could truly hide how she felt anyway. He was reading her as easily as he had read his book.

"I'm intensely uncomfortable around all Vampyres, but even more so around you." She forced a deep breath into her constricted lungs. "Is what they say about you true?"

He lifted one sleek eyebrow. "To what are you referring?"

She met his gaze. "That you were a priest when you

were human. The Inquisition killed your family, and that was when you became a Vampyre—and you went after all of the officers of the Inquisition until everybody who had been involved was dead."

Something glittered deep in his eyes, a fierce, hot spark of reaction, until his eyelids lowered again to cover the expression, and he looked as cool and collected as he had before. "Yes."

It was the smallest betrayal of feeling, that spark, but she had seen it, and her perception of him altered again.

What kind of rage and pain drove a young man to end life as he knew it, so that he could bring justice to those who had killed his family?

For some reason, she glanced down at the book where he had laid it on the table. The name of the author and title were clearly stamped in black on the old leather cover: René Descartes, *Meditations on First Philosophy*.

The book was worn and had clearly been read often. So, not only did he have excellent taste, and evidently sincere feelings for at least one of his attendants, but he enjoyed philosophy too. The business of compartmentalizing him into a box labeled "monster" was quickly getting more complicated than she had expected.

Clearing her throat, she fumbled for something appropriate to say. "I know it happened a long time ago, but I'm sorry for your loss."

"Thank you," he said. "And I'm sorry that circumstances have forced you into being here, when you are clearly so uncomfortable. I will be blunt with you—you are of no use to me if you are forced into doing something you cannot come to terms with. We will not be able to maintain a liaison if you cannot banish your fear, or at the very least control it."

Her hands tightened into fists, and her breathing roughened. He wasn't going to change his mind, was he? Not after she had spent the last of her cash just to get here?

"I'm sorry if it seems otherwise to you, but I do want to be here," she said tightly. "And if you need for me to prove it, I will. The first night of a patron-attendant liaison is supposed to involve the first blood offering, isn't it?"

His eyes narrowed. "Yes."

"So, bite me." Oh, dear. That sounded so much ruder than she had meant for it to. If Xavier was a painting by Monet, nuanced and elegant, then she was a picture drawn in crayon by an angry kindergartner.

He lowered his hands, uncrossed his legs and rose to his feet, all in one sinuous, graceful movement. His steady gaze never leaving her face, he walked forward and crouched in front of her chair. Everything he did was at an unhurried pace, all with the same incredibly beautiful economy of motion. He simply flowed like water.

If a wild lion had walked up to her, it could not have been a more powerful experience. A deep shaking started in her limbs and intensified as he took one of her fists and lifted it. Gently but firmly, he pulled her fingers out and turned her wrist up.

His slim fingers felt cool and light on her overheated skin. Bending his head at a slant, he watched her face as he raised her wrist at the same time. In the firelight, his eyes had turned the shade of green bottle glass, bright and glittering, and his skin appeared tinged with a faint wash of color.

She couldn't look away. How she had ever thought he was plain-looking, she didn't know. He might not be conventionally handsome, but everything about him, from the power of his presence to his quiet dignity of manner, was unspeakably striking.

Then he put his mouth on the delicate, thin skin at her inner wrist. His lips were cool as well, but not unpleasantly so. Resting his mouth on her like that . . .

It felt almost as if he kissed her.

Any moment now, his fangs would pierce her flesh. Somehow, she managed to swallow the small moan that wanted to escape, biting her lip until her teeth broke through the skin. Why was he doing everything with such excruciating slowness?

She wanted to shout at him. Stop dragging this out. Just do it.

When he raised his head again, a pulse of anxiety shot through her. She managed to whisper, "What's wrong?"

"Even though everything inside of you has clenched in protest against this, you would still let me drink," he said.

His voice had gentled again, and to her horrified surprise, her eyes dampened. She said between her teeth, "That's our bargain, and I'll keep it."

"Such fierce determination." He smiled, folded her fingers back to her palm and set her hand in her lap. "I will not bite you, not when the very thought of it causes you such distress."

"If you're not going to bite me, why did you do that?" Her chest heaved as she sucked air, and she flung out an unsteady hand to gesture at him kneeling at her feet.

"To test your resolve. Your commitment, if you will."

"But if you don't take an offering, how can we create or maintain a liaison?" she asked, near to tears. "You need blood. I'm supposed to give you blood. You're supposed to protect me."

"You can still give blood." He rose to his feet and walked back to his chair. "I don't need to drink directly from your vein. We have all the necessary equipment, and Raoul is a licensed phlebotomist. Of course, that means you would forego any of the benefits that humans gain from a Vampyre's bite, but I assume that will not be a problem for you, at least for the time being."

"No. . . ." Her forehead wrinkled. She hadn't slept in a bed in a week, and it had been over twenty-six hours since she had last eaten. An exhausted kind of fog had been slowly but steadily filling her mind, but suddenly it all cleared away and the fear had subsided enough so that she could truly think.

She asked, "Why did you ask me here?"

He smiled, and for the first time since she had met him, he looked genuinely approving. "That is the right question to ask, but it is not the right time for me to give you an answer. How old are you?"

Taken by surprise, she told him, "Twenty-four."

"You appear to be in excellent health."

"I am."

"Do you exercise?"

"Yes, usually I run three times a week, and I like to do weight training at the gym, but I haven't had the chance—"

"Good," he said, cutting off her flow of words. "You need to know, this is a very busy time for me. After the Vampyre's Ball, Julian holds a series of council meetings while senior members of the demesne are still in the area. Usually every year, he hosts some kind of visit from the Light Fae as well, which means I will not have much time to give to your training, at least in the beginning."

Relief banished a huge amount of her fear, until she felt almost normal. "I understand."

The light touched the corner of his mouth and the strong line of his forehead. "While I am otherwise occupied, Raoul will be in charge of your training. I warn you, physically it won't be easy."

She straightened her spine. "I'm not afraid of hard work."

He smiled again. "If, at any time, you feel the need to end our liaison, you may do so. If you stay, you will do as you're told. It's as simple as that. All of my attendants receive a monthly stipend. While we have an arrangement, I will cover your medical needs, and of course your room and board. Everyone gets time off each month. Should we develop a long-term liaison, eventually I would care for you in retirement as well, although these days, we have a more mobile society than we used to, and people are more likely to want to change professions and lifestyles than they used to."

"Has that happened often?"

"Not with any of my attendants, but it does happen." He paused. "Tess."

It was strange to hear him say her name, intimate in a way that she couldn't define. She looked at him curiously. "Yes?"

"I will never bite you without your permission." His voice was soft, even courteous. "I will never take anything from you that you do not want to give, but make no mistake—there are some Vampyres who would."

Dread had become a familiar acquaintance of hers by now. It pulsed again, sullen like an aching bruise. "I understand."

His gaze turned hard and piercing. "It's important you do, because if you choose to leave, some might approach you and offer a liaison merely because you have resided within these walls for a time. I would advise against doing that. Anyone who would choose to offer for you would not have your best interests at heart."

She swallowed. "I see."

"One more thing. If you are not able to give a direct blood offering, freely and willingly, by the end of the trial year, our liaison will be over."

She clenched her jaw, but she couldn't keep quiet. "Forgive me, but isn't that a contradiction? First you said you wouldn't take anything I didn't want to give, but now you just said otherwise."

He lifted one eyebrow, and when he spoke, his voice had chilled. "There is no contradiction. Everything you do here will be by your choice, and you are always free to go. I will not coerce you into doing something you do not want to do, but there are also requirements of this job that you must fulfill if you want to stay on permanently. You don't get a free pass, and you don't get to change my rules just because you might not like them. I will give you ample opportunity to come to terms with the blood offering, during which time, I expect you to get over it and move on. Does that clarify things for you?"

Folding her lips tight, she forced herself to breathe evenly until her unruly temper had subsided enough for her to answer. "Your job, your rules. Got it."

"Good. Now there is one more thing you will do for me

before we're done for the night. Come with me." He rose to his feet.

Curious, she stood to follow him, but he only led her to the large desk across the room.

Standing to one side, he gestured to the chair. "Please sit."

Complying, she glanced at the large dark screen of the desktop in front of her. It was easily a ten thousand dollar machine. A discreet, thoroughly modern keyboard tray had been added to the antique desk. "What now?"

"Now you will prove to me that you can really do what you claim you can do." While he talked, he pulled an iPhone out of his pocket and moved his thumb rapidly over the screen. "The Nightkind demesne website is Evenfall dot gov. You said you can break through a firewall, so go break through it."

She had lost count of how many times her adrenaline had surged over the last twenty-four hours. Gripping the edge of the desk, she said, "No, wait. I didn't say that."

"I asked if you could break through a firewall." His hard gaze bored into her. "You said you were good at it."

She shook her head. "That was your choice of words, not mine! I just agreed because at the time I didn't want to get into a big discussion about it."

He cocked his head, and his expression carried a cool challenge. "Are you saying that you lied in the interview?"

"No!" Frustration made her voice go shrill. "Look, you have to understand what you're asking and what can actually be done. There's no such thing as breaking through a firewall, because there is no wall."

"Explain." He crossed his arms.

Running her hands through her hair, she tried to come up with the right words to adequately describe a complicated technical concept quickly. "You don't break through a firewall like you would smash a window to get inside a house. A firewall is a complicated list of configured rules that either lets things pass through or blocks them. One way you can breach a system is if you discover something has been misconfigured. Do you understand?"

"I understand perfectly. You've got ten minutes." He held the phone up to his ear. "She's starting now."

Son of a bitch. He meant it.

Son of a bitch.

Galvanized into action, she yanked out the keyboard tray and toggled the screen on, as she muttered under her breath, "Ten minutes? Excuse me, but you're fucking nuts. It takes time to look for this kind of thing."

"Nine minutes now." He didn't sound in the least perturbed by her agitation or her swearing.

Her mind raced through various possibilities. She had one potential rabbit in her hat that she might be able to use on such ridiculously short notice—she would bet everything in her inaccessible bank accounts that he was on the inside of the Evenfall security network. That would mean the network firewall would be configured to recognize his IP address and his email program.

Maybe she could get lucky. The quickest way to bypass firewall security was from the inside, through a client-side attack. If she could hack his email, she could send a rough, simple malware program to exploit the breach. He said he wanted her to "break through" the firewall. He didn't say how, or what she should do when she did, or that it had to be an elegant job.

"Six minutes."

"Shut up," she hissed. Her fingers flew across the keyboard.

She hadn't hacked in a while. It felt good, running hot against the clock. It felt crazy, and she wanted to laugh like a lunatic, except she had already sworn at one of the scariest men she had ever met, and she thought she should keep her mouth shut for a few minutes.

He said, "Time."

She sat back. "You've got mail."

Sleek as a panther, he moved up behind her. She was intensely aware of his closeness as he leaned over to look at the screen. As he did so, the cell phone he held in one hand buzzed. He thumbed it on. "Yes, Gavin?"

On the other end, she could clearly hear a strange male voice demanding, "Did you leave your email program running while you set her to hack into the network?"

"Of course I didn't," said Xavier. "I locked it down."

"Well, I want to fucking know how she fucking sent a blast email to fucking everybody from your email address."

She pulled back so Xavier could take control of the desktop, open his email account and click on his new mail.

In big red letters, the body of the email said:

YOU SUCK.

"This went out to everybody," Xavier said.

"Fucking yes. All six hundred and thirty fucking people in the fucking network."

Xavier told the man on the other end of the line, "I'll call you back in a few minutes."

"You'd better."

After that, silence filled the room. Angling her head away, Tess slowly slid the chair a few inches farther away from him. Out of the corner of her eye, she saw his hand come toward her. He took hold of the back of the chair, and as he pulled her closer again, he swiveled her around to face him.

When she lifted her eyes to his face, they felt as heavy as a ton of bricks.

His gaze was rapier-sharp.

She felt one of her shoulders creep up toward her ear. In a quiet, shaky voice, she said, "You didn't give me any time to finesse."

"No, I didn't, did I?" he said. "You just tied Evenfall's IT administrator into gibbering knots."

His voice had turned gentle again. While she suspected that gentleness of his was not always a safe or good thing to hear, this time he didn't appear to be angry with her. Not quite angry. She didn't think.

When the silence became too prolonged, she said, "So . . . Did I pass your test? Am I still staying?"

"Oh, indeed you are," he told her. Finally he looked away, and only then did she realize how intense his gaze had been, like a spotlight, and how much the pressure eased from her chest when she was released from it. "Tomorrow you can explain to Gavin just how you did what you did, but for now, I believe I've asked quite enough from you for one evening. That will be all for tonight. Raoul has seen to your needs?"

Relief tried to turn her legs to noodles. She swallowed and said, "I— Yes."

"Then I'll say good night."

As he stood back, she rose to her feet and almost turned to go, but then paused to look at him again. "Xavier?"

He looked at her, slim eyebrows raised, looking as surprised as she was that she chose to linger in his presence. "Yes?"

A Vampyre's gaze was supposed to be mesmerizing, but he hadn't used it to force her into doing anything. According to his promise, he never would. Until she had reason to do otherwise, she might as well take him at his word.

She met his gaze. "Thank you for this opportunity. I really mean it. I'll work hard and do everything you or Raoul ask of me."

He smiled again, and it must have been her imagination that said there was something slightly wistful about it. "Very good, Tess."

Awkwardly, she returned his nod, and she left the room with a huge sense of relief and an equal amount of disquiet.

Outside in the hall, Raoul waited. When she appeared, he escorted her to the attendants' house without saying a word. If he had heard anything of what had happened in the study, it didn't show in his bland expression.

The tension from the last fifteen minutes faded and exhaustion rolled over her, as inescapable as the tide. Lightheaded and shaky, she could have sworn she could still feel where Xavier's lips had rested on the thin skin of her wrist.

If she hadn't been so afraid of him, so tensed for the bite, it might have been . . . pleasurable.

If he weren't a Vampyre intent on feeding from her, his actions could have been construed as . . . caring.

She rubbed the area with a scowl.

She was grateful he had refrained from taking blood, and she was still frightened of him, but mostly he just confused her. He prompted her to think of things she didn't want to consider. While she had caught glimpses of his sharp, powerful personality, overall, he had shown her a depth of courtesy, thoughtfulness and feeling that she simply had no idea what to do with, even when she had been challenging or downright rude.

No matter how much she wanted to, she couldn't put him in a simple conceptual box. He didn't fit. He was too big, too complicated. The very fact that she couldn't simply label him and be done with it made her uneasy. It hinted at an unknown future, one where she learned new things and made adaptations, and became a stranger to herself.

She shook off the uneasiness. She could handle learning and adapting, as long as it meant survival. For now, supper was waiting and she could take time to settle into her own room, and put all thoughts of Xavier del Torro out of her mind.

L eft alone, Xavier paced the room in long, quick strides, while his mind raced. As he reached the sitting area, he glanced at the book he'd been reading, but a quiet contemplation of Descartes's intelligent, ordered philosophy wasn't in his foreseeable future.

To save wear and tear on the book's spine, he closed it without bothering to mark the page. He and Descartes's writings were old friends, and he would reread all the old passages soon enough.

He went back to his desk and checked his email. Already there were fifty-six replies to the blast email. Like an apologetic cough, the program emitted a discreet ding and the number of unread replies updated to seventy-two.

Something shook through him, and he burst out laughing. He dialed Gavin's number again, and Gavin answered without a greeting. "Never mind, I figured out how she fucking did it. Your computer is compromised. Are you coming to Evenfall this evening?"

"Yes, I'll be leaving soon."

"Bring it with you. I'll wipe the hard drive and reinstall everything while you're here."

"Remember what I said," Xavier told him. "I don't want you to say a word to anyone about how this happened."

"Don't worry, I won't fucking say a fucking word. No matter how many fucking email complaints I get. Jesus Christ, I just got ten more— Come on, people. All the email said was YOU SUCK. It didn't contain a bomb threat." Gavin sounded completely out of patience. "Look Xavier, I want to meet her when I've got time, but for now, just keep her away from my network, you hear?"

"Understood." Disconnecting from the call, he powered down his computer, walked over to his leather armchair, sat and tried to haul his thoughts into some kind of order.

They refused to comply. Rubbing his face with one hand, he thought of the angry defiance in Tess's eyes as her fingers had raced over the keyboard, and how, despite being so afraid of him, she had spat out curses as she worked, and he laughed all over again.

Underneath it all, a persistent, more insidious thread ran through his thoughts. The memory of the silken, warm skin at Tess's wrist wouldn't leave him. He closed his eyes, reliving the moment in the dark privacy of his mind, until a discreet tap came at the door.

"Come in, Raoul."

Raoul opened the door and walked in, carrying a tray with a bottle of bloodwine, an empty glass and a second glass filled with a normal Merlot. He set the bloodwine on the table near Xavier's hand. "Are you sure you don't want anything fresh to drink?"

"Not tonight, thanks. I need to leave soon. Julian, all twelve Nightkind council members and Melisande await." He paused. "So she is settled for the night."

"Yes." Raoul took the Merlot and sat in the chair opposite him with a small smile. "I would ask how she did with your little test, except I got the email."

Xavier snorted without replying. It would be a long time before he heard the end of the evening's adventure.

Raoul sipped his wine. He said, "Are you sure you don't want me to run a background check on her? She has an edge that I dislike. It's a little too desperate, for my taste."

The last of his humor died as he rested his head against the back of his chair and considered the idea.

You're supposed to protect me, she had said.

In that moment, she had been so upset he didn't think she realized what she had given away. Her dark eyes had gone wide, and her soft, sensitive-looking mouth had trembled.

There was a certain kind of nobility in her narrow bone structure, and that wonderful, aquiline nose, as if she was descended from unknown kings. Watching her gave him a subversive pleasure, and he had catalogued her every emotion to date.

Thus far she had evidenced an overabundance of fear, along with a spitting kind of defiance, as well as a rather naive outrage at the Vampyre's Ball, along with the wariness of a young, untamed animal.

Some of it had amused him, but that one moment of raw, uncensored distress of hers . . .

He didn't like it. It called all kinds of inappropriate responses out of him. He wanted to find out what had caused her such distress and to protect her from it. And none of that had to do with the reason why he had invited her here. Protectiveness was the very last thing he should be feeling toward her.

He frowned.

Raoul was right. Tess was desperate about something. A shadow of violence seemed to hover behind her words.

Perhaps she'd had an abusive boyfriend or husband, or she had gotten involved in something illegal. He tried to imagine her involved in the drug trade but couldn't. That would harm innocents and go against her moral code.

One by one, he considered various possibilities and dismissed them. Whatever the reason behind her distress, the chances were very slim that a non-magical human would have been involved in something dangerous enough to concern him.

Which was, of course, why he was interested in her. Most creatures of the Elder Races would think the same thing. After one glance, they would dismiss her utterly. That dismissal could be very useful to him.

Unbidden, the memory returned of her trembling body as he took her wrist in his hand The blood offering could have been such a beautiful gesture, the trembling evocative, sensual and indicative of surrender, yet the taint of her fear had saturated the air.

His mouth tightened. There were some Vampyres who would have embraced all of it, the trembling and the fear, and would have taken everything from her in a predatory glut.

He had lived for a very long time, and he was under no illusions about himself. He was every bit as much of a predator as any other Vampyre, but he had his own moral code, and none of his predatory instincts were triggered by the kind of fear that came from an innocent woman under his power.

No, his predator instincts were triggered by another kind of fear entirely.

"Go ahead and run a routine check on her," he said. "I'm not prepared to focus a great deal of time on this, but we should at least find out if she has a criminal record, so we can deal with it, if need be. If we gain her trust and loyalty, she should volunteer information about herself willingly soon enough."

The other man shrugged. "You got it.

⇒ FIVE ⇐

Having made his decision, Xavier dismissed the subject, picked up his glass of bloodwine and drank. Even though bloodwine didn't have the same nutritive qualities as fresh blood, he liked the taste, and on some nights, he simply had no interest in the courtesies and interaction involved in feeding from one of his attendants.

He said, "I'll be leaving for Evenfall before the hour's end, and I might not get away before daylight. I'll text you if I'm staying on."

Raoul frowned. "Want me to come with you?"

For a moment, he was tempted. Raoul had a cool head, which would be particularly welcome, since tensions between Julian and the council were at an all-time high. But after a moment, he shook his head. "I want you here to keep an eye on Tess."

Raoul drank his wine too. "The others can babysit her, and Diego could start her training tomorrow, not that I expect that to change your mind."

"You are correct. It does not."

Raoul's mouth tightened. "What good am I as head of

your security if you don't let me do my job? Half the council would like to see you dead, if they could manage it."

He poured himself another glass of bloodwine. "Surely not half."

"Okay, Justine and Darius, then. Along with any of the other council members they might be able to coerce or cajole into killing you."

"I can look after myself," Xavier said. "And you will do a perfectly fine job of looking out for everybody here, which is all I require." He met the other man's gaze. "If you would let me turn you, I might decide otherwise."

Raoul emitted a sharp sigh. "That's not going to happen."

He shook his head. "Then I see no other alternative. I'm not about to risk any of my fragile human attendants, not with all the Nightkind council members under one roof."

Raoul made a disgusted sound. "You and your damned protective instincts."

Xavier narrowed his eyes. "Yes, me and my damned protective instincts. You are of no use to me dead. Instead, I want you to focus on what you might make of our new arrival."

"For what it's worth, I think she's a mistake," Raoul said.

"Why?" He was genuinely curious. "You do not see the promise in her?"

"Oh, I see the promise all right. I also see problems." Scowling, the human tossed back the last of his Merlot.

"Such is life, old friend." He shrugged.

Sooner or later, either the promise or the problems would win out. Time always told the tale.

After finishing his bloodwine, Xavier wrapped his desktop in a blanket, stowed it in the backseat of his black Lexus SUV and drove the curving coastal road to Evenfall.

Built in 1800 and sprawling over four acres along the Pacific coastline, Evenfall had been built with old-world crafting techniques and was modeled after a classic Normandy castle in every aspect, including a moat, drawbridge, defensive towers, a great hall and three interior courtyards.

Every night Evenfall was lit all over, a behemoth beacon in the dark, and strong floodlights illuminated the foaming waves crashing on the rock-strewn beach. As Xavier approached, the castle towered against the backdrop of a crescent moon.

Decades ago, the largest interior courtyard had been converted into a parking lot. It was large enough to accommodate all the daily—and nightly—traffic, even during the busiest times of the year. There was also a second parking lot underground, with a modest gravel drive that led up to a metal door with security cameras set on either side of the arched entrance.

When Xavier pulled up to the door, it opened silently to reveal a lowered bar and a guard station located just inside. The guard raised the bar and waved him through, and moments later he pulled into a parking space.

Leaving the computer in the SUV for Gavin to retrieve, he made his way through the lower levels to a stairwell that led up to a narrow gallery, concealed with a privacy screen. The gallery overlooked the Nightkind council chamber, where a shouting match was in progress.

"I don't give a good goddamn what your mother says!" Julian's deep-throated shout filled the open area like the roar of an infuriated lion.

"I'll just text Mommy and let her know you said that, shall I?" Melisande shot back.

The Nightkind King and the Light Fae heir to the throne stood several feet away from each other on the council floor, facing each other like gladiators in an arena.

Scattered in a rough circle around the pair were the twelve members of the Nightkind council, each Vampyre the head of a major house. Xavier took careful note of their positions and expressions. Their geography and body language was telling. Most maintained a healthy distance from the confrontation while they watched with closed expressions, including Marged and Dominic, the two that Xavier considered the most compliant.

Two of the Vampyres looked notably different from the

others. Darius, a strongly built man with hawkish features, stared at Julian unblinkingly, the predatory hunger in his eyes naked and apparent. The other one, Justine, a beautiful redheaded woman, watched Julian as well, her face filled with avid amusement.

Xavier turned his attention to the Light Fae princess. Melisande's famous angular, golden-skinned features were suffused with rage. Standing six foot tall in sparkling silver stilettos, she wore a dark gray Donna Karan suit with a tuxedo jacket that flowed over her narrow body. Her long pointed ears were hidden by the thick, curling blonde hair that tumbled down her back. If looks could kill, her glare would have sliced Julian into several pieces.

Julian threw out his hands. "What self-respecting hundred-and-sixty-year-old woman says 'Mommy'?"

"Oh, fuck you, Julian," Melisande snarled. "Just because you're demon spawn and you have no clue what a sincere feeling is doesn't mean you get to sneer at those of us who have real family ties."

"For God's sake, Melly, you're a B-movie horror actress, not a diplomat," Julian snapped. "Go home to Mommy, and tell Tatiana to send someone more qualified."

"And my mother is head of a major movie studio as well as being Light Fae Queen. Unlike you, most of us have the capacity to do more than one thing at a time." Melisande crossed her arms. "Are you sure you want me to go home? Because if I do, I promise you can kiss all of this year's trade proposals good-bye."

Xavier leaned one shoulder against the wall as he rubbed the bridge of his nose. Neither Julian nor Melisande could stand to be in the same room together without driving each other into a frenzy.

Julian, he said telepathically.

On the council floor, Julian lifted his head to look toward the gallery where Xavier stood hidden. Julian's eyes had turned red. *Where the fuck have you been?*

I got here as soon as I could, Xavier told him calmly. *You're flaming out in front of the whole council. Has it occurred to you that this is exactly what Tatiana—or somebody—wanted to have happen?*

Julian lowered his head like a maddened bull, his jaw angled out. *If Tatiana sent Melly to drive me crazy, it's working. I'm going to strangle her before the night's out.*

Look to Darius, Xavier said simply. *And Justine. You're being played.*

Julian turned toward Darius. After a moment, he said between his teeth, "My apologies to the council. Clearly we've gotten off topic. Everybody take a break. We can pick up again in an hour."

While Julian stalked out of the room and most of the council members moved toward the exits with undisguised relief, Xavier kept his attention on Justine, who glided smoothly up to Melisande's side. The two women looked at each other silently. They had gone telepathic.

He watched sharply as Melisande threw her hands up in a classic gesture of frustration. Justine laid a hand on Melisande's arm and gave her a warm, sympathetic smile.

Julian wasn't the only one being played.

Moving swiftly, Xavier pushed away from the wall and raced down the stairs. Within moments he was shouldering his way into the council chamber, and he came up on Melisande's free side.

"Melly," he said. "It's good to see you. It's been too long."

Melisande turned to him, her tense expression lightening into a smile. "Xavier, it's good to see you too. How are you?"

"I'm well, and you?" All too aware of Justine's hardening expression, he kissed Melisande's offered cheek.

"Oh, I'm fine, thanks." She blew out a breath between even white teeth. "I was just telling Justine how embarrassed I am. When I came up here, I was so determined not to lose my temper or let Julian get to me. Then within five minutes we're shouting ridiculous things at each other in front of everybody. We rub each other so wrong, we lose all common sense."

"I know you can move past this," he told her quietly. "Your history with Julian is just that—history. You're too intelligent to let it get in your way for long."

Melisande squared her shoulders. "I appreciate you saying that. You always were the voice of reason."

He smiled, touched her hand and turned to incline his head to Justine. "Good evening, Justine. You're looking beautiful as always."

"Xavier." Justine gave him a narrow, cold smile. "Ever the loyal dog, aren't you? I always did prefer cats. You interrupted us. Melly and I were just having a private word."

"You know how these things go." Xavier returned her smile with one just as cold. "There's never anything private that happens while the council is in session."

A buzzing sound came from the direction of Melisande's jacket pocket. Slipping one hand into her pocket, the Light Fae woman frowned. "Forgive me, I need to take this call."

"Certainly," Xavier said. "I would be happy to keep Justine company." As Melisande walked away, he turned to the other Vampyre. "And how are you doing this evening? Sowing seeds of dissent, as usual?"

Justine was far older than he and came from the violent, shadowy beginnings of Britannia. Eyes glittering, she said, "Why, Xavier, I have no idea what you're talking about."

Xavier angled his head and took a step closer as he said softly, "Oh, I think you do. I'd heard that Tatiana was thinking of sending Melisande to handle the annual trade negotiations. I wonder where she got that idea. Then Melisande and Julian fight in front of the council. So typical of them, don't you think? And you step in to offer comfort. What does come next, Justine? Perhaps you save the trade agreements, while Julian becomes even more alienated from the council and you become more indispensable."

"I was wrong," Justine said. When she smiled again her fangs had descended. "You're not a dog, you're a spider. Always spinning your little webs, sending out your little spies and gathering up your little snippets of information.

Too bad it's all in a lost cause. Julian never did have total control over the council, and now after his split from Carling, his days as Nightkind King are numbered."

Xavier stepped closer to her, until the tips of their shoes touched, and smiled into her reddened gaze.

"I don't believe any cause is lost," he said. He took her hand, raised it to his lips and her angry smile slipped. "Everyone has a chance at redemption, even you. All you have to do is make different choices."

Snatching back her hand, she hissed at him. "Don't prattle your failed priestly sentiments at me, fool."

He murmured, "I was not talking about religion, but redemption of another sort entirely. Of course, making different choices is all but impossible for some, but I'm warning you, Justine. If you keep going down this path, it can only end badly for you."

"You're going to regret interfering with me," she said, just as softly.

The quick, light tap of approaching footsteps broke them apart. Xavier turned, along with Justine, to face Melisande as she came up to them.

Melisande said without preamble, "I'm going to take my sister Bailey's advice and head back to the city."

"Oh darling, I don't blame you," Justine said. The red had faded from her gaze, which began to gleam with triumph. "This has been completely unacceptable."

"Don't worry, I'm not giving up yet," Melisande said briskly. "It's just for one night so that I can clear my head. No offense, but I can't think straight when I'm in the middle of this great, hulking pile of rocks. It brings back too many memories."

Before Justine could say anything else to do more damage, Xavier smiled at Melisande and said, "I have a great idea. Come home with me and we'll spend the rest of the night talking about old times—but we'll focus only on good stuff, I promise."

The Light Fae woman's expression softened and she

returned his smile. "What a perfect solution. You're close by, and your home is beautiful. I'd love to stay overnight. Will I get the chance to say hi to Raoul?"

"Of course," Xavier told her. "He'll be delighted to see you."

"How wonderful all the way around," Justine said, giving him a venomous look. She linked her arm through one of Melisande's. "I'll come too, shall I?"

Frustration made him grit his teeth. He didn't want Justine anywhere near his property. Not only had he just taken on an unschooled attendant, but he also had five trainees whose names and faces were virtually unknown, and he meant to keep their identities hidden. Also, for every good word he might try to put in with Melisande about dealing with Julian, Justine would be whispering poison in her other ear.

"I don't recommend that," he said to Justine. "A visit to my home might not be good for your health."

"But why ever not?" Justine opened her eyes wide, while Melisande tilted her head, her expression sharpening.

While Melisande wasn't stupid, she also didn't understand the full scope of the tensions within the Nightkind demesne at the moment, and now wasn't the time to enlighten her. Staring at Justine, he waited the merest heartbeat to let his threat sink in.

Then he smiled and said, "I don't have a total house shutdown at sunrise, and I know many Vampyres have a problem with that."

A look of revulsion flickered over Justine's perfect features. "Don't tell me you have one of those revolving systems."

"I do, indeed."

Melisande said, "Justine, please don't feel obligated to come if it's going to make you uncomfortable."

"Nonsense," said Justine. Her gaze met Xavier's with a clash that was almost audible. "Pass up the chance to see inside our reclusive Xavier's private retreat? I wouldn't miss this opportunity for the world."

"Of course you wouldn't," said Xavier grimly.

Both Melisande and Justine left to make last-minute arrangements. Xavier texted Raoul as he waited.

Prepare for houseguests until sundown tomorrow. All trainees need to stay in total seclusion.

Raoul responded almost immediately. Who's coming?

Melisande and Justine. Trade negotiations with the Light Fae have been suspended for the night. You have a half hour to get ready.

A pause.
Then Raoul texted back: Bloody hell.

By the time Tess had unpacked her suitcases and set them on the floor of the closet, a knock sounded at her door and she went to answer it.

Outside in the hall, a short man stood holding a dinner tray. He had an intense gaze and appeared to be in his sixties. According to his looks, he could be older than Raoul, but of course that would depend on how old he had been when he had become Xavier's attendant.

He gave her a nod. "I'm Jordan. I do the cooking. Raoul asked me to bring you a supper tray."

"Hi, I'm Tess." She took the tray, staring at the food. The main dish was covered, but the side plates weren't. One plate contained a green salad with a variety of different colored beets and a simple olive oil dressing. The other small plate held a slice of carrot cake. There was also a small green bottle of Perrier, another small, unopened individual bottle of wine, and silverware wrapped in a linen napkin. The scent of roast chicken coming from the covered dish made her mouth water. "This is fantastic. Thank you."

"You're welcome." Jordan hesitated. "We're all night owls

and tend to stay up late, so you'll have to speak up if the
music or the TV bothers you."

She shook her head. "Thanks for the warning, but I'm a
pretty hardy sleeper."

Usually. When she wasn't having nightmares of being
endlessly tortured by a vengeful Djinn.

"I'll let the others know. Bon appetit."

As he left, she pushed the door shut with one foot, carried the tray to the bed and removed the lid from the main
plate to reveal succulent slices of moist roast chicken,
mashed potatoes with gravy and dressing. Real, homemade food.

She dove in and didn't come up for air until all of it was
gone.

As the nutrition hit her system, it gave her a burst of
energy and the fog cleared from her mind. Gathering up
the tray, she took it downstairs to the large, well-appointed
kitchen, washed her dishes and found the appropriate
drawers and shelves for everything except for the tray itself
and her used linen napkin. After some hesitation, she left
those on one end of the counter.

Then she went exploring, and ran into a large number of
young men engaged in a variety of activities. Some watched
TV and a few played Ping-Pong in the large family-style
room in the basement.

Still more worked on laptops, although she never got a
glimpse of what was on any of their screens. To a person,
they closed their laptops before she got too close.

In fact, except for Jordan, Raoul, and an older Hispanic-
looking woman with graying hair who introduced herself
as the housekeeper, Angelica, all of the other attendants
she met were young, fit-looking men.

Was that strange?

She was inclined to think that was a little strange, but
then she was running short on sleep and so many other
weird things had happened that day, she decided to let it go
for the moment.

After so many introductions, she didn't remember anybody's name except for Diego's, mostly because Raoul had mentioned him before.

"You're the one who searched my car," she said to Diego as they shook hands.

"So I did," he said. He was a handsome man who appeared to be in his thirties, but then she wasn't sure about anybody's real age on the estate. His dark, restless gaze swept over her, taking in her appearance. "Are you settling in all right?"

"Yes, thanks. Jordan brought me a supper tray with the most amazing carrot cake for dessert."

He nodded. "Jordan's a great cook. And don't worry about the dessert. You'll be working off the calories soon enough."

It was her turn to glance down his lean, muscled body. He looked like an athlete in the peak of condition. While a regular blood offering to Xavier would give him a lot of enhancement, she bet those bicep guns and washboard abs came from good old-fashioned, hard training.

"Looking forward to it," she said. "Hey, it is okay if I walk around outside?"

"Sure it is, chica. Use the gym, swim in the pool, walk the beach. You're home now. Just don't help yourself to Xavier's wine cellar without permission." His gaze went back to his closed laptop.

Taking the hint, she backed away. "Okay, thanks."

She went upstairs, grabbed her jacket and slipped out the front door. The lawn was wet and the breeze felt damp on her face, even though the night sky had turned clear with just a thin film of cloud on the horizon. A moment later, an underground sprinkler system kicked on, and she smiled. Lawns that were this beautiful took some upkeep.

Exploring the gym could wait until daylight. Keeping to the paths, she made her way to the edge of the oceanside bluff. A wide, simple set of stairs had been carved into the rock. With a sense of incredulity and pleasure, she descended to the beach.

The ocean was a vast dark blue, lightly touched with

ripples of silver, while the beach was a deep, shadowy ocher. She felt the urge to pinch herself. The scene was too idyllic. There had to be a catch.

Well, of course there was a *catch*.

It was an idyllic scene, with Vampyres. Or at least one courteous, yet quite autocratic Vampyre.

Tucking in her chin and wrapping her jacket close, she strolled down the beach and let the stress of the day melt away.

A shout came from some distance, and she turned to look behind her. A man stood at the top of the bluff. As she watched, he leaped down the stairs and raced toward her.

It was Raoul. When he came near, she said defensively, "Did I do something wrong? Diego said I could walk the beach."

"Usually, you can, but not tonight." Raoul's voice was grim. "Get back to the house now. Run."

Her heart kicked. Man, her adrenal system had been overworked for days now. Jogging along the sand while he kept pace beside her, she panted, "What's wrong?"

"We're getting company."

He didn't say anything else until they reached the attendants' house. When she turned to ask him questions, he opened the door, put a hand to her back and propelled her inside.

She went without resisting. After experiencing his calm, unflappable behavior earlier, his attitude now seriously scared her.

The other attendants had gathered in the large living room, some sitting and others standing. It was the first time she had seen all eleven together. Everyone watched Raoul, expressions tense.

Without preamble, he said, "The council has broken off for the night. Melisande is coming to stay here until tomorrow evening, and Justine is coming with her."

While Tess didn't recognize either name, she watched a ripple of reaction pass through the others.

Diego said sharply, "Justine. She's coming here?"

"Correct." Raoul turned to Jordan. "Justine usually travels with two attendants, and Melisande will have a couple of bodyguards with her, which means you'll be preparing food for at least five people." He said to everyone else, "Only senior staff is allowed outside this house until they leave. Tess, the senior staff is Diego, Jordan and his assistant Peter, Angelica and her assistant Enrique, and myself."

"I'll get weapons," Diego said.

Weapons? Tess tilted her head. For *houseguests*?

Another of the young men—Marc, she thought his name was—said, "I'll help."

"Hurry," Raoul said.

The two raced out the door.

Raoul turned to Tess. "I know you don't understand what's going on, but you don't have to understand to follow orders."

"Someone dangerous is coming," she said dryly. "I got that much."

"Yes. Melisande is the Light Fae heir. She's being accompanied by a very old Vampyre who sits on the Nightkind council. Be clear about this—Justine is an enemy. The only reason why Xavier would allow her on the property is because he wouldn't have had any other choice."

She gave him a jerky nod. "Got it."

"The rest of you, go over the protocol with Tess." He strode out, and Angelica, Jordan and two others followed him.

Slowly Tess eased out of her jacket while she eyed the others who were left. Aside from her, there were four young men. The door opened, and Marc came inside, carrying several handguns that he passed out to the others.

She raised her eyebrows. "You didn't bring a handgun for me?"

He looked at her. "Do you know how to shoot?"

Her mouth tightened. "No, but I can learn fast when I have enough incentive."

He shook his head. "Raoul didn't say anything about arming an untried, unknown trainee who could be a danger to herself and others. If you've never fired a gun before, you're not getting one from me. Besides, this is all just a precaution."

She ground her teeth a moment before she replied, "It looks like a pretty serious precaution to me."

"Of course it is. Justine has never been here before, and she's dangerous, but trust me, Xavier is too. She'll have two attendants, but we have twelve people, all of whom know how to handle themselves, except for you. Plus the Light Fae princess will be here, along with her attendants and bodyguards. It would be very foolish for Justine or any of her people to get violent. In fact, it would be tantamount to a public declaration of civil war. Frankly, the greatest risk is for her to try to mesmerize one of us and pump us for information."

Tapping a foot, she thought through what Marc had said. He sounded intelligent and remarkably educated, and he'd certainly delivered a good, concise overview of the situation, but something didn't add up.

If everyone—except her—knew how to handle themselves, why did they all have to stay hidden behind closed windows and doors? If they were using this as a rationale, shouldn't she be the only one who needed to be cloistered?

But she didn't want to question Marc too closely, or come across as too challenging. He wasn't in charge and he hadn't created the rules. He was only telling her what he was supposed to, and she didn't want to start an argument on her first night.

"Fine," she said. "Raoul said you guys would go over protocol with me."

"It's simple," Marc told her. "It's standard protocol for everyone to be armed when a hostile entity is on the property. When you're trained and this comes up again, you'll be armed too. Raoul said senior staff will handle this, so we stay in, lock up the house, and we don't invite anybody in. No Vampyres, and no visiting humans. Nobody gets inside. We close all the window coverings, and we keep them shut—day and night—until we're told we can open them again. Aside from that, we sit tight and relax."

"Relax," she said.

"There's nothing else for us to do." He shrugged. "It's a situation. It's being handled by people who know what they're doing."

While they had been talking, one of the other men— Tess couldn't remember his name, Scott or Brian—had been keeping watch out the front window.

He said, "They're here." Tess joined the others as they peered out. Three gleaming vehicles, all of them black, pulled into the parking lot, and several people climbed out.

Xavier was immediately apparent, with his slim figure and erect carriage. He walked toward the second vehicle as a tall, striking blonde woman climbed out along with two other Light Fae. The woman was dressed in a dark-colored, elegantly cut suit, while her silvery high heels caught the light and sparkled.

Recognition struck. Tess felt like reality took a sharp skid sideways, sending her hurtling into a dream. She murmured faintly, "Is that Melisande Aindris, the actress? Didn't she star in that zombie movie *They Ate New York*?"

Marc glanced at her. "Yes. Her mother, the Light Fae Queen, owns Northern Lights Studios."

"I knew that," she muttered. "I just forgot."

Three more figures emerged from the third vehicle. Tess recognized one of them as well, the beautiful redhead who had kept her female attendant on a leash at the Vampyre's Ball.

"And there's Justine," said Marc.

The redheaded woman spun in a slow circle, looking around the property. As she turned toward the attendants' house, Marc snapped the blinds closed.

"Show's over. The blinds and curtains stay shut now, until we get the all clear." Marc looked at Tess. "You know, you might as well go to bed. As far as we're concerned, nothing else is going to happen tonight."

Bristling at the thought of being sent to bed like a child, Tess lingered downstairs for close to an hour, but the others settled down to watch TV or open their laptops again. The only difference from earlier was that they did so with weapons close to hand.

Eventually inactivity allowed for exhaustion to creep back in. It weighed down her limbs and eyelids, until she muttered a good night to the others and went up to her room.

Troubled, she put on a nightshirt that came to the top of her thighs, brushed her teeth, poured a glass of water and climbed into bed.

All of her instincts felt askew.

Who was the monster now? Justine, Xavier, or both?

Certainly they were both old, dangerous and incomprehensible to her, but while they might be enemies, that didn't make one of them good and the other one evil. It was possible, even likely, that they were simply two different kinds of evil.

While she tried to puzzle it out, a black tide crept over her and washed it all away, and for a few hours she forgot all her fears and uncertainties.

Then her nightmares returned. First one of her foster fathers, the one who had loved to swing his belt, chased her around a huge, shadowy house. Then Malphas appeared to greet her with an angelic smile.

"Tess." He strolled toward her. "You know how this story ends."

"No," she said.

"Oh, yes."

She tried to run, but her feet sank into a deep mud, and then he caught her and set her world on fire.

$=$ SIX $=$

Drenched in sweat, she plunged awake, surrounded by darkness in a strange room.

No. Her chest heaved. Malphas couldn't have caught her so soon.

As she looked around wildly, reality asserted itself. The red illuminated numbers on the bedside clock read 3:16 A.M. She was in her new room at Xavier's estate, her sheets damp with sweat. The room felt airless and hot as an oven.

Kicking off the covers, she climbed out of bed and felt for one of the vents close to the floor. Hot air blew out of it. She was going to cook if she didn't get the heat turned down.

She slipped on her robe, left the room and searched for a thermostat. Lights shone from another part of the house. Very dimly, she could hear sound, perhaps music, either coming from another area in the house or perhaps from one of the other buildings, while the area around her bedroom was shadowed and quiet.

When she found the thermostat, the temperature had been set for seventy-two degrees, which was far too hot for her at night. After only a brief hesitation, she thumbed it down to sixty-five then reluctantly went back to her small, closed-in room.

She didn't have to stay in the bedroom. No doubt the basement would be much cooler, but she knew if she went downstairs, she would run into someone again. She was tired of dealing with so many strangers and all the odd tensions from the day and evening, and she needed privacy badly.

Reluctantly, she closed the door, but that made the heat even worse.

Now that she was fully awake, she could hear the sounds more clearly. Music played from the direction of the main house. She walked over to the small sink to splash cold water on her face and arms as she fought an almost overwhelming desire to peek through her curtains.

That was against The Protocol.

But why was that The Protocol? Was it to keep hostile Vampyres from mesmerizing anyone inside the attendants' house? If so, why couldn't they open the windows and doors at daybreak, when all the Vampyres would be cloistered from the sun?

Raoul had been so urgent about getting her back to the house, and Marc had been very clear. They were to remain in seclusion and not show their faces outside until they were told otherwise.

Was that to keep them safe, or to keep others from seeing them? But why keep them hidden from view, even in the daytime? It wasn't as if keeping a household of attendants was a secret practice.

Earlier she had felt like something was slightly off at the estate, and that feeling washed over her again. She couldn't put her finger on exactly what it was. She didn't know enough yet, but something didn't add up, and wasn't that typical—she had gone looking for a safe shelter and ended up in a place that felt full of hidden pitfalls and unexpected dangers.

And the temperature in her room was simply unbearable. A trickle of sweat slid between her shoulder blades.

She sidled over to one of her windows, not the one that

faced toward the main house, but the other one that faced the cluster of pines bordering the top of the bluff.

How stupid would it be if she kept the curtains closed but cracked the window for a little fresh air, just long enough to cool down her room?

It might be pretty stupid. But she couldn't make herself believe that anyone was paying attention to whether or not she cracked open a window. There was one hostile Vampyre in residence on the estate, with possibly two attendants, and they all had much better things to do than focus on this unobtrusive corner of the property. Besides, as concerned as Raoul had been, she was quite sure he was having Diego and the others watch their visitors closely.

Having talked herself into doing what she wanted to do anyway, she slipped her hands around the edge of the curtains and felt along the top of the window until she found the latch. She tried easing the window up, and it slid open quietly.

Cool, fresh air blew in around the edges of the curtain. Sighing in relief, she slid down the wall to sit on the floor between the bed and the nightstand. Just a few minutes more and she would shut the window again. Nobody would ever know the difference.

Now she could hear the music more clearly. Were they using the ballroom? She didn't dare open the curtains to look—she was stretching things as it was—but in her mind's eye, she imagined Xavier, Justine and Melisande in that jewel of a room, elegant and deadly.

Why had Melisande and Justine come, and why had Xavier allowed it? What were they saying to each other?

When she heard voices, it took a few seconds for her to realize they weren't in her imagination.

Where on earth were they coming from? While she didn't move the curtains, she knew from memory there wasn't anything outside the window except for a narrow strip of land with pines and shrubbery along the top of the bluff. Beyond that lay the beach.

Rolling onto her knees, she edged close to the open

windowsill and strained to listen, and that was when she realized the voices came from the beach. By some trick of acoustics, the wind carried them up the bluff.

". . . and I'm glad you came." Xavier's calm, quiet voice was quite distinctive.

A shiver ran along Tess's skin. Just hearing his voice affected her profoundly in ways she didn't understand.

"I'm glad I came too," a woman said. Her voice was beautiful and melodious, and even though Tess was hearing it outside of a movie theatre, it still sounded familiar. "I love your place. It's so lovely and peaceful here. Los Angeles is such a rat race."

"You're welcome to visit any time, Melly," Xavier said. He sounded warm, even affectionate. The difference from how he had spoken with Tess was shocking. "We would love to have you come back. I've missed you."

"Thank you. I've missed you too."

A short silence followed. Were they hugging?

Oh lord, they weren't kissing, were they?

Slowly and carefully, so that she didn't make any noise that sharp Vampyre hearing might pick up, Tess leaned forward until her forehead connected with the wall. She wanted to bang her head repeatedly.

Please don't let this be some sort of romantic assignation, she thought. I don't want to hear that. I really, really don't.

She started to realize how trapped she was. She couldn't shut the window, because she wasn't supposed to have it open to begin with, and no matter how quietly it might slide back into place, Xavier might hear it.

And, with the window open, the sound might carry too much if she moved around or tried to slip out of her room. After all, if she could hear them, they would definitely be able to hear her. Both the Vampyre and the Light Fae woman had senses that were so much sharper than hers.

Easing down to the floor, she sat with her knees up and her back to the wall, and put her head in her hands.

"I know I shouldn't have lost my temper earlier,"

Melisande said. "And in front of the whole Nightkind council too."

"Well, Julian shouldn't have lost his temper either," Xavier replied. "The most important thing is that you both move on from it."

"He's always been inflexible, but I don't remember him being so scathing." The Light Fae woman sounded utterly miserable. "Or at least he wasn't when we were together, until the very end. He always believed I cheated on him, but I didn't."

In the darkened bedroom, Tess started to chew on a fingernail. This wasn't a romantic assignation at all, but listening to them felt just as uncomfortable. She really hated that a part of her had perked up and gotten curious.

"I've always been sorry that things ended between you the way they did," Xavier said. "You were good for him."

"Was I? Thank you for saying that, but he would probably disagree with you."

"Julian and I don't always agree with each other. You lightened him up, and he laughed. He doesn't laugh anymore."

There was another pause, and when Melisande spoke next, she sounded very sober. "He's in real trouble, isn't he?"

"Things have gotten tense over the last year, especially since he's broken from Carling."

Who's Carling? Tess wondered. Was she another ex? Julian, you dog.

Melisande asked, "Can't they repair their relationship, now that Carling has found some way to heal herself? She *is* better now, isn't she? While she might be retired from the Elder tribunal, she's still Julian's sire."

Tess finished biting off one fingernail and started on another. She didn't know many details about Elder politics, but she did remember the high points that had hit the major news channels.

The previous summer had been full of upheaval for several of the Elder demesnes. The Lord of the Wyr had taken a mate, the Dark Fae King had been killed, and Julian had banished one of the original founders of the Nightkind demesne. From what Xavier and Melisande were discussing, it sounded like that might have been Carling.

"Whether or not Julian and Carling can mend fences remains to be seen," Xavier replied.

Melisande laughed softly. "You're always the soul of discretion. You have this knack for saying things without really saying anything. I can tell things are strained between Julian and the Nightkind council, and I know you weren't happy with the thought of playing host to Justine tonight. I apologize for creating the situation."

"Don't worry about it, Melly. You weren't the only one responsible for what happened, and even if you were, it was worth it to get the pleasure of your company for one night. Besides, I can handle Justine."

He sounded so unruffled, so confident. Tess remembered what Marc had said.

Justine is dangerous, but Xavier is too.

Either the cool night air or her own thoughts caused her to shiver. She reached up to grope along the surface of the bed for her throw. When her fingers encountered the soft chenille material, she pulled it toward her.

The throw slid off the bed and brought one of the pillows along with it. The pillow hit the nightstand and knocked into her water glass and the alarm clock. Both items hit the hardwood floor with a loud clatter.

Tess froze and broke into a light sweat. She didn't dare even breathe.

So, okay. That happened.

Maybe they wouldn't notice. They were closer to the water, and things must sound quite different on the beach.

Melisande said, "What was that?"

"Nothing important, I'm sure," Xavier said. He sounded almost bored. "Let's head back to the house before Justine comes looking for us. We can open a bottle of Chateau Briot. Tell me, are you going to New York for the Sentinel Games?"

"Those Games are the Elder Races event of the century. I wouldn't miss them for the world. Are you going?"

"I hadn't committed yet, but I've just made up my mind to go."

"We must get together while we're there. I'm leaving in a week."

Still talking, they moved away until Tess couldn't hear them anymore.

She couldn't bear to leave the window open any longer. Kneeling, she eased the window shut and groped for the alarm clock and the glass to set them on the nightstand again. A large puddle of water had sprayed over the floor.

Tess, she thought, you might be geek-smart, but you are not as bright as you claim to be. Try to get smarter before you die.

Tossing the pillow and the throw onto the bed, she eased over to the bedroom door. Earlier, she had noticed a linen closet down the hall that held plenty of extra sheets, towels and washcloths. Grabbing a towel, she headed back into her room and closed the door.

"You forgot to latch the window," Xavier said.

From inside her room.

Shock bolted through every one of her nerve endings. Even as she managed to swallow her scream, she leaped backward like a scalded cat and her back hit the wall with a *thump*.

The bedside light clicked on, and light assaulted her eyes.

The window was wide open and the curtain pulled back. Xavier sat on her bed, his back propped against the headboard and legs stretched out and crossed at the ankles. He was dressed simply in the white shirt and black trousers that he had worn earlier, but even that plain outfit seemed impossibly formal and extremely masculine against the backdrop of the rumpled bedcovers.

He regarded her coolly, his lean face hard.

She felt raw and exposed, as if she had left her skin behind when she had leaped backward. He had made some excuse to Melisande, come back to the attendants' house and climbed through the second-story window, all in the time it had taken her to go down the hall to the linen closet and back again.

This, she thought. This is why Vampyres scare the shit out of me.

Staring down at the towel she twisted between her hands, she said, "Oh, that window? I must have—I must have forgotten to latch it when I had it open this afternoon."

"Were you not told of the protocol that should be followed whenever an enemy might be on the estate?" he asked. The small, thin scar beside his stern mouth looked whiter than it had when she had noticed it at the Ball.

"The protocol." She cleared her throat, while in her mind's eye she was starting to see the words in capital letters: THE PROTOCOL. "Yes. Yes, I was told."

He rose to his feet with the same pure, liquid grace as before and walked toward her. "Did you open the window afterward?"

She pursed her lips, while her hands shook, and—oh my God, why did he keep coming toward her? Angling her head away, she sidestepped toward the puddle. Dropping the towel on the water, she pushed it around with one bare foot.

His hands came around her upper arms, and he turned her toward him. He said, "Did you. Open the window. Afterward."

Her head might have moved up and down a bit.

"Do you know how I know that already?"

This time she shook her head. Her gaze focused on the fourth button on his shirt. He smelled like a woman's perfume. If he and Melisande hadn't kissed, they had at least hugged.

Not that it was any of her business what they did. Still, she couldn't help but notice. It was very nice perfume.

He said between his teeth, "Because I know the others would have done a sweep of the house to make sure it was locked down as soon as they received word that a dangerous Vampyre and her attendants were going to arrive."

It was actually pretty terrible how he never raised his voice. She looked down at his hands, still gripping her upper arms. They were slim and strong, with long fingers and lean wrists.

While his touch seemed to brand itself into her skin, he wasn't hurting her. That might possibly change at any second. She lifted her gaze and met his. "I broke your rules, and I'm sorry."

His voice lowered into a growl. "You're not sorry."

"Well, I'm afraid that's true." She felt her head start to nod again and made herself stop. "I'm not really, exactly sorry I opened the window. I'm just sorry you noticed." She paused then forced herself to continue. "I'd also like to point out that you're touching me without my permission, and I just wanted to remind you of the promise you made. You know, the one where you wouldn't coerce me or do anything to me against my will."

One of his eyebrows rose—just one—and he looked angrier and more imperious than anyone else she had ever seen. Finger by finger, he lifted his hands away from her arms, moving so slowly and deliberately, it was as good as a shout.

I choose to do this, the gesture said. You do not compel me.

Her insides had turned to a quivering mass of jelly. Moving with extreme care, she took a step back.

He followed, and his piercing gaze held her like a trap. "Do you know why those rules are in place?"

He was crowding into her personal space, but she thought she'd better not point out again that he did so without her permission, because that seemed like a card that should only be played rarely. "I'll take a wild guess. They're probably for our own good?"

"Quite. Now can you please explain why you disregarded that?"

Unable to stand still, she squatted to fold the damp towel. "I woke up and it was something like eighty degrees in my room."

"And?"

"And I thought, well, just for five minutes, the one and only hostile Vampyre on the entire estate won't notice if a window in the far corner of a secondary building was cracked open. For five minutes. And even if she did notice, she wouldn't be able to get inside without an invitation. I was just about to close it again when I heard you and the Light Fae princess talking, and I realized I couldn't shut it until you left, because otherwise you might hear me. Then like a complete moron, I knocked stuff off my nightstand, and you found out anyway."

Shifting his weight so he stood hipshot, he crossed his arms. "What did you hear?"

"Not much." She shrugged, while her mind raced. Had any of it been confidential?

"Be specific."

"You like and miss each other. She's sorry she lost her temper. Things are strained between her and Julian, and I guess between Julian and the Nightkind council." Her gaze darted up to his face again, but his expression was a closed book. "You're not happy at having Justine here, but I already knew that. Raoul said earlier that she's an enemy."

"You didn't miss much, did you?"

"I guess the wind was blowing in the right direction. I didn't want to . . ." She caught herself up before she said something untrue, because after the first few minutes, she had actually wanted to eavesdrop. Not that she was proud of it. "I didn't mean for it to happen, and I'm really sorry about that."

He gestured impatiently. "Stop squatting."

Warily, she rose to her feet.

His quiet voice stung like a whip. "Justine might not have been able to enter without permission, but her attendants could have. They could have climbed in here almost as quickly and quietly as I did just now, slit your throat and be gone again inside of ten minutes. And before you tell me how unlikely that is, I will tell you that exact scenario has happened before. Vampyres have been known to take vengeance against other Vampyres through attacking their attendants."

Appalled, she lifted her chin. He was right, of course, and she would take whatever he had to say without flinching. Much. She said again, "I'm sorry. Were they your attendants?"

"No, they were someone else's, and it happened over thirty years ago." He studied her expression then said, "While it may surprise you to hear this, I'm not actually angry that you broke the rules."

The world shifted under her feet again. "You're not?"

"You thought things through, considered potential risks and took action that was independent of any orders that you'd been given. And while I understand that it was entirely accidental, you also acquired a great deal of information. Those traits are all very useful to me." He paused. "In fact, I only have a few real problems with what you did."

She regarded him with a great deal of wariness, because once again, this conversation had run away from her. "What are they?"

"You assumed you knew better than we did and were stupidly careless. And you got caught."

Her mouth opened and closed. She had never experienced anything quite like this lecture before, and she didn't know what to make of it.

He turned brisk. "Melisande, Justine and I will be leaving promptly tomorrow at sundown. As you undoubtedly already overheard, after the council meetings I'll be traveling to New York, so I will see you in February. I'll expect an excellent progress report, so try to stay out of trouble while I'm gone." He gave her a slow smile. "Or at least try not to get caught."

She opened her mouth again, but nothing came out.

He slipped a couple of fingers under her chin and gently eased her mouth shut. "To avoid unnecessary conversation with any of the others, I'm going to leave the way I came in. You will lock the window when I'm gone."

He didn't phrase it as a question, but she nodded anyway.

Even though he said he was leaving, he didn't move, nor did he drop his hand from her chin. Forgetting to be afraid, she watched him curiously as his gaze roamed over her face. He touched her lips with his thumb, and a slight frown came between his eyebrows. Then his eyelids lowered, hiding the expression in his eyes.

She held her breath. The pressure against her lips from the ball of his thumb was so slight that if she wasn't looking directly at him, she wasn't sure she would have felt it.

It wasn't quite a caress. She didn't know what it was.

His hand dropped away, and he inclined his head to her. Then he walked to the window, folded his lean body to slip through the open space and dropped out of sight with a boneless, catlike grace.

The room echoed with emptiness. She went to the window and looked out. He stood underneath, hands on his hips. As he watched, she closed the window and latched it. He nodded to her and walked toward the main house, where the music still played.

She watched until he had left her angle of sight and pulled the curtain closed.

Only then did it occur to her that he might have been fighting his Vampyre instincts as he held her chin and touched her mouth. But that didn't feel right to her. He hadn't looked as if he had been engaged in an internal struggle, and she hadn't felt any real threat from him.

Instead he had looked troubled, perhaps even sad.

Even as the thought occurred to her, she frowned. That couldn't be right. Why would looking at her sadden him? It reminded her of earlier, when she had thought she'd caught a hint of something wistful about him.

She had to let it go. Xavier was much too complicated for her to figure out after only a few meetings. For now, she needed to crawl back in bed and be grateful for the fact that, despite everything, she hadn't managed to get herself kicked off the estate.

⇒ SEVEN ⇐

Mid-February

Tess hit the training mat so hard it knocked the breath out of her. Wheezing, she rolled onto her stomach and struggled to suck some air into her cramped lungs.

Raoul stood over her, his arms crossed. "That's a wrap for the day."

She coughed. "Give me a few minutes. I can go again."

He shook his head. "We're done here. After you recover, please make up the time on the shooting range."

Please do this. Please do that.

Raoul had turned out to be a sadist with the most impeccable, old-school manners.

Please schedule an hour before breakfast for your morning run.

Please remember we will be focusing on weapons training on Monday. Please join me on the shooting range at one o'clock, after lunch.

Please protect your left side while you block me. You're very clearly right-handed, and your entire left side is much too weak.

It was like no other training she had ever heard of, and

she was in a class of one. He threw her, beckoned her to attack him from a different angle then threw her again. He kicked her, pinned her to the mat, gripped her in head-locks, slapped her against the wall, and gave her knives in practice bouts only to take them away from her with a confidence-crushing ease, and he did all of it so politely.

"Shooting range," she said. "You got it."

Still prone, she watched his shoes turn as he walked away.

Diego's head came into view, angled sideways. Squatting, he deposited a cold bottle of water on the mat beside her.

"You saw all that, did you?" It was still hard to talk, and her voice came out strained.

"Hard to miss it, chica. Watching you crash and burn has become a daily thing."

When she felt ready, she pushed onto her knees. "I would almost say I can't remember the last time I was pain-free, except I can—it was the night I arrived here."

"That's right, Xavier left right after you got here." He shook his head. "Normally people start feeling the benefits from a blood offering right away, but it must not have taken hold for you yet."

She didn't even want to get into that subject. Shaking her head, she screwed off the top of the water bottle and drank. "I guess I was naive, because I thought I was in shape."

"You weren't bad. Thing is, around here 'not bad' isn't good enough." He looked at her sidelong. "Are you sorry you came?"

She ran the cold bottle over her hot forehead. "I don't know how I feel." A quick glance around the large area told her that she and Diego were the only ones around. She confessed, "It's almost like Raoul wants me to fail. Like he wants me to reach the point after another hard, bruising fall when I'll throw in the towel and quit."

Diego glanced around too then shrugged. "Maybe you're right. He does seem to be riding you pretty hard."

"Well, if he is, to hell with him," she said between her teeth. "I never quit anything just because things got rough. I don't know how."

"Good attitude, chica, except for one thing. There's lots of easier ways to live life. You don't always have to go the hard way." Before she could react, he slapped her lightly on the back, straightened and walked back to the weights.

Scowling, she finished off the rest of the water and headed out to the shooting range. Maybe Diego was right. The problem was, she didn't know anything but the hard way.

After living her childhood in a series of foster homes, she had worked multiple jobs to get through school and had graduated with two bachelor's degrees, one in computer science and the other in accounting. Nobody had ever given her anything. She'd always had to fight to succeed, and this would be no different.

As she had promised Xavier, she did everything Raoul asked of her. When at first she couldn't run for an entire hour every day, she ran and walked as fast as she could, often battling a stitch in her side.

Then came the daily weight training sessions, both on machines and with free weights, and swimming, three times a week. After cardio and muscle-building exercises came the training sessions—hand to hand, small weapons training and the shooting range.

At the end of some days she could barely climb up the stairs to crawl into bed. At least severe exhaustion had stopped the nightmares with Malphas, because as soon as her head hit the pillow each night, she slept like the dead.

As for Malphas, despite being an all-Powerful Djinn, either he was completely out of touch with how a mere human might be able to hide, or retrieving her hadn't become that important to him—yet.

At the end of January, she had received her first stipend for a thousand dollars. When Raoul summoned her into his office, which was located off one end of the gym, and he handed her the receipt, she stared at the number for a while, too shocked to say anything.

Everything she needed had already been bought and paid for. She had even been given new clothes for training, along with three pairs of excellent running shoes. The stipend was just for discretionary spending.

Raoul asked, "Do you want the money deposited into a bank account?"

She shook her head numbly. If it went into one of her accounts, she wouldn't be able to touch it. Worse, the account activity might attract attention.

"Very well," hé said after a few moments. "Until you decide what to do with it, I'll keep a running total of what you're owed."

"Actually, could I have it on a prepaid Visa card?" she asked. At least then she would have the money readily at hand, in case something untoward happened and she had to leave. "I might want to order some books, or maybe a portable stereo for my room."

"Of course. I'll get one ordered for you."

The card arrived at the end of that week, and Raoul gave it to her one night after supper.

She didn't order anything. Instead, she tucked the card away in her underwear drawer. If the position fell through, that anonymous Visa card was her lifeline away from the estate. She intended on collecting as many of them as she could get. Even if she lasted only as long as the trial period, when the year was up, she would have twelve thousand dollars to help her relocate somewhere else.

She liked the shooting range. It was the only time during the day that she could stop straining her whole body, all except for her arms and shoulders. Even then, sometimes those ached so much it was all she could do to aim two-handed with a small Glock 17 that weighed less than two pounds. She also discovered she was good at target practice, and she liked the work with the handguns, although she struggled with the larger automatic weapons.

Throughout her training, people drifted in and out of her lessons, some joining her for the morning run while others participated in other activities, until gradually she grew acquainted with the other eleven inhabitants of the estate.

There was Raoul, of course, the polite sadist who was clearly the acknowledged manager in Xavier's absence. Raoul's deputy was Diego, who was responsible for all the vehicles and for maintaining the indoor pool. There were also Angelica and her assistant, Enrique; Jordan and his assistant, Peter; and Marc, Jeremy, Aaron, Scott and Brian, the five she had been cloistered with until Melisande and Justine had left the estate.

Angelica, the only other female, was a reticent, gray-haired woman of Hispanic descent with a rounded form that was nevertheless toned with muscle. Tess wanted to ask her why there were so few women on the estate, but there never seemed to be a good time to talk with her.

To a person, they were all uniformly friendly toward her and also a bit distant, and she was under no illusions whatsoever. She didn't fit in, and probably, as far as they were concerned, she wouldn't truly belong until at least after her trial year was over.

That was okay. She had never really fit in anywhere, certainly not in any of her foster families. She didn't need to fit in or belong. She just needed to survive.

Midafternoons, right around the time when she could hardly walk anymore, it was time for the other lessons—Elder Races history, politics and inter-demesne conflicts. Memorizing the different races and their predilections, strengths and weakness. Information about each Councillor on the Elder tribunal. The power structures in each demesne, along with the heads and their heirs.

After supper came the lessons in etiquette. The ideal attendant was the invisible one who anticipated her patron's needs and fulfilled them without needing to be asked.

One never spoke until one was spoken to. Always serve drinks from the left, food—for those visitors who partook of food—from the right. The dagger set at the top of every supper plate was symbolic (of what, she hadn't yet figured out, and no one had told her); no one ever used them, or if they did, it was considered gauche and the height of rudeness.

An attendant might disregard any request or order from another Vampyre (or anyone else, for that matter) outside of the house, but if that Vampyre was a guest in her patron's house, then as an extension of her patron's hospitality, she must do everything in her power to make that visiting Vampyre (or other creature) feel at home.

Out of the entire six weeks of training, that was the one time she balked.

She said, "You've got to be kidding me. Everything."

Raoul said, "Everything that your patron would wish you to do, you should do."

"Oh, come on." She gestured with a stranger's arm that was slim, tanned and rippling with toned muscle. Between the insane amount of training and truly excellent nutrition, the entire landscape of her body was changing dramatically. "Sex. Blood. *Anything*?"

He gave her a severe look. "What do you think Xavier would want for you to do?"

She hesitated, as she remembered the talk she'd had with Xavier in his study.

I will never bite you without your permission. I will never take anything from you that you do not want to give.

Feeling only slightly chastened, she muttered, "You're saying he wouldn't want us to give in to another Vampyre's demand for sex or blood, but would the other Vampyre know that? What if they didn't care and pushed for it anyway?"

"That would be a most extreme mistake on their part," said Raoul, his face stern. "If any guest tries to press you to do something you don't want to do, you must tell me or Xavier immediately."

She watched him narrowly. "But what about what happens in other Vampyre households?"

Raoul lifted a shoulder in a very Gallic shrug. "To each house, its own rules."

"That sounds almost like a motto."

"It's an ancient saying and lies at the root of Vampyre diplomacy. Old Vampyres are not only Powerful and opinionated, but they have lived through huge societal changes. What is normal for them may not be so in modern society."

Even though it was considered the height of bad manners to put her elbows on the table, she did it anyway and propped her head in both hands. "What if they're trafficking? Slavery was pretty prominent once, and a societal norm."

"That's another matter entirely." For once Raoul didn't admonish her for her incorrect posture, and he seemed happy enough to just talk, as he leaned back in his chair opposite hers. "You're no longer talking behaviors or who has the authority to dictate what customs to follow in a house. If someone is breaking the law and they get caught, they have to face the consequences."

But how often were they caught? She scratched her fingers against her scalp. "Thinking about all of this makes my head hurt. I feel like I'm training for war and a house party all at the same time."

"That's a fair description," he said. "Sometimes relations get strained between Vampyre houses, or between creatures from different demesnes, and occasionally violence might break out. While that's relatively unusual, if a human is caught in the middle and doesn't know how to handle herself, she's as helpless as a six-week-old puppy. No patron with any kind of conscience would allow for that to happen."

Conscience. There was another concept that messed with her simple idea of what a monster should be. Irritably she pushed the thought away. "So all of this is just an extended version of basic training."

"In some ways, yes." He regarded her with an unfathomable expression. "And like basic training, we've barely scratched the surface. It will be some time before you're suitable to be taken out in public."

She bristled for more than one reason, but mostly because, despite her attempt to keep up emotional barriers, she was starting to look for Raoul's approval, and his words stung.

Clearly everyone else in the household thought highly of him, and she was beginning to respect him as well. He was always patient, always courteous, and indefatigable. But despite the fact that she threw everything she had into every single day, she had almost never heard a word of praise from him.

Her mouth tightened. "And here I thought I was doing rather well."

She had meant to sound flippant, but it fell flat. He met her gaze, his face devastatingly dispassionate.

"You are, by far, the weakest link in this household." His voice was just as dispassionate as his expression, which made his words all the more cutting. "You are much weaker and slower than the rest of us, and far less trained, and at best, your loyalties are undefined and uncommitted. As long as you refuse a direct blood offering, you will retain the worst of a human's frailties. With Xavier's bite, you would become faster and stronger. The hour-long run that you struggle to complete every day would become merely routine, and all the aches and bruises you've suffered in the last few weeks would heal overnight. While I like you well enough, and I don't necessarily think you're a bad person, I see you as a dangerous liability."

She would not let his words hurt. Balling her hands into fists, she breathed evenly until the heavy ache in her gut passed. After a moment, she said, "Xavier has already told me that if I can't let him take a direct blood offering, freely and willingly, by the end of the trial year, I'm out. Now I even understand why. It's for all the reasons you just listed. But it's also early days yet. Despite everything you've thrown at me, I'm still here. I'm still training."

He studied her. "Fair enough. I think we're done for the day."

She stood with poorly disguised relief. "See you in the morning."

"And you."

As soon as she reached her room, she brushed her teeth, fell into bed and was out like a light again.

Six A.M. came hard these days, but one good thing about rising early for a run—she was a good fifteen minutes into her hour before she fully woke up.

If she weren't so sore, she would grow to love those early morning runs. It was the only time since she had arrived that she went outside the walls of the estate, and it was quickly becoming hypnotic.

That early in the day, sunlight had barely begun to filter through the tall redwood trees on the east side of the curving, remote road, and to the west, more often than not fog rolled off of the ocean like a crowd of ghosts. Whenever any of the others joined her, usually they wore headphones and listened to music, but she didn't have an MP3 so she listened to the sounds of the wind and the ocean, and the rhythm of her own breath.

After a quick shower, she dressed in plain black exercise pants, tennis shoes and tank top, breakfasted on a hefty helping of oatmeal, raw walnuts, fresh fruit and prescription strength Aleve, and arrived at the training area in the gym, ready for another day.

As had happened several other times, this morning Raoul greeted her with a nod and gestured her over to where Marc and Jeremy were sparring with knives. Relieved at the small reprieve, she reached his side.

She noted, and not for the first time, that everybody else maintained their physical regimen while working at their jobs on the estate. Of all the attendants, she was the only one that trained all day long, and she was all too aware it was because she was so new and had so much to learn.

For several minutes, she and Raoul stood watching the two men who fought with such swiftness and ferocity she had difficulty tracking their actions. They were totally engaged, their faces hard with concentration.

Thinking of the conversation from last night, she had to swallow past an unexpected lump in her throat. "I understand exactly what you were saying last night, especially when I watch them." She kept her voice quiet. "They're wicked and beautiful and completely fearless, while I'm struggling to avoid getting pinned to the mat."

Raoul didn't disagree. His gaze fixed on the other two men, he said, "Your first choice must always be to run away. If you see danger or violence, avoid it at all costs. If at first you can't run, you fight to get away. Then you run. Kill if you have to, but run. Marc and Jeremy are at a different level entirely."

She crossed her arms and cupped her elbows. "How do you get there from here?"

She half-expected him to spout a trainer's rhetoric. Train every day, work your ass off, don't make excuses or slack off, blah blah blah.

Instead, Raoul turned to give her his full attention. When at first he didn't speak, she turned to face him as well, growing self-conscious at his intent, thoughtful expression.

He said, "To get to where Marc or Jeremy is, you have to change the conversations in your head."

She frowned uneasily. "What do you mean?"

"When you face a confrontation, you have to decide if whether you live or die is part of your agenda. Either you fight to survive, and that's your goal, or you fight to put your opponent down, no matter what the cost. Those are two separate conversations, and the decision for them has to come from here." He tapped her on her breastbone with the back of his knuckles. "That basic choice affects your capacity to act in the world. You can train as much as you like, but you won't ever become what they are until you decide to."

When Raoul deemed they had watched enough of the fight, he turned away and beckoned for her to follow, which she did thoughtfully. They reached a separate training mat, and as Raoul turned toward her, she faced him.

"Making a decision is all very well and good," she said. "But you also have to factor in your opponent, and whether or not he's a Vampyre or some other kind of Elder Races creature that is much faster, stronger and more Powerful than you are. That would take strategy and tactics."

Raoul raised his eyebrows. "Of course."

She put her hands on her hips. "So, when do you start teaching me how I can possibly take down those stronger, more Powerful creatures instead of just focusing on these basic maneuvers?"

He smiled. "As soon as you can surprise me."

"That's it, you just want me to surprise you?" She gave him a wary squint. "You don't want me to pin you, or score some kind of hit?"

"That would be asking far too much of you," he told her gently. "Now, on your guard, if you please."

If you please.

Yeah, that was never a good sign.

She took the appropriate stance, as he had taught her, and he slammed her down onto the mat. Even though he was just a human, he could move so fast, she often never saw him coming.

As lithe as a normal athlete in his twenties, Raoul straightened and turned away to wait until she recovered.

Then she rolled to her feet, and they went at it again.

While listening to the others talking over lunch, she found out that Xavier was due to return some time that night, and her nerves bunched into a jangled mess.

Even though she had no real idea what Xavier did in the business of running the Nightkind demesne, she knew he was a very busy and important man. He would have any number of matters to attend to once he arrived home.

No doubt she was far down on his list of things to do, but sooner or later, he would turn his attention to her once again. She might not be exactly comfortable here, but her days had fallen into a certain rhythm that she had started to depend upon. Xavier's return threatened to throw all of that into chaos.

With a sense of weary relief, Xavier drove his Jaguar through the gates of his estate shortly before eleven that evening. The house was ablaze with lights, the lawn a softly shadowed green carpet that fell away to glimpses of the ocean that gleamed darkly in the moonlight.

The scene was beautiful, welcoming and peaceful.

As he pulled to a stop, the front door opened and Diego jogged lightly down the steps to the car, greeting him with a ready smile.

"Good evening, sir."

"Hello, Diego." Xavier smiled at the other man. Diego was handsome, thirty, energetic and ambitious, but thankfully he was also likeable, which helped to balance out the rest. "How are you?"

"Good, thanks. And you?"

"Glad to be home." He realized he had automatically taken the car keys from the ignition, and he tossed them to the other man. "Please take my things inside."

"Of course."

Angelica, Jordan and Raoul were waiting for him just inside, their faces warm with welcome. He had kept up-to-date on all the daily happenings via text messages, emails and phone calls, but it was still heartwarming to see their pleasure at his return.

He touched Angelica's arm. "How are you? Well, I hope?"

She nodded, her lined face wreathed in a smile. "Yes, it's been very peaceful here, as always."

"I'm glad to hear it. I could use some peace right now." He turned his attention to Jordan. "And you?"

"About to go on vacation, sir." Jordan grinned. "Only two more days now."

"Very nice. Where are you going?"

"I'm going to spend a week in Mendocino."

"That'll be a nice break for you. I'm glad you're getting away for a while." After he finished speaking, he met Raoul's gaze.

Smoothly, Raoul turned to Jordan and said, "Please bring a bottle of Cabernet Sauvignon and a bottle of blood-wine to the study."

Jordan inclined his head. "Right away."

The pleasantries over, Xavier walked into his study,

where a bright fire was already filling the room with warmth and light. The windows had been propped open, allowing a fresh breeze to flow into the room.

He enjoyed the combination of the fresh, cool night air and the warmth from the fire. Everything had been arranged just as he liked it.

As he strolled to his chair, he shrugged out of his jacket, tugged off his tie and unbuttoned his shirt at the neck and wrists, and rolled up his sleeves. The book he had been reading before he had left lay where he had left it, on the table beside his chair. A sense of comfort stole over him.

Raoul followed, closing the door behind him. "How was New York?"

"Interesting, and a much needed change of pace after all the council meetings last month. Dragos spared no expense on the Games. He's quite the showman when he decides to be." He rubbed his dry eyes and relaxed with a sigh. "I got Melisande to agree to the last of the trade proposals."

Raoul raised his eyebrows. "That will have pissed Justine off."

"The thought has given me a great deal of satisfaction, after everything she did to sabotage this year's council sessions."

"You've made a bad enemy of her."

"She's made a bad enemy of me," he said softly.

"I mean it, Xavier." Raoul's expression was serious. "By blocking what she tried to do with Melisande and the council, you've gone from being an annoying inconvenience to a serious impediment to Justine's goals. She won't forgive or forget that. You need to watch your back."

As he talked, Jordan tapped at the door and brought in their drinks. Raoul poured bloodwine for him, and the Cabernet Sauvignon for himself.

Xavier gestured with one hand. "Enough. I'm sick to death of all of it. Tell me how things are going here."

While Raoul talked about the mundane day-to-day events, Xavier leaned his head against the back of his chair and closed his eyes, sipped his bloodwine and listened. It was a thoroughly pleasant way to unwind, until Raoul brought up Tess.

Interest sparked through his growing laziness. He asked, "How is she doing?"

Raoul remained silent for so long, he lifted his head to look at the other man. Not that he gained much information by doing so. Raoul could be entirely inscrutable when he wanted to be, which was one of the many reasons why Xavier valued him.

Finally, Raoul said, "She's tenacious."

Amused, he smiled. "Is that the best you can say?"

Raoul didn't return his smile. "I think she's a loose cannon."

Remembering how Tess had hacked his email and, later on, how she had broken his rules and eavesdropped on his conversation with Melisande, he gave an infinitesimal shrug. "I like loose cannons. They think creatively, and shake up the status quo."

"I'll tell you what I told her this morning," Raoul said. "I see her as a dangerous liability. She is by far the weakest link in this household. She's weaker and slower than any of us, and her loyalties are undefined and uncommitted at best."

His smile faded, and he stared into the bright golden flames of the fire. While Raoul's assessment was fair, there was something about Tess that might be worth the time and effort they poured into her. Some indefinable thing, maybe the very tenacity of which Raoul spoke, along with that delicious spark of defiance.

"I remember you emailed me when her background check came back," he said. "It was clean."

"Yes, it was. Aside from the fact that she worked at one of the major casinos in Las Vegas, there was nothing of note in it. But then standard background checks reveal very little." Raoul shrugged, and his wry gaze met his. "After all, neither you nor I have been convicted of any crime either."

"True enough, my friend." His smile returned to tug at the corners of his lips.

"I also took the liberty of searching through all the Las Vegas newspapers for anything that might seem odd, or for any mention of a reported theft from the casino where she worked, but I didn't find anything."

"Good enough. Anything else?"

Raoul shook his head. "Even though I've made things hard on her, she's done everything I've asked of her. That's it."

He mulled things over. Her fear of Vampyres—of him—had been so palpable he wouldn't be surprised if she was holed up in her room that very moment, worrying about how their next meeting would go.

While he had been looking forward to relaxing for the rest of the night, it might be a kindness to meet with her first and get it over with. If nothing else, they could establish next steps. Besides, after dealing with so much politics over the last five weeks, with the veiled smiles, insincere platitudes and outright aggressions, the thought of looking into her dark eyes and seeing the honesty of her emotions sounded downright refreshing.

Would she still be as afraid of him as she was when they had first met? He thought of the plush softness of her lips underneath his thumb. She had not backed away when he had touched her. Instead, she had stood watching him, her dark gaze curious.

He shouldn't have touched her. He shouldn't have wanted to, and he certainly shouldn't have thought about it so often over the last six weeks.

But he had, and she had let him. Perhaps that meant she would be calmer now, more open and friendly.

For the moment, he kept his decision private and savored the anticipation as he turned his attention elsewhere. "How are the others doing?"

"They're ready to go out," Raoul told him. "Aaron knows it and he's patiently waiting. Marc and Jeremy are champing at the bit. The only thing Scott lacks is self-confidence, but he'll acquire that soon enough when he gets into the field. Brian's perfect in every way. I couldn't ask for a better agent."

"High praise. Please set up a schedule of one-on-one meetings with everyone, will you? It's time they each get their first assignment."

"Certainly." Raoul sipped his wine. "You know they'll be happy to get a chance to visit with you, and they'll be ecstatic at the thought of getting in the field. Anything else?"

"Yes," Xavier said. "Would you fetch Tess for me? I want you to be ready with your phlebotomy equipment in case she needs it. I should have done this the night she arrived. One way or another, it's time for her to offer blood."

"As you wish." Raoul set aside his glass, stood and left.

Xavier finished his glass of bloodwine while he waited. The study was one of his favorite parts of the house, quiet and peaceful and filled with the kind of books he loved that prompted reflection. His only regret was that he didn't get as much time to spend in it as he would have liked.

A quick rap sounded at the door, and it opened before he could invite the newcomer in. Raoul would never do such a thing. He suppressed a smile, folded his hands together and watched his tenacious, problematic trainee approach.

Tess looked very different, and he absorbed the changes with a blink. She wore the loose black training pants that were de rigueur at the estate, along with a formfitting black tank top. Her dark hair had grown a touch longer. The ends now kissed along the graceful wings of her collarbones.

She had also lost some weight, and healthy muscle flowed under the tanned skin of her slim arms. She didn't move quite as fluidly as one might expect from the changes in her physique. Instead, she held herself with a certain stiffness that indicated she was more than a little sore. Xavier knew from experience that Raoul could be a demanding taskmaster, and it was clear that he had not spared her.

Her face looked more angular as well, but not in an unhealthy way. The change was small but startling. It highlighted the proud lines in her bone structure, and he realized the casual eye would no longer travel over her in search of brighter creatures. She had been pretty enough in her own quiet way before, but now she had grown arresting.

He frowned, troubled by the realization.

As she grew closer, he could hear the sound of her heart pounding, and taste the scent of her fear.

Abruptly his disquiet turned to disappointment and anger. He snapped, "Have I given you any reason to believe you are in danger from me? Have I not done the exact opposite, and tried my very best to make you feel at ease here, in my own home?"

The look in her large, dark eyes turned wry. She didn't hesitate, but approached him at the same, steady pace as she had entered the room, even though her heart rate sped up even further.

When she reached the empty armchair, she sat and folded her hands together in a deliberate mimicry of his position. "What does reason have to do with fear?"

That drew him up short. He stared at her, eyes narrowed, while a muscle bunched in his jaw. Moments ticked by as they regarded each other. Her expression was resolute, her gaze steady. Raoul had the right of it; she was tenacious.

He did something that had become completely unnecessary over the last several hundred years, once he had died as a human man. He drew in a breath.

Abruptly, he grew aware of his own uncharacteristic loss of temper, and his anger turned onto himself. It had been a mistake to try to see her tonight, when he had only just returned.

"My apologies," he said, his tone abrupt. "I should not have sent for you tonight. I'm tired and low on patience, and I should have known better."

Startlement flashed in her gaze, and she lowered her eyelids. "It isn't your fault," she said. "It's mine. I'm sorry."

Was it her fault, he thought bitterly, when she faced a predator that could overpower her completely and feed on her until she died?

Or wasn't her fear the most reasonable reaction after all?

⚍ EIGHT ⚍

He couldn't remember the last time he was so irritated with himself. Slicing his hand through the air, he rejected her words with the gesture. "We should start over. Or better still, we should meet on another night."

He watched her lovely mouth compress and counted three of her quickened heartbeats. Then she said in a measured, courteous tone, "How did your trip to New York go? Good, I hope?"

Coming from her, it was a major effort at conciliation. Just as abruptly as his temper had flared, it faded completely. "It was good, thank you. How has the training gone these last six weeks?"

She glanced at him from underneath her lowered lids, a sly, wary look. "It's been eventful. A lot of hard work."

His mouth twitched. Watching her attempt polite conversation with him was rather excruciating, and he didn't know whether to be amused or irritated by it. "I'll have the real truth now, if you please."

"It's been bloody awful," she confessed in a rush. "I know he's a friend of yours, but Raoul is a sadist."

His eyebrows shot up. Whatever he had expected from this conversation, this wasn't it. "He is?"

She nodded. "Ibuprofen has become a staple in my diet, but I can now run for a full hour, although I slow down quite a bit toward the end. I can also strip and load four different guns, and hit the bull's-eye on the target nine times out of ten. And I still have no idea what the daggers at dinner mean."

He repeated, "Daggers at dinner."

"You know, the little ones that are set at the twelve o'clock position at each dinner plate on a formal table setting." She glanced with undisguised longing at the opened bottle of Chateau Sauvignon sitting on the table beside her chair.

He pinched his nose and smiled. "Do help yourself to some wine. I'll call for a fresh glass."

She sat straight and reached for Raoul's wineglass. "Thanks, don't bother. I don't mind using this one. It's not like anybody at the estate is sick."

"True enough." He watched her pour the wine into the glass. Its color wine was lovely in the firelight, red like rubies, like blood. "I've asked Raoul to prepare his phlebotomy equipment. It's past time you offer blood. Unless, of course, you wish for me to take it from the vein."

She drank half the glass at once. "If you're leaving the option up to me, I would rather not yet." Her dark gaze regarded him around the edge of the wineglass. "Unless you've changed your mind?"

"I do not change my mind about things such as this." He watched her for the tiny tells, and they were certainly there. The slender muscles in her throat flexed as she swallowed, and the way she held her mouth changed. Her expression seemed too complex for mere relief, but perhaps contained a hint of disappointment as well.

Was she disappointed that he did not live down to her worst expectations, or was she disappointed in herself for not agreeing to a direct blood offering? Given her tenacious nature, she must be battling a serious revulsion for the act. Troubled, he frowned down at his clasped hands.

"The daggers at the dinner settings is a very old Vampyre custom, dating back to the early Roman Empire," he said. "It is meant as a gesture of courtesy from the host."

"But what does it mean?"

"Often weapons were forbidden in palaces when a ruler was in residence. The dagger was a symbol of trust, a way of saying to the guest, you may go armed in my presence, and we are still at peace."

She nodded slowly. "So it would actually end up being a really terrible thing to pick it up. Kind of a betrayal against the host?"

"Yes, except on one occasion. The dagger was also used by the guest to prick herself to offer blood in a show of fealty to a Vampyre lord. At large gatherings like a banquet, it simply wasn't feasible for the host to take a direct blood offering from everyone personally. This way, a cup was passed from guest to guest. They could prick their fingers, add a few drops to the cup and pass it on. At the end of the round, when the cup had made it back to the Vampyre lord, he would take it and drink."

She frowned. "Was this a ritual for humans, or for Vampyres?"

He stretched out his legs and crossed his ankles. "It was for both. For example, Julian could insist on a blood fealty from all the heads of the Vampyre houses along with human officials that live within his demesne, but the ritual is no longer enacted. Still, the dagger is laid out in formal situations as a tradition. In some households, quite a bit of money is spent on the daggers, encrusting them with jewels and gold. They're pretty baubles, nothing more, and are usually about as dull as a letter opener."

She had listened intently, her eyes wide with fascination. "Thank you for the explanation."

"*De nada*," he said. When she lifted the bottle of wine and looked at him in inquiry, he gestured for her to help herself to a second glass.

Silence fell between them as she did so, and they sat for

a few minutes, each wrapped in thought. He noted that her fear had subsided somewhat as they talked, and he watched the flames in the fireplace as he considered that.

Finally he stirred and sighed. "You present some interesting challenges, Tess Graham."

She straightened in her chair. "I'm sorry. What can I do to make it better?"

"That is what I am trying to decide." He set his empty glass aside. "I've already told you that you must make a proper blood offering freely and willingly by the end of the trial year, and that is not an arbitrary requirement. There are reasons why it is necessary."

"I think I understand," she said. "Without your bite, I can't give as much blood as the others, or as often. Also, it would give me increased speed, strength and healing capacity, wouldn't it?"

"Yes, among other things. Regular blood offerings also establish a connection between us—it's nothing like telepathy, mind you. It just increases my awareness of where you are in a crowd, which can be a handy safety measure." He rubbed his forehead. "But I'm afraid your capacity to give a blood offering won't be enough."

Her expression turned wary again. "What do you mean?"

Meeting her gaze, he said, "You have to do more than confront your fear. You have to conquer it."

"I—I'm afraid I don't understand."

He leaned forward, rested his elbows on his knees and frowned at her. "You walked into this room directly toward me, despite the fact that every instinct you had was telling you to run the other way. Didn't you?"

She shifted uneasily under the weight of his stare. "Yes."

He would have smiled, except that it saddened him too much. She was certainly brave enough. An edge of bitterness entered his tone. "I respect the courage it takes for you to do so, but that's confronting your fear. It's not conquering it. As you grew closer, I heard your heart rate accelerate, and I could taste the pheromones of your fear in the air."

He paused to read her expression, but he could see no real comprehension on her face. She merely looked trapped and frustrated.

"I'm sorry," she said.

"No," he said. "This is not about sorry. I cannot in good conscience set you loose in a room full of predators. Many of them have far fewer principles than I do, and a few have absolutely none at all. They would circle around you like sharks drawn to a pool of blood. Even if my reputation held off most of them, you would certainly not go unnoticed, and that defeats any purpose you may serve for me. It is not acceptable. Do you see?"

The comprehension he had been looking for dawned in her eyes, and it looked very much like dismay.

"I do now," she whispered. She squared her shoulders. "I'll change it. I just have to figure out how."

Such tenacity. Her surface emotions might be all over the map, but underneath it all, she had a spine of steel.

Oh, he liked her. Far more, in fact, than was good for his peace of mind.

"Are you sure you want to?" he asked gently. "You may have chosen to come here, but I do not think you have yet chosen to stay."

Her eyes widened, and he saw that he had scored a hit. He liked that she didn't rush to answer him. Instead, her gaze turned troubled and she studied the remaining wine in her glass for a few moments.

Then she looked up and leaned forward, her angular expression firming into determination. "Yes, I want to."

"Very good," he said. He smiled, and even though she was still uneasy in his presence, she returned it. Then he turned brisk. "Starting tomorrow evening, we will add two more things to your training schedule."

"You want me to do more?"

Her dismay had returned, but he ignored it. "You will begin daily meditations and focus on a series of biofeedback exercises. There are techniques you can learn that will help you to control your body's reaction to stress, especially your heart rate. That should help to dampen the fear pheromones."

Her gaze sparked with interest. "I would love to learn that. What's the other thing?"

He adjusted one shirtsleeve. "I will take over your etiquette lessons. Prolonged exposure should help you master your aversion to Vampyres, at least enough so that you can mask your true feelings."

He did not have to look at her to gauge her reaction. He heard it in the loud *thump* of her heart. Still, she replied without a second's hesitation, "That makes sense. Thank you for taking the time to work with me."

Buried underneath all her tension and nerves was the heart of a lion. He smiled and heard himself asking, "Do you dance?"

"Probably not in the way that you mean," she replied in a dry voice. "I've never taken formal dance lessons. The only kind of dancing I've ever done is in a nightclub."

Bah. She meant modern dancing, which was little more than hopping around and waving one's arms to disco music. Watching a crowd of people on a nightclub dance floor was like watching a school of fish smacking their fins in shallow water. It was all flapping and splashing, and entirely devoid of dignity.

He glanced at her, amused. "You are correct. That is not what I meant. I will teach you to waltz. Perhaps also a minuet. Those should cover the times when you might attend a function and be asked to partner someone."

"How often would something like that happen?"

He shrugged. "Not often, but it is a situation that has arisen before. Someone might be alone and require a dancing partner."

The spark in her eyes faded, to be replaced with a clear look of dread. "I suppose I should be prepared."

"Tess, you are good for my soul," he said. He gave her a completely serious look. "If I ever feel that I am suffering from an overabundance of pride, I shall look for you immediately so you can trample all over it."

"I'm sorry," she said, dismayed. Then she quickly tried to change course. "Or maybe I mean, you're welcome?"

He almost burst out laughing, and considering that he had come to mirth when he had started out in anger, this conversation had ended up having a great deal of merit after all. "On that note, I believe we're done for tonight. Please see Raoul on your way out, so that he can draw blood."

She rose to her feet, but didn't leave immediately. When he glanced up, she looked at him steadily. "Thank you again, for taking a chance on me," she said. "I promise, you won't regret it."

Oh *querida*, he thought. I already regret it.

But he would not say so and crush such sincerity, so instead he smiled and nodded. He watched as she left, easing the door closed behind her.

Alone at last, he poured another glass of bloodwine, but the drink had lost its savor, so he set it aside and lost himself in the soothing contemplation of the fire, and tried to let the silence wash away the strain of the last six weeks.

It wouldn't leave so quickly or easily. Scraps of memory from the last several weeks kept playing through his mind. The pressure on Julian right now was extreme, and therefore so, too, was the pressure on him.

There was nothing else he could do but hold steady in the storm. He sent out his people to gather as much information as he could, while his gut told him that they stood on the brink of some event.

The tension within the demesne was too high. Something must occur to release it, some event that destroyed the peace. Someone's temper would flare. Loyalties that were already tenuous would snap.

The two likeliest candidates for trouble were Justine and Darius. If they weren't the actual instigators, still, either one would be quick to try to seize power at the slightest provocation.

Both were very old Vampyres, much older than he. While Justine had come from Britannia, Darius had been turned only a few hundred years after Julian, during the decline of the Roman Empire.

Like all Vampyres, they retained the core identities they'd had while they were human. Darius had always been overly fond of the gladiator arena, and Justine's beautiful face hid a vicious wolverine.

Neither of them had ever truly embraced the idea of the Nightkind demesne. They had no interest in protecting or preserving areas for other creatures of the night, or banding together to create a cohesive political unit. They certainly had no interest in any idea or cause that was greater than themselves.

They were wholly self-involved, quick to violence and eager for self-gain. He would have long since killed them both, if he could have gotten away with it.

He tapped his fingers on the leather-covered arm of his chair. Perhaps the opportunity to do so would still come. He could hope.

A quiet tap at the door interrupted his increasingly dark thoughts. He said, "Come in, Raoul."

The other man entered, carrying a crystal goblet. The rich, heady scent of blood filled his nostrils as Raoul crossed the room.

Tess's blood.

Out of nowhere, ravenous desire struck, and his fangs descended. He clenched against it, watching as Raoul approached to offer the fresh blood to him.

For a moment he didn't trust himself to take it. Then he forced his hands out and very carefully received the goblet with its precious contents. It was warm from her body heat.

"How did she do?" he asked.

"Perfectly well," Raoul said. "Her issue isn't with giving blood; it's with you taking it. She said it was all quite straightforward and clinical, like giving blood at the Red Cross."

"Thank you," he managed to say. When the other man made as if to linger, Xavier told him, "Good night."

Hesitating only for a moment, Raoul inclined his head. "Good night."

As Xavier waited for Raoul to exit the room and leave him in privacy, his hands started to shake. Bloody hell.

He was not an animal. He was not.

He was a thinking and feeling, rational and ethical creature. He would not be ruled by this storm of feeling, whatever it was. Moving with care, he set aside the goblet and gripped the arms of his chair.

A direct blood offering was a powerful act. Drinking from the vein was intoxicating for the Vampyre, and those who offered up their blood were always in such a vulnerable position. Prone to euphoria and quick to lose control, they ran the risk of offering up everything to the one who drank from them, and some unscrupulous Vampyres did not resist.

Xavier would not, *did not* behave in such a manner. Not ever. He always took blood from the vein in the wrist, never the neck or anywhere else. Those other places were too intimate. Over the course of his long life, many humans had been desperate to give him everything—blood, body and soul—but he had never fallen into that oubliette of meaningless animal carnality.

Take, eat. This is my body, which was broken for you. This is my blood, which is shed for you. . . .

People broke faith and committed atrocities in the name of God. He had watched it happen time and again over the centuries. Once he had gone to war over it. He had walked away so long ago from his vows and the Catholic Church, but the profundity of those words from scripture had never left him.

Blood was life. It was sacred.

There was no deeper covenant than a blood covenant.

No matter how much or little material wealth one attained in this world, the only things one truly owned were one's soul, one's body. The blood in the goblet was the most powerful thing Tess could ever give to him.

And he wanted the blood more than he had ever wanted

anything, this most difficult, hard-won offering, because the intensity of her struggle was what gave the gift such sweet, sweet savor.

When he felt he had regained a measure of control, he picked up the goblet again. It was cooling and losing its potency. Once it had been removed from the donor's body and turned completely cool, it lost all nutritive qualities for a Vampyre.

The only way to preserve blood in a way that was nourishing for Vampyres was the alchemical process used to make bloodwine, and even then, bloodwine did not nourish as fresh blood did.

He would not disrespect Tess's offering by allowing it to be wasted, but neither could he bring himself to drink it.

After a few more moments of internal struggle, he growled, frustrated with himself, and launched out of his chair to stride through the spacious, silent house, out the back door and along the path to the attendants' house, all the while carrying the goblet carefully so that he didn't spill a single drop.

The night had turned opaque, the moon wreathed with filmy clouds. Most of his attendants stayed up well into the night, and the house was lit in various places. He could hear music playing in one part, while in the den, the TV was playing.

If he had walked in the front door, he would have been made welcome, but he didn't. He usually avoided the attendants' house, except when he had climbed into Tess's room to confront her. That house was their space, so that they had time away from the demands of their patron. Instead of entering, he prowled around to stand underneath her window.

Her room was darkened with the curtains drawn, but he could sense her inside, moving around quietly. Her heartbeat had turned languid; she must be preparing for bed. He cocked his head, listening intently. The closet door opened and shut, and there was the sound of running water. He held the goblet with such tense care his fingers began to ache.

When she had turned the faucet off, he said telepathically, *Tess, come to your window.*

Startled, frozen silence. Then the languid pace of her heart exploded into a furious rhythm.

For a moment, when she didn't move, he thought she might disobey and end their tenuous relationship. Then he heard the soft rustle of cloth, and the creak of floorboards. When she appeared in the darkened window, she looked shadowy, like the half-hidden, opaque moon, her skin pale like pearls and hair lustrous with darkness.

She looked down at him but said nothing.

He held the goblet up to show it to her. *Are you sure you want to give this to me?*

Because it mattered. It mattered what she said. While the struggle made the offering sweet, it was the act of the gift itself that was the vital part of the covenant.

She didn't respond for long moments. He stood motionless as he waited, until finally she moved to put her hand to the windowpane.

Yes.

He inclined his head to her, brought the goblet to his lips and drank.

Pure, undiluted power slid down his throat. Like the delicate skin at her wrist, it was warm and perfumed with her scent.

Such precious, beautiful life.

⇒ NINE ⇒

After Raoul had taken her blood, Tess strode back to the attendants' house and her room, cranky and unsettled.

Thank God that was over, at least for now. She had met with the monster again and walked away unscathed. Plus, she had finally given blood, and without the supportive properties of a Vampyre's bite to boost her system, the subject of her donating again wouldn't come up for another two months.

Except, she was really starting to have a tough time with the whole "monster" concept. While she certainly hadn't been comfortable in Xavier's presence, their conversation that evening hadn't totally sucked—so to speak.

He had been irritable, amused, patient and insightful. He had listened to what she said, and he had been respectful of her input and wishes. It was getting more and more difficult to think of him merely as a blood-sucking fiend.

She was still afraid of him. She never quite forgot what history had said that he had done, and what he himself had admitted to doing. He had a powerful presence, and that wasn't simply from the weight of his intelligence. He carried a gravitas that went far beyond the illusion of youth in his face. His eyes were old.

Tonight she almost . . . liked him.

Then she thought about what it might be like to be bitten, and her whole body tightened in revulsion. It was like trying to imagine letting a snake bite her. Or a spider. Vampyres were like spiders with human faces.

She felt too hollow to wait until breakfast to eat, so she stopped by the kitchen, where Diego and Angelica were fixing sandwiches. They nodded to her when she appeared, seemingly friendly enough, but as she rummaged through the refrigerator, she noticed that they had stopped talking.

Her mouth tightened. She was tired of the invisible barrier that separated her from the others. Instead of heating up some leftovers from the evening meal, which had been her original intent, she changed her mind, grabbed a banana from the bowl of fruit on the counter and headed up the stairs to her room.

Tiredness dragged at her body. According to Xavier, her days were going to get even longer. It was time to go to bed.

She didn't even bother to turn on the bedroom light. She could see well enough by the light of the moon. It took her less than a minute to eat the banana. It might not have been the starchy lasagna that she'd been craving, but it filled the gnawing hole in her stomach.

Brushing her teeth, she stripped off her clothes and let them fall to the floor, then reached in her closet for a soft T-shirt that she yanked over her head. Then she took a moment to run some fresh water into a water glass that she set on the nightstand by her bed.

Xavier's strong, rich voice filled her head.

Tess.

She froze in the middle of pulling her covers down. What the fuck?

Come to your window.

Panic bolted through her. They had just finished talking. She had met her duty as an attendant and given blood, damn it. What could he possibly want from her now?

When nothing else happened, her muscles unlocked and she started to think again. If he wanted to, he could have forced himself into any room in this house, but he hadn't. He could be standing in the middle of her bedroom, but he wasn't.

The panic eased up enough to allow for curiosity to bloom. She walked to the window and looked out.

He stood on the lawn just underneath her window, a graceful, solitary figure with such immense poise, just gazing at him did something to her.

Her heart rate picked up speed, and she wasn't at all sure it had anything to do with fear. His white shirt gleamed in the night, accentuating his lean male form.

He raised something to her. It was the goblet Raoul had used to put her blood in.

Are you sure you want to give this to me?

She put a hand to the glass as she stared at him. He hadn't just drunk it?

He understood. He wasn't just putting up with her phobia. He knew how difficult it was for her, and he respected it. Suddenly she knew that if she told him no, he wouldn't touch the contents in the goblet.

Those weren't the actions of a ravening monster. Those were the actions of a considerate man.

She relaxed slightly and told him, *Yes*.

It was impossible to really see his gaze, but still, she knew he watched her as he lifted the goblet to his lips and drank. She imagined his lips touching the goblet's cool rim, and it was almost as though he had touched his lips to her wrist again.

And it was all right. The respect and restraint he showed her made it all right.

When he finished, he bowed his head to her, turned and walked back to the house. She didn't leave the window until he disappeared from her sight. Then she climbed into bed and settled down to sleep with a sigh.

That night, her nightmare about Malphas returned.

W hen she opened her eyes at dawn, a few minutes before her alarm went off, she thought, Raoul was right. Xavier was right.

I have to change the conversations in my head.

I have to do more than just confront my fear. I have to conquer it.

Each training session, she had gritted her teeth and determined to get through it. Now, for the first time, she considered Raoul as an opponent. While he might be too formidable for her to take down (yet?), he had given her an accessible goal.

She lay in bed thinking until her alarm chimed. Then, instead of going directly to her morning run, she went in search of Diego, who sat on the patio facing the ocean while he drank coffee. As she joined him, he nodded to her.

"No morning run today?" he asked.

It was peaceful on the patio; she would have to remember that and come out here to enjoy it more often. This early in the morning, the air was chilly, and she zipped up her hoodie.

"I have something else I need to do," she said. "And I need your help in order to do it."

"Oh yeah?" The glance he gave her contained marginal interest.

"I need you to get me into the weapons locker." The weapons locker was a room off the garage that was locked with an electronic code. She wasn't sure who all knew the code, but she did know two things—Diego had access to the locker, and she didn't.

"I don't know, chica." His expression had turned wary as he sipped his coffee. "I would need to hear a pretty good reason to do something like that."

"I need a small gun and some duct tape," she told him.

The muscles in her thighs started to shiver from the cold. Much to her surprise, her body knew she was supposed to be running, and she felt twitchy and full of energy. "A nine-millimeter would do. I'm not asking for any bullets, I just want the gun. I'm going to use it as a prop. It's for my morning training session with Raoul."

"No bullets, eh?" He mulled the idea over, black eyebrows raised. "What do you need the duct tape for?"

"Staging."

A grin began to spread across his broad, handsome features. "Okay, chica, I'll bite. I've got some duct tape in the garage. But if I do this for you, I get to see what goes down."

She shrugged. "I don't even know if it's going to work. Just make sure you're in the gym during my training session, and you'll see it."

They walked together to the garage, and Diego keyed in the code for the weapons locker, selected a nine-millimeter and checked it himself to make sure it was unloaded before he handed it to her. She tucked it into the pocket of her hoodie and followed him into the clean, spacious garage.

A few of the attendants, like Angelica and Peter, didn't own a vehicle, but those who did parked their cars in the lot at the side of the main house. The garage building was reserved for Xavier's four vehicles—a gray Jaguar, a silver Mercedes, a black Lexus SUV and an Audi TT. She shook her head as she looked at them. "They're gorgeous."

Diego looked at the cars too. "Yeah, they're nice, but some of the really wealthy patrons have fleets of thirty or more, filled with cars like Bentleys, Rolls-Royces and Lamborghinis. Xavier keeps a modest house by comparison."

She remembered Xavier saying something similar and muttered, "It's more than luxurious enough for me."

He threw her a lopsided grin. "Eh, you don't know any better. You haven't seen those other estates yet."

He sounded like he might be envious, but she wasn't sure of what. If he were envious of anything, she would have thought it would be of the small fortune in horsepower they were contemplating, but instead he sounded almost disparaging of Xavier's lifestyle. He couldn't be envious of the other Vampyre households, could he?

"And you've seen them?"

"Sure, when I've been attending Xavier at some function or other. I'm not always stuck here, babysitting cars and cleaning pools."

The tinge of envy in his voice had been replaced with restlessness or dissatisfaction. Maybe even a little resentment?

Finally, she had encountered something in this place that was less than idyllic. But instead of being reassured at finding a dose of reality, she found it jarring, and she studied him thoughtfully.

The estate had a cloistered atmosphere. While everybody got time off in rotation, they had to make an effort to actually leave, but she had found that she liked the peace and quiet. She enjoyed the surrounding forest and the ocean, and so far, cable TV and access to the Internet had met all of her modest needs. For the first time, though, she realized that others might not be as content with the lifestyle.

Diego walked over to the neat metal shelves set against one wall and rummaged through a few drawers, as he said, "Xavier has a six-bedroom house. Chica, that's almost like living in a double-wide compared to some places I've seen. But hey, we each get our own room, so that's saying something, right?"

He located a roll of duct tape and handed it to her. As she took it, she gave him a level look. "They're nice rooms. We ate grass-fed prime rib last night. I have a thousand dollar Visa card from last month that I can use for fun money, if I want."

He seemed to realize that he had begun to sound churlish, because he backtracked with a quick smile. "Yeah, of course. It's all good. I'm just saying, you might think this is fancy, but it's not as fancy as it can get."

"I hear you." Eager to back out of a conversation that was going nowhere fast, she hefted the roll of duct tape at him as she backed up a few steps. "Thanks for helping out."

"No problem." He gave her an easy smile. "Can't wait to see what you've got planned."

Now that she had gotten what she needed, she dismissed Diego from her thoughts and focused on her next steps. Hurrying to the gym, she was pleased to find it empty, and she studied the various angles and possibilities from the mat where she and Raoul usually worked. Everything had to be planned perfectly. She couldn't afford even a moment's hesitation, and even then, it might not work.

Once she had everything arranged to her liking, she jogged slowly back to the attendants' house, showered and made it downstairs in time for breakfast.

Afterward, she met Raoul in the gym as usual. Others were already there. Scott jumped rope, sweat trickling down the side of his face. Aaron and Brian sparred with each other. Diego had positioned himself over at the selection of free weights, pumping iron without appearing to look once in her direction.

As they walked to their usual mat, Raoul said, "I noticed you didn't open the gates for your morning run."

If she'd ever had any doubt whether or not Raoul was keeping an eye on her through the discreet security cameras that dotted the property, his words banished it.

She shrugged. "I pulled a hamstring and thought it would be better to take the time to stretch this morning."

Aside from one quick, keen glance, he didn't make any further comment. He didn't have to; they both knew that if Xavier were periodically taking blood from her vein, she would have healed from any hamstring injury overnight.

Instead, he gestured to the mat, and they took their accustomed places. Adrenaline spiked her senses as she readied herself, bringing her weight to the balls of her feet, but her adrenaline spiked every morning just before Raoul started to pummel her, and besides, as enhanced as he was, she didn't think he had a Vampyre's sensitivity to pick up on anything unusual.

He paused, studying the placement of her feet. "Are you sure you don't need to do any more stretching first?"

"I'm sure," she told him. She brought her hands up.

"Very well," he said. "On your guard, if you please."

It was how he started every torture session. As soon as she heard the words, she whirled and sprinted toward the punching bag in another corner of the room.

What would he do? Would he chase her? He was so much faster—she would only get a split second from surprise. She lunged as hard and as fast as she could.

Then she heard him, coming after her. Dimly, she was aware of the others, talking and exclaiming.

Three more steps. Two.

His fingers brushed the back of her neck. She twisted away from the touch, dove, rolled and grabbed for the gun that she had duct-taped to the bottom of the punching bag.

Bracing her shoulders against the floor, she brought the gun up just as Raoul reached for her again.

He reared back, his gaze flaring.

She sighted down the gun, aimed at his heart and said, "Bang, bang. You're dead."

Silence fell over the gym. Raoul didn't move. His astonished expression settled into something calmer and much more deadly. "How did you get that?"

She tilted the nose of the barrel away from him and opened up her hand, loosening her grip on the gun. "It's not loaded."

Relaxing, he took it from her and checked the cartridge, then checked the chamber. "That didn't answer my question. You don't have the passcode to the weapons locker."

Out of the corner of her eye, she caught sight of Diego. He shook his head at her, grinning. She rolled to her feet. "Trade secret. Did I surprise you?"

Raoul gave her a speaking look, eyebrows raised. "What do you think?"

She knew he remembered their talk from the day before as well as she did. Training was all well and good, but in real life there weren't any rules to a fight. You either won or you didn't. This time, she had cheated, but she had also won.

She smiled. "I think I just changed the conversation."

Nothing changed about the rest of her day, and yet everything had. At lunch, most of the guys gave her broad grins, and Marc gave her a friendly wink.

As she helped to clear away the dishes, Angelica said to her, "Don't let it go to your head. You got lucky. You still have a lot to learn."

"I know," she told the older woman. "I'm working on it."

Angelica's only reply was a sniff, but her attitude toward Tess seemed to relax a bit too, and Tess thought she might have gotten a step closer to becoming part of the group.

Part of the family, really. The thought made her pause, but it was true. All the attendants really were like a family. They spent their energies working for the common good.

Maybe she had taken only one step out of many, but . . . It felt good. She liked it here. She liked these people.

For the first time since she had arrived, she considered what it might be like to stay long-term and plan for a future here. When she left Las Vegas and Malphas's employ, all she could think about was getting away and trying to find a bolt-hole in which to hide. Long-term plans hadn't factored into her thinking.

What if she did choose to stay?

She couldn't train full-time for the rest of her life, nor would she want to. Eventually she would have to take on other tasks, but maybe Xavier or Raoul could give her meaningful, interesting work. As she had worked to get through school, she had been so ambitious. When she had graduated, she knew Malphas was dangerous even as she took a job working in one of his casinos.

But making money had been her biggest priority. She had been so determined she would never again be as poor as she had been growing up.

She told herself she was being worldly, working for a pariah Djinn. She wanted to be able to afford nice things, to have a fashionable wardrobe and a fat 401(k), to go on vacations to Hawaii and Europe, and retire by the time she was fifty. Now, when she looked back, she could see how foolish and shortsighted she had been.

Here, she might have a place and people to belong to. It was good to be able to go down the path to the beach and walk along the shore, and at night the estate was peaceful, surrounded as it was by forest and wreathed in fresh ocean air. Once she thought she might miss the bright lights of Las Vegas, but she didn't. She liked the quiet and the seclusion of the forest that surrounded the estate.

She might have been a fool once, but she didn't think she was being one twice. She knew there would be much more involved in her position as she finished her training. She had to complete her pact with Xavier, and one of the simplest yet hardest obstacles for her to overcome would be to walk calmly into a room filled with Vampyres.

Also, training so hard, not only in hand to hand but with weapons, might be to cover unlikely eventualities, but those eventualities did occur. Some day shit would get real, and some kind of confrontation would happen. But even that thought didn't deter her. It was good to feel empowered, and to know that because of the work she did now, she might one day have an active hand in shaping critical events.

As the day wore on and evening approached, her good mood dissipated, and she grew more and more nervous.

Honestly, she didn't know how to feel about Xavier after the previous night. She only knew that just because something had changed, maybe even something important, it didn't take away her discomfort at being around him.

But discomfort wasn't the same as the kind of outright panic she had been in when she had first met him. Discomfort was an entirely different animal. She had already taken an important stride forward.

After supper, when it came time for her evening lessons, she walked into the main house to the formal dining area, where she found Xavier standing at one of the windows, looking out over the lawn.

Reflexively, her gaze flew to the outside scene framed by the tall window. The last of the daylight covered the foliage and emerald lawn in a transparent mantle of heavy gold, but the angle of the sunlight came nowhere near the window where he stood.

He wore black slacks, a white shirt and a gray jacket, and his dark hair was pulled neatly away from his quiet, reflective face. His shirt was open at the neck and he wore no tie. She was beginning to recognize that this was his casual attire, yet he achieved a certain elegance, due to his erect carriage and natural poise more than anything he chose to wear. She suspected he would embody that same kind of elegance even if he wore jeans and a T-shirt.

As she paused on the doorstep, he turned to walk toward her, fixing his intelligent, keen gaze on her face. She felt her damn heart rate speed up again, and what little poise she had fell apart completely.

She bolted into the room. "Hi, I hope I'm not late. Beautiful evening outside, huh? Not that you're able to go out to enjoy any of it, at least until the sun disappears—but maybe I'm not supposed to mention something like that. You know, it does seem a little like pointing out someone's pimples. . . ."

He seemed to move at a casual, unhurried pace, yet somehow he appeared directly in front of her, which brought her to an abrupt halt. Amusement tilted the corners of his eyes. "Trust me when I say this—that is not at all how you should enter a room. Ever."

"I just thought I might be late," she said stupidly, looking up into his smiling gaze. His presence was so large and intense, she was surprised to discover that he was only a few inches taller than she.

He put one slim, strong hand on her arm and gently turned her around. "Enter the room once again, and this time, do so slowly, if you please."

Ah, that phrase again. It would be her nemesis yet.

Intensely conscious of his touch, she walked back to the door. To her own frustration, she noticed her all too human reactions were out of control again. Her breathing accelerated, along with her heartbeat, and a fine tremor shivered through her hands.

Still, it wasn't quite from panic. Not quite from terror. She knew he wouldn't hurt her. She had no idea why she was reacting so strongly to him, and she had no words to describe it. He simply approached, and all her systems went haywire.

Baffled at herself, she plunged into talk again. "You should know, I'm beginning to develop a conditioned reaction to the phrase 'if you please.'"

"Are you?" The Vampyre quirked an eyebrow as he kept a smooth pace beside her. "And why is that?"

"Raoul says it all the time, usually just before he slams me to the ground or throws me into a wall." Reaching the doorway, she used it as an excuse to pull away from his hand as she turned to face him again.

He frowned, his lips drew tight and the small scar at the side of his mouth whitened. Her gaze lingered on it. She had seen that scar whiten once before. It was a tiny tell, and she wasn't sure what it meant, except that it revealed some kind of deeper emotion.

He said, "I noticed you were moving rather stiffly yesterday evening."

She knew where his thoughts went, and she met his gray-green gaze. "It's all right. I'm handling it."

He shook his head. "You should not have to deal with pain, or handle any discomfort."

The way he said it made her pause as her perception underwent another small but irrevocable shift. If Xavier refused to take advantage of his human attendants during a blood offering, then the act of the blood offering itself was all for their benefit, not for his. Theoretically, Raoul could draw blood from everyone, and Xavier could get his needs met quite well from a distance.

So he didn't say what he had because he needed or wanted the blood offering. He said it out of concern for her well-being.

Oh hell, he was going to make her give up the whole concept of "monster" entirely, wasn't he?

"I understand," she said softly. "And I'm on my journey

toward making that choice. But for now, do you know what I did this morning?"

He studied her. "Raoul told me what happened in the gym. You surprised him."

"Yes." She pointed to her own chest. "I did that. Nobody enhanced me, or gave me special powers. I thought the plan up, and I executed it. And because I've worked my ass off these last six weeks, I was fast enough to pull it off. Barely, but I did, and that feels nice. I know I'm not where I need to be yet, but for now I feel pretty good about where I'm at."

His lean jaw angled out slightly, but he refrained from saying anything further. Instead, he stood back. "Fair enough. Now, please go down the hall and come back in. Show me that you know how to walk, not bolt like a runaway horse."

She sighed but complied. As she walked into the room again, she found that he had moved some distance away. When she paused, he walked toward her, moving with his characteristic seamless, balletic grace. She watched warily as he gave her a slight bow, inclined his head and offered his arm.

"Good evening. May I escort you into dinner?"

She squinted one eye at him. "I'm supposed to be your attendant, not a guest. Attendants are supposed to be invisible and anticipate your every need, not be escorted in to dinner."

He sighed. "Well, I do not see any evidence of you anticipating my every need at the moment."

"Didn't you ask me to walk out and come back in?" she said. "And didn't I do it?"

He looked at her in exasperation. "For the love of God, *querida*, do not argue over every little thing. Just go along with this."

"I'm sorry," she said, stung. Gingerly she put her hand into the crook of his elbow, feeling the bulk of hard muscle move underneath the cloth of his jacket like a panther's muscles shifting underneath its fur.

He led her around the table, smoothly matching his longer stride to hers. "If you were attending me at a function, what would you do?"

"How many attendants do you have with you?"

They reached where one of two formal dinner settings had been laid, and she waited while he pulled out the chair for her, then sat.

He said, "For this hypothetical scenario, I have just you in attendance."

"Then I would keep pace a few steps behind you until we reached the room." She watched him walk to the place setting on the opposite side of the table and sit. "After you sat down, I would take the position just behind your chair, so I could serve you wine or whatever else you might need. If this was a function without a banquet table, where people stood to mingle, I would find a place against a wall to stand and watch until I'm needed."

"Very good." With a flick of his long fingers, he indicated the place setting in front of her. "Now, can you explain this to me?"

She barely refrained from rolling her eyes, because she knew he would not appreciate it. Reaching for patience, she told him, "Of course I can. This is what Raoul has been teaching me for the last month and a half."

"Then you should have no trouble demonstrating that knowledge to me, should you?" He sounded as if he might be reaching for patience too, although for the life of her she couldn't understand why.

A sigh escaped her before she could stop it. "Raoul and I have gone through table manners, a history of Vampyre customs, and what an attendant should and should not do for a wide variety of events. I just don't understand why you want to focus on this now, when I know all of it already."

"Do you, indeed?" he said. His diction seemed to become even more perfect. She wondered if that might be some kind of warning sign, as he cocked his head, his mouth held at a slant. "Then perhaps you can kindly explain how this place setting would differ should an Elf be present."

Her gaze fell to the place setting. The outside spoon was very slightly out of alignment, and she took her time adjusting it. Finally she had to make the grudging admission. "We haven't talked about Elven dining yet."

"I see." His gray-green gaze glittered as he looked at her. "What about Dark Fae formal dining customs?"

She rubbed her chin, her lips pursed. Then she shook her head.

"The Light Fae?"

"No," she muttered.

"What about the Demonkind? I do not refer to the Djinn, who naturally do not need to eat and will adapt to the predominant social custom of the occasion, but to the other Demonkind who may be at table."

Oh, for crying out loud. This was like some kind of modern version of *My Fair Lady*.

Only with Vampyres.

She made herself breathe evenly for a few moments. "You've made your point."

"Have I? How fortuitous." As he lounged back in his chair, all the subtle signs of aggravation disappeared. "Then perhaps we should get back to the task at hand, so that I can determine what you *have* learned before going on to teach you what you haven't."

Okay, that went too far. One small part of her mind— the wary part, the sensible part—started to whisper, *Don't say it, don't say it. . . .*

But the rest of her was too exasperated to listen. She flung out her hands and opened her eyes wide. "Who says 'fortuitous' these days?"

He just looked at her. The slanted angle of his mouth had returned, as well as the slight snap to his diction. "Apparently, I do. Now, if you are quite through, it might behoove you to remember that a successful attendant is nowhere near this argumentative with her patron."

The devil took hold of her tongue. There was no other explanation for it.

"Behoove," she said.

The angle of his mouth leveled out, and his voice turned exceedingly, dangerously soft. "Yes. *Behoove.*"

She opened her mouth. Shut it. Opened it again. *Don't say it. . . .*

Gray-green eyes narrowed, daring her to cross the line.

Then the rest of what he had said sank in.

A successful attendant. Meaning, of course, that she wasn't a successful one. She wasn't anywhere near it. She wouldn't let him bite her, and she couldn't keep her mouth shut.

Was this what he had meant when he had said that some people couldn't settle into the lifestyle of attendant, even when they wanted to?

Discouragement sagged her shoulders. With a groan, she bent her head and put her face in her hands. "I'm sorry. I'm failing completely at this, aren't I?"

≈ TEN ≈

Xavier covered his mouth with one hand as he regarded Tess's dejected figure. "I don't know that I would quite say you're failing *completely*."

"Thanks," she said, her voice muffled. "I find those words *so* encouraging."

Some undefined impulse brought him out of his chair. He walked around to her and when he reached her side, he leaned back against the table, crossed his arms and looked down at an angle at her bent head. "Perhaps we should take a moment to recall a frightened young woman I met at the Vampyre's Ball. Do you remember her?"

Her head lifted, and she looked up at him.

Those large, lovely dark eyes of hers were surrounded by shadows. She looked tired and worried. He smiled. "That young woman could not run for an hour, nor could she hit nine marks out of ten when shooting a gun. And she certainly could not have surprised Raoul so thoroughly, could she?"

Her gaze fell, and she pretended to straighten the spoon again. "Probably not."

Nor would that young woman have tested his patience so thoroughly or endured having him in such close proximity, but he decided not to push his luck by mentioning that.

Instead, he held out one hand to her, palm up. "I think we are through with etiquette for the evening. Now we will begin with the dancing lessons."

Her gaze focused on his outstretched hand. She hesitated, and for a moment he thought she would not take it. Then she put her hand in his, her gesture uncertain.

He didn't give her time to reconsider. Instead, he curled his fingers strongly around hers and tugged. Following his prompt, she rose to her feet. He tucked her hand into the crook of his arm and firmly led her away, toward the ballroom.

While they had talked—and argued—the sunlight had faded enough so that he could enter the ballroom. He turned on the lights then led her into the room, pausing only to look at her curiously as her hand tightened and she dragged at his arm.

Her sharp gaze darted from the windows to the gleaming expanse of the floor, and he realized what she was doing. She was making sure it was safe enough for him to enter.

Something startled inside him warmed. Not only did she pay attention to the details in her immediate environment, also she had good protective instincts.

"It's safe," he said. "But thank you."

The glance she gave him was as uncertain as everything else she had done that evening, but her grip on his arm relaxed, and they walked forward together until they stood in the middle of the empty, polished floor.

Earlier, he had set a portable stereo on the piano, already loaded with a CD filled with waltz music. He turned to face her, and while he was not quite able to ignore how her heart sped up when they came face-to-face, at least her scent didn't fill with such overwhelming fear.

"The waltz is a simple and elegant dance," he said. "And the music is beautiful. It's in triple meter."

"I'm not musical," she told him, looking down at their feet. "I don't know what that means."

"Don't look at your feet. Nobody looks at their feet when they dance. Look at me." He paused until her head lifted, and her wary gaze met his. "Triple meter simply means three beats to a measure. One-two-three, one-two-three. That's the rhythm of the dance. Spatially, visualize a box. We will be stepping around the corners of the box together. You move backward, while I move forward."

The angle of her head acquired a skeptical slant. "Why can't you move backward, and I move forward?"

Trust Tess to ask that question. He bit back another smile. "Convention. I'm the male, and you're the female. That means I lead and you follow, which is good for you, since I already know the dance."

"Well, you know how that old saying goes," she said.

"What saying is that?"

A spark of humor entered her gaze. "Ginger Rogers did the same thing Fred Astaire did, only backward and in high heels."

He had met Fred Astaire and Ginger Rogers once in 1934, when they had come to Evenfall to dance for the Masque at winter solstice. He chuckled. "Very true. I'll keep the pace and guide you around the corners of the box, like thus."

As she watched, he stepped back and positioned his arms as if he held a woman, one hand curved around his invisible partner's back and the other pretending to clasp her hand. Then he glided through the steps as he watched Tess.

Her eyes widened, and he stopped. "What is it?"

Color tinged her skin, along the proud curves of her high cheekbones. "You have this way of moving."

"What way is that?" He walked back toward her with a frown, disquieted again.

When he had invited her, he truly had not anticipated how much she might change. The strong angles of her face highlighted the shape of her eyes and the sensual curve of her lips.

She had become too striking. That meant more eyes would fall upon her and linger, more people would remember her, and that meant, in some situations, she might be in more danger.

He would have to consider the possible ramifications of that, another time. For now, he set the issue aside and concentrated on her.

She lifted her shoulders in an awkward shrug, and her gaze fell away. "You move with such grace and self-assurance all of the time. I'll never be able to match that."

"Nonsense," he said. "Not only have I been dancing for a very long time, but I was also engaged in fencing lessons and swordplay from the time I was a young child. I have a lot of experience, and you haven't. You will learn soon enough."

She shook her head and gave him a wry look. "Believe me, the way you move takes a lot more than just experience, no matter how many decades—or centuries—you have under your belt. Just now you looked as if you were floating."

If that had come from anyone but Tess, he would have been sure that was a compliment. As it was, he had no idea how to respond.

Instead of speaking, he dug in his pocket to pull out the remote for the portable stereo and keyed on the music, and the lovely, timeless strains of Chopin's *Grande Valse Brillante* swelled to fill the room.

A sense of peace and contentment filled him. He loved music, and he loved to dance. Teaching Tess to waltz was going to be a pleasure.

A half an hour later, he had revised his opinion drastically, as she stepped on his foot again. Instantly, they both stopped moving and glared at each other.

"Young lady, you are not an elephant," he told her. "Kindly refrain from imitating one."

"I'm sorry!" she said for the fifth time.

Or perhaps it was the sixth. He wasn't sure; he had lost count. It was certainly often enough that she had begun to say it through gritted teeth.

He forced himself to take a breath. While he might not need to breathe anymore, the action seemed to help him reach for patience. "Not to worry. We'll keep doing it until we get it right."

Rubbing the back of her head, she muttered something about dancing with the stars and Vampyres.

He cocked his head. "What was that? I didn't quite understand you."

"I—never mind." She squared her shoulders. "Are we going again?"

"Of course." He opened up his arms, and she stepped into them.

While teaching her to dance had turned into much more of a chore than he had anticipated, this one thing was purest pleasure: she came readily to him, and she no longer remembered to flinch from his touch.

Of course, he did not clasp her too tightly, but instead held her precisely at the correct distance. And her heart rate still sped up every time he looked at her, or reached out to touch her slender, muscular body. But mostly, he thought, her fear seemed to have subsided, and even though she seemed to have the dancing ability of a koala bear, for that reason alone, he counted the waltzing lessons a success.

They assumed the proper dancing posture, hands clasped. His right hand cupped the strong, graceful curve of her shoulder blade. She rested the fingertips of her left hand along the shoulder seam of his jacket.

He met her gaze as they waited for the right beat in the music. Then he nodded to her, and as they began to move, she stepped forward instead of back and trod on his foot again.

"*Madre de Dios*," he said. He said a few other choice things too. He hadn't realized that he had slipped into speaking Spanish until she started to snort and shudder. He stopped to glare at her. "What?"

"You sound like Ricky Ricardo," she told him. Her voice quivered, and so did her beautiful lips.

When he looked at her more closely, he realized she was laughing, and trying to muffle it. "Who is this Ricardo?"

"From *I Love Lucy*," she said. Then, when he still looked blank, she prompted, "The classic TV sitcom?"

"I do not watch TV," he said. Belatedly, a vague image of a redheaded comedienne came to mind. Once, she had been famous enough that her image had dominated the media. He dismissed it.

"Not ever?"

He shrugged. "I do keep an eye on CNN, MSNBC and other news channels."

"That's not real TV," she told him. She glanced down at their feet again as she muttered under her breath, "Tonight is a lot like *I Love Lucy*. Only with Vampyres. Naturally."

He decided to ignore that. "This conversation has turned irrelevant. You keep trying to lead, and you can't."

"It's a natural instinct to step forward, not backward," she pointed out.

"While I understand that, I have every faith you can overcome it and stop trampling your partner's feet." He paused and looked at her more closely.

Dark circles had appeared in the delicate skin underneath her eyes. If she had looked tired before, now she looked exhausted and entirely out of sorts. As he studied her expression, he realized that while his "day" had begun shortly before sunset, she had been engaged in some kind of training exercise since early that morning.

Contrition hit. "Tess, I apologize. We have been working you too hard."

Immediately her back straightened as she bristled. "I'm fine. Let's go again."

"I think not. Thank you for your time. We're finished for tonight." He inclined his head to her and turned away.

"Please." Slender fingers caught at his sleeve. "I want to try one more time. "

He stilled and looked down at her hand. It was an imprudent gesture, of course, and when he had been a young man, it would never have been permitted. One did not lay hands upon a member of the nobility without permission.

But those early days of his youth were centuries gone. Now so many humans were brash and heedless. Strange vulgarities such as "yo mama" and "motherfucker" were actually considered legitimate interactions, along with backslapping, head rubbing, fist-bumping, hugs and other importunities.

He had learned to tolerate without flinching most minor encroachments upon his person, and if anyone else had so heedlessly laid a hand on him, he wouldn't have given it more than a passing thought.

Except, this was Tess who had voluntarily laid a hand on him. Tess, who, when they had first met, had difficulty remaining in the same room as him. Just now she had reached out so naturally, so thoughtlessly.

A quick, bright reaction flared. Triumph, perhaps, along with pleasure. He schooled his expression to conceal it as he turned back to her, covering her hand with his. "Very well, one more time, but then we're through. You need to rest, and I have other matters to attend to."

Her forehead crinkled. "We were going to start meditating so I could learn some biofeedback techniques."

Some tense, buried emotion lay underneath her words, and he studied her more closely. She was anxious, yet struggling to hide it. Frowning, he thought back over their conversation that evening. It had not exactly gone smoothly. She had tried his patience, and had evidenced her own frustration and discouragement more than once.

Then he remembered what she had said about Raoul slamming her to the ground or throwing her into the wall, and his frown deepened. If his suspicion was correct, the other man had been trying to discourage her from staying. It appeared they might have been hard on her in more ways than one.

"There's no harm in starting the meditation tomorrow evening," he said gently. "We're undertaking a journey, not running a race. Overall, you've been working quite hard and doing a very good job. I'm pleased with the progress you've made."

Her tired eyes brightened. "Really? You're not just saying that?"

He shook his head. "I'm not just saying that."

"Thank you."

"You're welcome." He inclined his head. "And now to try this one more time. Are you ready?"

"Yes."

They took the waltz position, which was another thing she did very well. She held her head high, shoulders back. He pulled out the stereo remote and keyed the music to start, then dropped the remote back into his jacket pocket and took her hand.

They waited, and as the first strains of music filled the ballroom, he met her gaze and mouthed, *Backward.*

She took a deep breath, nodded and they stepped into the waltz together.

For a full minute and a half they achieved a thing of beauty. Her slender body moved lightly and gracefully through the steps, at one with his. Her expression lit with excitement, and he smiled to see it.

Then she stepped on his foot.

He stopped immediately, and before the dismay in her eyes could dampen her expression, he said, "Well done!"

She had opened her mouth, he knew, to apologize, and his words caught her off guard. "You don't really mean that." Her voice wavered upward at the end, turning it into a hopeful question.

"Of course I do. I think that time you got a chance to see how the waltz really feels, which will make tomorrow's lesson go more easily. And I never say anything I don't mean." He took one of her hands and bowed over it. The courtly gesture was decidedly out of date, but it felt good to indulge the impulse. "If I were you, I would take the compliment and call it a win."

Still bent over her hand, he tilted his head to glance up at her and caught her wry smile. "If you insist."

"I will tell Raoul that your presence will not be required until lunchtime," he told her as he straightened. "Enjoy your morning off. You've earned it."

Her smile widened into real pleasure. "Thank you."

"*De nada*. Good night."

"Good night."

After watching her step out of the ballroom, he turned off the stereo and the lights. Whistling Strauss's *Blue Danube* underneath his breath, he went to look for Raoul.

He found the other man in the gym, immersed in paperwork in his office. When he appeared in the doorway, Raoul looked up from his work. "How did it go?"

Fortuitous. Behoove.

A ripple of laughter waltzed silently through his soul. He admitted, "There were some frustrations."

Raoul barked out a laugh. "That bad?"

"Actually, we ended the evening on a positive note." Crossing his arms, he leaned against the doorway. "I've given her the morning off. We need to adjust her schedule. We can't expect her to start at dawn while also working late into the night."

Raoul lounged back in his seat, swiveling to face him. "Of course. I should have thought of that already. It'll be no problem to begin a few hours later."

Xavier paused as he regarded the other man. Raoul had been with him for a long time, and they knew each other well. "I want you to stop trying to drive her away."

Raoul gave him a sour look. "Did she complain?"

"No, she didn't. She made a joke about it, but I could still read the subtext."

"Well, for what it's worth, I'd already decided to stop this morning after she ambushed me." Raoul twirled a pen between his fingers. "She wants to take things to the next level, and I'm going to oblige."

"Good. That's good." He nodded absently as his thoughts turned in another direction. "You're the one who orders supplies for everyone, so you must know what size clothes she wears, yes?"

"Of course." The other man's expression turned guarded. "Why do you ask?"

He turned decisive. "I want you to order a ball gown for her."

Raoul's eyebrows took a slow, incredulous hike up his forehead. He repeated, "Order a ball gown."

"Yes, one with a long, full skirt. Make it a dark blue one." Tess would look good in dark blue. He remembered the quip she made about Ginger Rogers and Fred Astaire, and added, "Don't forget to order high heels either."

Tossing his pen onto the desk, Raoul rose to his feet and strode over to him, enunciating, "What. Are. You. Doing?"

"What do you think I'm doing?" Xavier's eyes narrowed at the other man's attitude. "I'm teaching her to dance."

"She doesn't need a dress to learn how to dance!"

He shook his head. "Raoul, nobody waltzes in exercise pants."

She needed to learn how to deal with the long skirts and high heels, along with everything else, should the occasion call for it. Oh, lord. He braced himself at the thought.

Raoul stuck a finger under his collar. "It was one time. In the last forty years, as far as I know, an attendant has been asked to dance with a guest one time, and yet now you're squandering hours and hours of *your* time to make sure that Tess knows how to waltz." He paused to let the sarcasm in the room marinate for a few seconds, then added, "Should the subject ever come up in her lifetime."

Xavier focused on the opposite wall. "I don't see that there's an issue."

"I know what you're doing," Raoul said.

"Do you? Please do enlighten me." He was very interested

to hear what the other man had to say, because he didn't have a clue what he was doing.

"You're beginning to invest time and trouble in her—a ball gown, Xavier. Really? Soon you'll grow attached, and your protective instincts will kick in. Then you'll never be able to send her out on assignment." Raoul spread both hands wide. "Which is assuming we get that far, and frankly, right now, that's a bit of a stretch, since she hasn't made the most basic of commitments to you yet. And that means all of this will have been for nothing."

Patiently, Xavier heard him out. When Raoul paused to take a breath, he said calmly, "I disagree with you on several counts."

Raoul glared at him. "Such as?"

"You're assuming an end goal that has never been decided upon. Yes, I saw potential in her, but I never committed to sending her out on any assignments."

Pausing, Xavier considered again how her appearance had changed, and how memorable she had become, and the same thread of disquiet rippled over him again. He had good instincts. They had been honed by personal disaster and tragedy, and he had no intention of ignoring them now.

He continued thoughtfully, "There are any number of factors that may keep me from sending her on assignment, including the fact that she came to me very publicly through the Vampyre's Ball."

"Many people ask for interviews, and it never goes anywhere," Raoul pointed out. It was not for the first time, since they had begun to discuss Tess's potential merits and shortcomings.

"That may be so, but *I* don't ask for many interviews at the Ball, and there are those who take note of every move I make," he said. "And even if I did offer her the chance, we don't know that she would accept. The only thing I ever offered her—and she accepted—was the chance to become an attendant. That's all we have the right to expect, and right now she's showing signs of becoming an excellent one."

The other man frowned. "Fair enough."

He met Raoul's gaze. "I also disagree with what you said about her not having made the most basic commitment, because I think she has. She's done everything you've asked, and she's done everything I've asked as well, and we've not been easy on her. She's taken every bruise and every fall without complaint, while you've worked her to the bone."

"True, but she hasn't made a direct blood offering, has she?"

"No, but I like the fact that she hasn't." Changing position as he leaned back, he faced the opposite side of the doorway. "I like that it's difficult for her, because it will have significance when she does it. You know as well as I do that most of the humans at the Vampyre's Ball would have given a blood offering without a second's hesitation to any Vampyre who asked for it, while the act itself would reveal nothing about their abilities, character, or their capacity for loyalty. As a ritual, it's become outdated and meaningless." He murmured, almost to himself, "And it shouldn't be."

Raoul heaved a sigh. "I hate it when you're right."

One corner of his mouth lifted in a smile. "That is your cross to bear, since I am right so often."

"Yes, well . . ." Raoul turned back to his desk and sat down. "And none of that pertains to teaching her how to waltz, but fine, I'll order a ball gown for her to practice in. A cheap one."

He contemplated the toe of one shoe. "A blue one."

"A cheap, blue one," said Raoul, as he scribbled it on a Post-it note. "Along with cheap high heels."

He heaved a sigh. "Raoul, don't do that to her feet. You do want her to be able to run in the mornings, don't you?"

"Fine." Raoul crossed out the Post-it note with strong, dark lines and wrote another one. "Good high heels. Are you satisfied now?"

He smiled. "I am, thank you. Have you scheduled meetings for me this evening?"

"Yes, the first one, Marc, will be in to see you at midnight, if that's okay? I've scheduled one meeting per hour, for each of the five men."

"That sounds perfect."

"Do you know where you'll send Marc? I think he would do well with a challenge."

"I thought he could keep an eye on either Justine or Darius," he said. Unlike Tess, one huge advantage of all five men was that they had been recruited in secrecy. That widened his choices considerably in choosing how to use their services. "Let me know who you would recommend to send to the other. I want an extra pair of eyes on both of them right now."

"That assignment might be too weighty for Scott," said Raoul, tapping his pen against his lips as he thought. "I'd like to see him get an assignment that builds on his confidence. Right now, I'd have to pick Brian."

"Good enough."

He left Raoul's office and the gym, and strolled back to the main house. The night was sparkling clear, with thousands of stars sprayed along the wide, dark expanse of sky like crystals sewn on velvet.

Tess would look good in a dress made of black velvet too.

He glanced at the attendants' house. Her room was in darkness. Detouring from the path to the main house, he walked over to the attendants' house, listening carefully to filter out all of the sounds made by the others.

She was in her room, and her breathing had turned deep and even. He imagined how she looked. Did she wear a nightshirt, or did she sleep nude? When he had entered her bedroom before, she had worn a dark red shirt that had come to the tops of her thighs.

The bedcovers would drape around her slender form in a gentle canopy. Her hair would spill onto the pillow like black silk, and the lines of her angular face would be relaxed and peaceful.

He would like to see her look peaceful. Unguarded.

But it was none of his business how she looked when she was alone, asleep in bed. Despite all his clever arguments, Raoul had the right of it. He was in danger of growing too attached.

Turning, he made his way back to his own silent house.

⇒ ELEVEN ⇐

Late the next morning, after everyone else had started work and Tess relished the quiet of an empty house, she made a pot of coffee and sat down to read through several newspapers.

Even though print newspapers were dead, apparently Xavier's household hadn't gotten the memo. Daily, twenty or more newspapers from all over the world were delivered to the estate, including all major human news outlets and several Elder Races newsletters and papers that she had never heard of before she had come to work for Xavier.

One of her duties was to keep abreast of current events, but she didn't mind doing it. She wanted to read all the news she could get her hands on, and the papers saved her the trouble of trying to figure out how to glean information from the Internet without leaving any kind of discernible trail.

Ten minutes later, she rested her elbows on the dining table, propped her forehead in her hands and stared in horror down at the *Boston Herald* spread out before her.

U.S. SENATOR'S SON DIES

Eathan Jackson, twenty-one-year-old son of Massachusetts senator Paul Jackson (R.), died off the coast of Florida Saturday afternoon in what officials are calling a "freak boating accident." A senior undergraduate at Harvard, the younger Jackson was taking a long weekend break with his girlfriend and two other friends. The four had gone sailing on an otherwise cloudless day, when a sudden squall capsized their boat.

Jackson's girlfriend and friends were able to employ an inflatable emergency dinghy until help arrived, while Jackson disappeared from sight. His body was discovered several hours later. . . .

Pain filled Tess's chest like a gigantic bruise. As tears pricked the back of her eyes, she rubbed her face and thought, Freak squall, my ass.

Eathan had been a spoiled, ungrateful boy who had carried around a sense of entitlement wherever he went, but he hadn't deserved to be killed for it. She had always hoped there was something finer in him that would emerge as he matured.

Now he wouldn't have the chance. He was dead, and she knew in her bones that Malphas had killed him.

It had been an entirely unnecessary murder. While the senior Jackson was a politician of some repute and sat on several Senate committees, Eathan hadn't known any state secrets or carried any kind of deadly, magical Power.

He wasn't a player, in any sense of the word. He hadn't even finished college.

Killing him had been an act of pure, deadly spite.

All the tentative hopes and dreams she had begun to nurture about building a new life vanished like so many illusions. Malphas hadn't forgotten or let go of anything. He simply hadn't gotten around to finding her. Yet.

But he would, and when he did, he would be so much more spiteful toward her than he had been toward Eathan. Eathan had just been a mark that got away. She had actually worked for Malphas, and she had owed him a certain amount of loyalty.

It wouldn't matter that she had never promised to stand idly by and watch while he trapped people into making crippling gambling debts just so that he could enslave them. She had taken away something he wanted, and he was never going to let that go.

Wiping her eyes, she noticed the time. She was late for her session with Raoul. She tried to care, but after so many weeks of trying so hard, she felt as if something had broken inside.

Still, if she didn't show up, he would come looking for her. Forcing herself to move, she pushed upright and cleaned the table, bound her overlong hair back with a rubber band and got to work.

When she entered the gym, Raoul was waiting for her. He said, "You're late."

"I know," she said. "I'm sorry."

She tried to inject something that sounded like genuine emotion into her voice but knew she had failed from the look on his face.

"What's wrong? Didn't you get enough rest?"

She shook her head. "I'm fine."

His gaze was too keen and made her uncomfortable. "Are you sure? Xavier pointed out we've been pushing you too hard, and he's right. That doesn't mean I'm going to stop pushing you, but you can say if something gets to be too much."

Her gaze fell to the training mat. It was the wrong time for him to show her kindness. She would not cry. She wouldn't.

Forcing words to come steadily out of her tight throat, she admitted, "I'm having an off day, but it will help to focus on something."

"Very well." He started to stroll in a circle around her, not to engage, she could tell, but simply to move. "Yesterday, you said you wanted to change the conversation. Why?"

Other than following him with her gaze when he was in

sight, she didn't bother to move. After all, he hadn't told her to be on guard, or said "if you please."

Thinking of Eathan, she replied, "Because I don't want to just run away my whole life. Sometimes you need to stand and fight."

"Agreed." He came to stand in front of her. "As long as you remember, in most cases you really should fight to run away. Even when you complete the blood offering—and your speed, healing and strength have become enhanced— the reality is, at your best, your abilities will always be at the level of a newly turned Vampyre or a younger Elf. Many Elder Races creatures will still be faster and stronger than you."

She noticed Raoul said "when" and not "if" she completed the blood offering. He was beginning to believe in her. Seemed like rotten timing, all the way around. She clenched her fists and bit the inside of her lip until it bled.

"They won't necessarily be smarter," she said through her teeth. "Or as well trained."

"That's what I can give you," he said, smiling. "I'll teach you weak points for each race, along with kill spots. Eventually we'll get members of each race in for practice bouts. Take trolls, for an example. If a troll manages to get ahold of you and he's intent on killing you, you're dead. But even as an unenhanced human, you move so much faster than trolls do, you should be able to get away— unless they set a trap. They can be cunning like that, so you have to watch out for it."

As he talked, gradually she calmed enough to be able to focus. "What is a troll's kill spot? Do they have one?"

"Unless you have high-density explosives, they have just one—their eyes. Everything else about them is as hard as granite. A high-density explosive can stun one and dam- age their joints enough so that you can hack one apart with an axe, but that's a massively slow, cruel and inefficient way to kill one." He pointed to one of his eyes. "But if you aim for the eye, you can hit their brain. That's quick and gets the job done."

She gave him a leery look. He spoke with crisp dispassion, and as matter-of-factly as if he had dispatched a troll before. With his intimidating array of fighting skills, Raoul would have been a terrific assassin.

Maybe he had been one, once.

Except . . . He had said he'd worked for Xavier for forty-eight years, and he was now seventy-five. That meant he had come to Xavier when he was a young man of twenty-seven. Back then, he wouldn't have been nearly as proficient, which meant he had to have learned a lot of his skills while working for Xavier.

Once the thoughts had wormed their way into her head, they wouldn't leave. Tucking them away to consider at another time, she said, "Realistically, I'm not going to come up against any fighting trolls, am I?"

"You never know, but probably not." He shrugged. "Usually they're pretty peaceful. I'm just using them as an example. For the most part, we're going to concentrate on creatures that you'll see most often, because those are the ones you would be most likely to engage."

She cocked her head. "Like Vampyres?"

He smiled. "Like Vampyres. They are famously dangerous, but they also have quite a few vulnerabilities, such as they can't enter your house without your permission. That doesn't apply to public places, like hotels or hotel rooms. It also doesn't apply to any rooms you may occupy when you're a guest in someone else's home, so you need to know what your boundaries are and what's safe."

"So if I'm a guest in a Vampyre's house, they can get to me wherever I am," she said.

"Yes, or if you're a guest in someone's home, and they've already given permission to a Vampyre to enter, you can't revoke it. The older, more Powerful ones can mesmerize with their eyes or their voice, but that's one of the things a blood offering will help to protect you from. When you develop that connection with Xavier, another Vampyre won't be able to mesmerize you. Of course, you can kill a Vampyre with direct sunlight, but a total SPF sunblock or a well-made cloak will usually buy them enough time to find shelter. Any Vampyre with a grain of sense buys clothes made of UPF 50+ material that will block up to 98 percent of UV rays."

"What about UV lamps?"

"Don't bother, unless you want to piss one off. They cause burns and pain, but they're not strong enough to incapacitate." He made a slicing motion across his throat with one finger. "Decapitation works, and a penetrating blow to the heart, like a sword thrust. Brain damage also works, but it's got to be severe enough to be lethal. In other words, like the troll, you can shoot a Vampyre in the eye, and as long as the shot goes directly through the brain, it will kill them."

She rubbed the back of her neck. "I feel funny talking about this, you know."

His lean face creased as he laughed. "None of this is privileged information. It's not as though I'm imparting state secrets."

The phrase caused her mind to wing back to earlier that morning, when she had discovered Eathan's death, and she winced. But now was not the time to focus on that either, so she forced herself to concentrate on the subject at hand. "When Xavier interviewed me at the Vampyre's Ball, he asked if I used drugs."

"That's a whole other subject," he told her.

She shrugged. "It sounded like it could do some damage."

"Yes, but it tends to happen over a period of time. Luckily, most often, the problem can be caught before any damage gets too severe. When it doesn't get stopped in time . . ." He shook his head. "The results are ugly."

As she listened, she tucked her fingers into the pockets of her pants and hunched her shoulders. "How do you mean?"

"If Vampyres feed regularly on blood that has been tainted with hard drugs, it warps them and turns them bestial. Given enough exposure, the damage becomes permanent." He turned to the door. "I can see we're not going to get to any physical training today. Come on, let's walk outside while we talk."

She followed him out into the sunshine. "But like you said, most of the time the damage can be stopped before it turns permanent, so it isn't really a danger, is it?"

"That's true, but the trick is, the Vampyre has to want to stop it." He led her to the path that went down to the beach. While a steady breeze blew off the water, the day was sunny and warm, and he turned his tanned face up with evident enjoyment to the sun's strong, bright rays. "People persist in believing that becoming a Vampyre will solve all their problems, and it simply isn't true. Vampyrism isn't a panacea. Who you are as a person is who you will be as a Vampyre."

"I don't understand," she said as she fell into step beside him.

They walked along the beach, while the wild cry of seagulls sounded from overhead. "If you're an alcoholic when you're a human, you'll still be an alcoholic when you're a Vampyre," Raoul told her. "You still have the issues that drove you to drink in the first place, only drinking alcohol itself won't have any effect on you."

"I've heard of that." She squinted against the bright sunlight. "Vampyres can't get drunk from alcohol they consume directly, right?"

"Correct. Just as they can't get nutrition from consuming food. They need blood to carry the nutrients, or the alcohol, in such a way that their systems will absorb it."

"So they can get drunk if they feed from inebriated humans?"

"Yes, they can, and the same principle applies to drug addiction. If you're an addict as a human, you'll be an addict as a Vampyre. Getting turned doesn't erase personality problems. It only wipes out physical diseases. But once a drug addict become a Vampyre, he can't feel the effect from taking drugs directly."

"Oh, wow." She thought of the possible consequences and shuddered.

"As I said, it can be ugly. It's against Nightkind law to turn a drug addict, but it still happens. There's a whole subculture of addicted Vampyres that infest the tunnels that run underneath San Francisco. Every once in a while, Julian gathers enough resources to burn them out, but either they know of places to hide that his forces can't reach, or the problem simply continues to multiply. Addicted Vampyres pay or prey on drug-addicted humans. Sometimes they supply the drugs, or turn the humans as payment, or if the Vampyre has become too bestial, they might tear them apart. It's a twisted, feral place underneath the city." He waved a hand. "But enough about that. There's one more way to kill a Vampyre. Have you ever heard of brodifacoum?"

She looked sidelong at him. "No, should I have?"

He shrugged. "If you're an environmentalist you might have come across the term. Brodifacoum is a highly lethal anticoagulant poison that's been used in a number of pesticides."

"Anticoagulant," she said.

He met her gaze. "A derivative of brodifacoum has been developed that affects Vampyres. The progression of the poison is the same as it is for humans. First it attacks a Vampyre's small blood vessels then it leads to internal bleeding, shock, convulsions, unconsciousness and eventually death."

"It makes them bleed to death?"

He nodded. "I've seen it, and it's a grim way to die."

She winced. "There's no cure?"

"No real cure to speak of. The only thing that can be done is to try to flush out the poison as quickly as possible and not let it get absorbed into the system. That involves a major blood draining and a massive infusion of untainted blood. Once the poison has been absorbed and causes internal bleeding in all the major organs, it's invariably lethal." He cocked a sandy eyebrow at her. "Not that you'll be handing out drugs or poisons in the middle of a fight, but at least now you have a basic overview. Let's head back."

They turned to retrace their steps, and after a few minutes, Raoul continued, "We're going to focus more of your training on missile weaponry—gun training, knife throwing and archery. That doesn't mean we'll neglect the close combat sessions, but if you can avoid going hand to hand, you'll have a greater chance of hitting kill spots with a higher chance of survivability. Most creatures are vulnerable around their eyes, and your best asset is your hand-eye coordination." He cocked an eyebrow at her. "You know, you could become a hell of a sniper, if you chose to."

She had finally earned a compliment, from Raoul? Trying not to show how much pleasure it gave her, she said, dryly, "Good to know, although it's not a career choice I'd ever considered before."

He chuckled.

Looking down the shore into the distance, she tried to sound casual as she asked, "What about the more exotic Elder Races creatures, like the Djinn? What's their kill spot?"

The laughter died from his face. "They don't have one, not physically, anyway. If you ever run the risk of tangling with a Djinn, you run away. *I* run away. I've heard of them being killed before, but that's a rare, dangerous event. It calls for a coordinated attack from a team of creatures who are far more Powerful than either you or I."

The darkness of disappointment overtook the sun's bright light. Her shoulders sagged. "That's what I thought."

When they got back to the gym, they worked through the details of a new schedule that started later in the morning, took into account the time she would be spending with Xavier in the evenings and incorporated more time on the gun range, and introduced archery. Then Raoul sent her off for an afternoon run.

She let herself out the main gates and started down the road, which was striped with intense sunlight and dark shadows thrown by the surrounding, towering redwoods. Watching her feet as she ran, she stepped in light, then darkness, then light again.

Her thoughts followed a similar pattern.

Light: Malphas hasn't found me yet. Maybe he won't. He doesn't know how humans think, or how we can behave.

Dark: You know that's a lie. It's just a matter of time. He got to Eathan, didn't he?

Light: Eathan wasn't trying to hide, and I am. I'm virtually living off the grid here. I don't go anywhere, or use my bank accounts. I haven't given my Social Security number to anybody, I never do anything meaningful on the Internet or use similar passcodes, and I never let myself develop any kind of search pattern that has anything to do with Las Vegas, or gambling, or Djinn.

Dark: Stop trying to fool yourself, and plan for it to happen. He'll find you, and when he does, he might do more than just kill you. He might hurt people on the estate, just for sheltering you.

She slowed to a stop, staring blankly down the deserted road.

Turning in a semicircle, she looked back the way she had come. The estate had disappeared, and cool forest surrounded her. Because of how the road curved, she couldn't see more than a hundred yards in either direction.

Her answers weren't down either stretch of road, anyway. She already knew what she needed to do.

After a moment, she resumed her jog, but at a slower pace. After all, she didn't need to push herself. It didn't matter how fast or how far she ran now. When a half hour was up, she turned and made her way back to the estate. She keyed in the code that would open the gates and stepped back onto the grounds. As the gates swung closed behind her, she walked at a sedate pace back to the attendants' house.

She could just see the corner of the ballroom, and it was

as beautiful from the outside as it was from within. Now that she knew she had to leave, she could spare herself another evening spent in Xavier's company, but surprisingly, that idea didn't hold any appeal.

For a few fleeting moments last night, she had felt as if she winged weightlessly over the floor. Xavier's hold had been both assured and gentle. As soon as she had relaxed and trusted it, he swept her along in the dance and the world turned around them.

She forgot about her clumsy feet, or that she was in hiding. She forgot he was supposed to be a repulsive monster. She didn't feel a single bruise or aching muscle.

All she felt, all she heard was the music. All she saw was the slow widening of his smile that lit his intent gaze and turned his intelligent, naturally reflective expression into something much more keen and transcendent.

She really wanted to find out if they could achieve ninety seconds like that one more time.

After staying for six weeks, she thought, a few more hours won't hurt.

I can leave in the morning.

That evening, for dinner the attendants had Spanish paella, with rabbit, chorizo sausage, shrimp, clams, mussels and calamari, and for dessert, they had a simple, delicious homemade ice cream. All five of the other trainees—Marc, Jeremy, Aaron, Scott and Brian—were absent, and nobody mentioned where they had gone, but everyone else was present and ate a hearty meal.

Tess sat beside Angelica at one end of the farm-style table. As was her usual habit, she kept her attention on her food while she listened to everyone else talk. This time, instead of focusing on how the conversation seemed almost deliberately innocuous, she noticed instead the teasing banter and genuine warmth.

At the end of the meal, she glanced sidelong at Angelica and said quietly, "I haven't really taken the opportunity to get to know you, and I'm sorry for that."

Angelica turned to her with a look of surprise that

melted into a warm, crooked smile that deepened all the lines in her face and made her beautiful. "You're a good kid," the older woman said. "And you've been busy. We've got time."

She nodded without replying, because, of course, they had no time, and she would be gone before breakfast. After she helped clean up, she went upstairs to her room to make sure she hadn't dropped any food on her shirt. Tidying her hair by putting it into a short braid, she brushed her teeth and headed for the main house.

This time when she reached the dining room, it was empty. A small pile of old books had been stacked by one of the place settings, and a note rested on top of them. She picked it up.

Written in a strong, slanting hand, the note said, *Please begin reading these. I will join you in the ballroom at sundown.—X.*

Of course, he must be a very busy man, doing whatever he did for the Nightkind demesne. Setting the note aside, she examined the books. Most were written in English and dealt with the different etiquettes for several Elder Races, but a few were in French. He had remembered that she could read French.

One book was much more modern than the others, a heavy trade paperback on biofeedback techniques.

Choosing that book, she settled into a chair and began reading. Most biofeedback therapies were done in a clinical setting, with electronic and thermal sensors, but one section concentrated on exercises one could do outside of a clinical environment to change one's thoughts, emotions or behavior.

Funny, how it all came back to the same thing that Raoul had said to her—she had to change the conversations in her head. Deep, steady breathing could slow the heart rate. Focusing on things other than what produced a strong fear response could calm panic attacks. So could positive imagery.

She poked her tongue into one cheek. Was it positive

imagery to think of all the ways you could kill a Vampyre when you met one, or all the ways in which they were vulnerable?

Well, she wouldn't learn biofeedback with electrodes plastered to her head, so she ought to be able to think of whatever image worked for her too.

Not that she would be around to practice, anyway.

She read until the light faded outside and dusk darkened the page. Setting aside the book, she rose to her feet and went to the empty ballroom to look out at the ocean. On warm evenings, the tall, Palladian-style windows could be opened all around the room to allow for fresh air to blow in.

She had to agree with Raoul. This room was the jewel of the house.

Something ached. Was she actually sad at the thought of leaving?

Frowning, she turned from the window just as Xavier strode into the room. Tonight, he wore all black, simple slacks and a thin sweater that looked as if it might be silk. The clothes molded to his lean, strong form and emphasized his natural elegance more than ever.

Her pulse quickened, but it wasn't from fear. While she certainly respected how dangerous he was, she no longer believed he would hurt her. So why did her blasted heart rate pick up again?

She had no time to puzzle over it. As soon as he saw her, he gave her a small smile and a slight, archaic bow in greeting that seemed as natural to him as breathing. "Ah, good, you are here. Follow me, please."

He turned to walk out again. Caught off balance, she hurried to catch up with him. "Where are we going?"

"You'll see."

He led her up the stairs, bounding lightly up them two at a time and down the hall opposite the master's suite to the first bedroom where a light was shining. Once there, he stepped back from the open doorway and gestured for her to go in.

Puzzled, she complied. "What are we doing?"

"You are changing outfits," he told her.

A large garment bag from Nordstrom lay across the queen-sized bed. A smaller Nordstrom bag rested beside it. In the smaller bag, she could just see the tip of a shoe box, and she turned to stare at Xavier. "You bought me a dress? And shoes?"

Completely unmoved by her incredulity, he shrugged. "As I said to Raoul, people do not waltz in exercise pants. You need to wear the right outfit to learn how to dance properly, otherwise you will not know how to contend with the skirt or the shoes, and your poor partner's feet will never recover."

"But—but—"

"No buts." He looked both cheerful and adamant. "Change. I will see you down in the ballroom."

But you shouldn't have spent the money. I'm not staying.

The words tangled up in her head. She hadn't planned on telling him she was leaving until after the dance lesson, and before she could decide how she wanted to respond, he closed the door and left her alone.

She needed to go after him and tell him, if only she could find the right words to say.

But her feet discovered they had a mind of their own, and they propelled her to the side of the bed. Her hands became independent thinkers also, as they unzipped the garment bag.

Her mind followed suit, as she thought, Well, a quick peek wouldn't hurt.

Pulling apart the edges of the bag, she stared down at the dress. It was a beautiful, deep midnight blue gown ruched at one hip, with a long gauzy skirt. While the gown itself was strapless, it came with a fitted lacy bodice overlay in the same color.

She pulled the shoe box out of the bag and opened it. Delicate, nude-colored sandals lay inside. In a daze, she pulled out one sandal and checked it. It had a bit of a heel, but it wasn't too high, and it was her size.

She couldn't remember the last time she had worn pretty clothes, and this outfit was simply beautiful.

Oh, hell.

≈ TWELVE ≈

Of their own volition, her fingers went out to stroke the gauzy skirt of the dress.

She could try on the outfit, just to see if it fit. If it did, they could try a dance or two. If she tucked in the price tags but didn't remove them, they could return everything to the store.

And really, in the end, what did it matter if she went through one more dance lesson in her training outfit, or in the dress?

Not giving herself a chance to dither any longer, she toed off her running shoes and stripped, then shimmied into the gown, strapped on the sandals and stepped in front of a tall oval mirror set in a stand in one corner of the room.

If the dress was really hers and she would actually consider keeping it, she would make some changes. While it was the right size across the shoulders and hips, the waist was a bit loose and the length of the arms was a touch too long, but a good tailor could easily fix those issues. The color was simply lovely. It brought out a sheen in her dark hair and highlighted her healthy tan, and the whole outfit emphasized all the right curves in her body.

And she adored the sandals. It felt strange to be out of running shoes, and she'd gotten out of the habit of wearing heels, but the sandals were light, comfortable and made her feet look feminine and slender.

One part of her mind said severely, What on earth are you doing, Tess?

She stuffed a gag in it, left the room and went downstairs.

She heard music before she actually reached the ballroom, a single-note melody that sounded somehow pensive. Whatever it was, it wasn't waltz music. When she reached the doorway, she found Xavier sitting at the baby grand, his head bent as he watched the keys, and she realized the music wasn't a recording. He was playing, although not seriously, as he fingered out the notes with one hand.

"I have no classical education," she said as she walked toward him. "But whatever you're playing sounds lovely."

He stopped, and his dark head lifted as he turned to the doorway. When he caught sight of her, he rose to his feet quickly.

The intensity of his scrutiny made her self-conscious. The severe part of her mind spat out its gag and snarled, The dress is only a prop, fool, and it's not even yours. And why on earth would you care about his opinion anyway. . . .

That was all it got a chance to say before she gagged it again. As she walked toward him, she asked aloud, "Will this do?"

"It will do splendidly," he said. His voice was warm, the expression in his gaze lit with something that looked like pleasure. "Now you can know what it feels like to really waltz." When she came close, he held out a hand and she offered him hers. Instead of leading her out onto the floor, he bent to press his lips lightly to her fingers. "And you look beautiful."

The severe part of her mind broke free of its restraint

and took control of her vocal chords. In a quiet voice, she said, "Which is completely irrelevant, of course, but thank you."

He looked up, over her hand, and gave her a slow smile that was remarkably sweet and sexy, and completely devastating. "I'm afraid I must disagree. A beautiful woman is never irrelevant. She can be the most compelling, most gloriously dangerous creature in all the world."

Sexy. With the last of her fear banished, for the first time she could see it, sense it, almost reach out and scoop it up in her hands.

He was sexy.

Shaken, she withdrew her fingers and gave a little laugh. In an attempt to deflect that devastating, intent scrutiny of his, she reminded him, "You didn't say what you were playing just now."

"It is a Chopin piece, one of the Nocturnes," he said. "I think it's one of the most beautiful pieces of music he wrote. But I wasn't really playing it, just picking out the melody. Would you like to hear the real thing?"

Pleasure was a deadly thing. It weakened the resolve and skewed one's motives. But she couldn't resist. She found herself saying, "Yes, please."

He inclined his head and sat, sliding to one side on the bench in a clear invitation for her to join him.

Oh, hell. How had this evening turned into such a slippery slope?

Gingerly, she eased onto the seat beside him. There was no sheet music. Whatever he played here, he knew by heart. He gave her a sidelong smile, positioned his long-fingered hands over the ivory keys and began.

The acoustics in the ballroom were wonderful. Haunting, exquisite music swelled to fill the space.

Her emotions careened all over the map. The long, unwinding strings of sound reached into her heart and plucked out its own melody. Somehow, by one of the strangest set of circumstances she'd ever heard of or experienced, she had come to this place and time.

The details lay scattered in her mind like a strange necklace of pearls strewn over an unknown woman's vanity. She wore a beautiful dress on a serene moonlit night, sitting in the jewel of a gracious house, and a Vampyre who was both dangerous and kind played Chopin for her ears alone.

Once she left the estate's cloistered protection, she would probably be dead within the week. For now she set it aside, threw all her barriers down and opened herself wide to surrender to this singular experience.

When the last notes faded from the air, she wanted to grab them and demand they stay, but even if she heard the song again, it could never be quite the same as that first time, filled as it was with the unique newness of discovery and the surprise of pleasure that had been previously unknown. Those strings in the heart could be plucked only once.

The moment fled into memory. She thought, when I die—if he dies—no one will ever know what just happened. Beside her, he sat still, waiting patiently.

She opened her eyes and looked at him, and it didn't matter that her gaze was damp with tears and he was the one who had done that to her. Instead, she wanted to thank him for it.

Those old eyes of his, set in that noble, young face. She shook her head and gave him a small, twisted smile. "I don't know how to reconcile in my mind everything I know about you."

Instead of asking what she meant, he looked down at the piano and touched one ivory key but didn't press it. "You asked me once if I had done everything that had been attributed to me, and I said yes. May I tell you a story?"

She nodded as she looked away and wiped one cheek. Of course he knew to go there. He was a very clever man.

He pressed the key, and a single note sounded. It seemed forlorn and incomplete without its companions. "My mother died having me," he said. "It was a tragedy, of course, as such things always are. My older brother and sister had come some years before me, but still, she was too young to die in such a way. She had been the light of my father's life, and he was heartbroken."

"I'm sorry," she said. It seemed inadequate, or out of place somehow.

He gave her a sidelong look and a smile that made it all right. "Thank you, Tess. My sister, Aeliana, was thirteen, and for all practical purposes, she became my mother. My father withdrew emotionally and preoccupied himself with managing his estates, and my brother was absent more often than not, but Aeliana raised me and let me know in a thousand ways that I was safe, wanted and loved. Unfortunately, she looked quite a bit like me." This was accompanied by another sidelong, self-deprecating smile. "But all the same, she was lovely. She had a strength and sweetness that shone out of her like a beacon, and people were drawn to her because of it."

His sister wasn't the only one who had that quality.

His sister, the one who had been murdered by the Inquisition. She knotted her hands together in her lap. Despite a somewhat innocuous beginning, he was not telling an easy story.

His quiet voice continued. "I was the third child and a second son, and I would never inherit. It was always understood that I was destined for the Church. My father believed I would make a fine statesman, perhaps bishop one day, or if God allowed, even cardinal. With the right piety and championship from senior officials within the Church, along with generous contributions from the family, God could afford to allow quite a bit of good fortune to fall on the del Torro name." He shrugged and smiled at her. "It was how we thought at the time."

"Did you mind?" she asked.

"No, not at all. So many modern stories focus on the angst of this kind of thing and glorify one's right to choose one's own path, but truly, I was fine with it. I liked to learn, and at that time the Church was at the center of human education. So, I was raised as a typical young nobleman and taught to hunt, and fight and fence. I was good at all of it, and I enjoyed it, until it came time for me to join the Church, where I found the discipline and study suited me. I came to realize I loved God, and I committed to the life and said the vows. And I meant them."

Now that she had caught glimpses into his personal life, she could picture him as a young, earnest ascetic. Fingering one of the keys herself, she asked, "You didn't miss any of those other pursuits?"

His mouth took on an ironic twist. "The reality of it was, I didn't have to give very much of it up. I was not a poor country priest. God really could afford to allow good fortune to fall upon a rich nobleman's son. I was housed in a comfortable, monied monastery near our main home in Valencia, and I became secretary to the bishop at that time, and I saw my family, especially Aeliana, regularly. It was a good life. I . . . believed in it. I believed in dedicating myself to a life that was filled with the holy scripture and mixed with politics. I was not rebellious or insincere. In many ways, I really was very much a product of my time."

"I find that hard to believe," she murmured. If he had been so typical, he wouldn't be so feared now, nor would he be sitting here, telling her the story of what happened centuries ago.

He quirked an eyebrow at her but didn't pursue that. Instead, he said, "Then there was the Inquisition. At the time, the Inquisition had turned its focus onto matters of Power, and magical creatures were declared an anathema. Those of the Elder Races were to be pitied, because they were godless, soulless creatures, but Vampyres were a different matter. Vampyres chose to become what they were, and thus they fell from God's grace and were damned."

She shook her head. Hadn't she done something very similar, when she had called all Vampyres "monsters" in her mind? "What about those who might have been turned against their will?"

"That didn't matter. They must have done something to have deserved it."

"They blamed the victim?" Outrage stirred. Even though it had all happened so long ago, his words had given it an immediacy that made it seem current.

"Cause and effect. God blessed those who were good and punished those who had sinned. The Church could forgive most sins and bless the petitioner, but some sins were mortal offenses."

"It's barbaric," she muttered.

"Of course it was. Meanwhile, things happened to the del Torro family. My father died of some kind of lung disease, perhaps pneumonia, and my brother, Felipe, inherited the title—it was just a minor lordship, mind you—and the estate. Still, Felipe was an explorer and was gone much of the time, while Aeliana remained home and managed the estate. Then Felipe died when his ship went down somewhere near the Canary Islands. There was only Aeliana and me, and Aeliana had fallen in love with a man who was a gentle soul, who also happened to be a Vampyre. That was the beginning of the end."

She touched a black key and whispered, "It was bad."

"I'm afraid so." He touched her hand briefly. "But I don't need to make it so, for you."

Needing to see how much he felt of the old pain, she turned toward him and searched his gaze. He met her scrutiny with the same quiet dignity with which he told the story.

"Everything happened quickly after that, over a span of about four months. I may have been book bright, but I was a young, naive fool. I didn't want to leave the Church, and while Aeliana couldn't inherit the title, I thought she deserved the estates. I had met Inigo, the man she had fallen in love with. He was from a nearby community of twenty or so Vampyres. While I . . . liked him, I was troubled by the fact that he was a Vampyre. At that time the Inquisition had not made any moves against Vampyre communities and I didn't see the danger until it was too late. I couldn't see him as damned, but I didn't have time to agonize over the morality of the Church's opinion or how I felt about it. Worried, I talked to my bishop about it in the confessional."

He fell silent. She whispered, "Oh, no."

"He was supposed to be my spiritual leader," he told her softly, and somehow his wry, knowledgeable gaze hurt more than anything. "I was hoping for some kind of guidance or advice. Of course, I didn't see things the way I would now—how tempting such a rich estate would have been to some, or how certain Church officials would have seen it as vulnerable, with its only male heir committed to the Church and unable to inherit. Also, I had never been in love. I couldn't conceive of how strong a force love might be, or how transformative. Aeliana asked Inigo to turn her, and he did just after they married. I found out afterward, about both."

The story carried her forward, with the inevitability of a train wreck.

"Once the decision was made, the Church acted quickly, for that time. There weren't any trials, not for Vampyres. It was extermination. Inquisition officers seized the estate in the name of the Church. I found out afterward, when a servant who had been with my family for years came to tell me the news. There were no bodies to bury, of course. All the Vampyres had turned to ash." He paused and took a deep breath. "He said the women had been brutalized by the soldiers before they'd been killed, and everything in that young, naive boy broke that day."

She didn't think before she acted. She put a hand over his as it rested against his lean thigh, and his fingers closed around hers in a strong grip. "They killed her and took everything? You didn't have anything?"

"Nothing. I had no legal recourse either, as I had renounced all worldly possessions with my vows. Even my horse was technically the Church's."

"What a colossal betrayal," she whispered.

He gave her a small, ironic smile. "I stole my horse, and a sword. I stole other things too, to sell, so I could make passage to Italy to where Julian resided at that time. He had been a famous commander of a Roman army, and I needed to know how to go to war. We made a bargain. I swore I would come back to serve him once I had done what I needed to do. He turned me, and taught me. Then he set me loose in the world and said, 'Come back when you're finished.' It took me ten years, but I came back to him."

She asked from the back of her throat, "Did you kill everyone responsible?"

His gaze turned fierce and hot, as it had the first time she had asked him if the stories were true, although his soft, even voice never altered. "Oh, yes."

"And you've been serving Julian ever since."

He inclined his head. "He's my sire."

She nodded. There were so many things she wanted to ask him. How had he put the pieces of himself back together?

Somehow the core of him had survived.

He wasn't a monster. He was courteous and thoughtful. Self-disciplined and well-mannered. How had he coped with such a shattered faith?

She became aware of her hand, wrapped in his. Growing self-conscious, she tried to let go, but he tightened his grip and said, "I told you all this, because you have the right to know who your patron is. You should be able to reconcile in your mind all of those things you know about me, and you should know that no one who is under my care will ever come to harm like that again. Not ever. I swear it."

Realization crushed down. He had taken so much time and effort, all to reassure her, when she had every intention of leaving anyway.

They weren't going to make the dance lesson after all. She couldn't go on without saying anything. Now it was her turn to grip his fingers. She met his gaze and said, "I have to leave in the morning."

Surprise flared in his expression then settled into coldness, and he pulled away from her touch. "I see. My apologies, if I've offended you in any way."

What? No!

She grabbed the sleeve of his jacket before he could stand. "Your story didn't offend me. I was incredibly moved and saddened, and I wished I could do something to protect that boy from all the horrible things that happened to him."

The coldness eased somewhat, but while he didn't pull away, his body remained stiff. "Thank you," he said. "But then why leave? I thought we had made progress. You're no longer afraid, and you seemed pleased enough last night. When did you decide this?"

She put her face in her hands and rubbed eyes that had gone dry and gritty with tiredness. "This morning. I was going to tell you. I should never have put on the dress and shoes, but they were so pretty, and I wanted to see if we might be able to waltz again before I told you. Just ninety seconds more."

He took both of her hands and pulled them down, and she saw that he had moved to straddle the bench to face her fully. Searching her expression, he asked, "What happened?"

She hesitated, her mind racing. She didn't want to tell him, in case that provided some kind of buffer. But what if it didn't? He had a right to know what kind of danger she had brought to his estate, so that he could guard against it. She couldn't betray him, or the others, by leaving them in ignorance.

"I've made a powerful enemy," she said. "And he's vindictive. I thought I might be able to disappear, or if he found me, just being in your household would be enough to back him off, but this morning I realized I was being stupid. Just me being here has put you and everybody else in danger."

He looked calm, but his gaze had turned deadly. If he had looked anything like that at the Vampyre's Ball, she would have been terrified. As it was, her breath shortened.

"Who is it?"

She realized he still held both her wrists in a gentle, entirely unbreakable grip. "I think I've told you enough."

"It's Malphas, isn't it?"

Hearing Xavier speak his name aloud shocked her, and her heart began a slow, hard clanging in her chest. Tightening her hands into fists, she pulled at his grip. Somewhat to her own surprise, he let her go. "How do you know that name?"

He gave her a quizzical look. "We ran a background check on you. You worked at a casino in Las Vegas. It was not difficult to find out who owned the casino."

"Oh, God." Black spots danced in front of her eyes. She bent forward, putting her forehead to her knees. "Can he trace that? I know that Djinn can get into computer systems somehow, and spy on Internet usage. He can trace that, can't he?"

Xavier put a hand at the back of her neck, his touch steady and bracing. "Slow, deep breaths. No, don't come up so fast. Give it a moment. Some Djinn have the ability to get into electronic systems, but only a few are tech savvy enough to understand how to read the bytes of information. Since he hasn't shown up here, I think we can assume Malphas hasn't tracked the interaction."

"Okay," she said, breathing slow and deep like he said. The black spots disappeared. "You can let me up now."

The pressure on the back of her neck eased, and she sat upright. He rubbed her back, still watching her closely. "Better?"

She gave him a quick, stiff nod. "Yes."

He gave her a smile that she could tell was meant to be reassuring, but his gaze was still deadly. Over the centuries, that broken naive boy had turned into something entirely honed and dangerous. Somehow, though, she could tell that the expression wasn't meant for her. It didn't frighten her, but a shiver ran down her back anyway.

He said, "This is where you tell me everything."

"I don't know," she replied. She rubbed her arms. "I have to think."

His smile widened. "Tess, you can't possibly believe I'm going to let you walk out those front gates now, can you?"

Lifting her chin, she said, "Yes, I do. Any time during this trial year, either one of us can call it quits."

He laughed, a quiet sound that shivered along her skin. "That was then. This is now."

"What do you mean?" She stared at him, wide-eyed. "You can't change our agreement like that.".

"I can do anything I want," he told her. "And I will, including changing the terms of your stay. You've already said you intend to leave, which means we have no agreement."

"What are you saying?" The bottom dropped out of her stomach. "You can't keep me prisoner here."

"Can't I?" He looked entirely ruthless.

Her voice rose. "What happened to those fancy promises you made about not making me do something against my will?"

He shook his head. "But you don't really want to go, do you?"

She glared at him and tried to force a denial out, but he had her with that one.

"You might as well start talking," he told her. "If you don't tell me what happened, I'll go to Malphas and ask him."

"Don't!" Without thinking, she clutched at his lapel.

He took her by the shoulders and pulled her close, his hard, glittering eyes boring into hers. "Talk."

"Who are you?" she said, staring. "Where has the soft-spoken, courteous man gone?"

"He's right here in front of you, and he's very angry. He just doesn't know if he's angry at you yet." He gave her a thin-lipped smile. "Now, what is it going to be? Are you going to tell me what happened, or will Malphas?"

She knew who she was looking at. This was the man who chose to become a Vampyre in order to go to war for ten years. She said, calmly, "I can't talk you into letting this go, can I?"

He shook his head slowly, his gaze never leaving her face.

"Fine. *Fine*." She still held his lapel, and he still gripped her shoulders. They were much too close. She pushed against his chest, and this time he let her go. Swinging away, she rose to her feet and started to pace. "Remember how I said I was good with money? Malphas hired me to keep his books."

While he still straddled the bench, he watched her with an unnerving attention. "Were you cooking them?"

"Oh no, there's nothing on paper." She waved a hand in the air, reached the edge of the ballroom and stalked back. "He looks like he's completely in compliance with the gaming commission, and he pays taxes on all casino profits. That's not the issue."

He sat back and crossed his arms. "Then what is?"

She glanced over her shoulder at him. "What I saw and heard happened around the edges of casino life. People showed up for private appointments with Malphas, people who had racked up really large debts. I saw their expressions afterward, and I overheard things I wasn't meant to hear."

"Dear God, you eavesdropped?" said Xavier. His expression turned ironic. "I don't know why I find myself shocked. You are far more talented at gathering information than I ever gave you credit for."

She swung around to the end of the baby grand that was opposite from where he sat, wanting the illusion of something between her and his too-still figure. "Oh, I didn't mean to, and nothing happened quite like what happened the night you and Melisande were talking. I just . . . I caught snippets of conversations here and there. I really tried not to notice what was happening or put two and two together. That was my first job out of college, and it paid damn well." She laughed bitterly. "But I was flattered and excited that I could pay off my student loans so quickly, and I wanted it to be okay."

"Tess," Xavier said. "What the fuck was he doing?"

That brought her up short. Normally he was so courteous, the expletive seemed doubly shocking.

"He lured people into placing bigger and bigger bets, and they got more and more into debt. Then he would meet with them, and when they left, they looked sick to death, yet their debt would be forgiven." She looked down at her blurred image in the polished dark wood of the piano. "On the surface, you might think that was no big deal. Casinos write off tens of millions of bad debt every year. But none of the people I saw looked like they had been given a reprieve. I heard one of them say he was going to be sick, and another one told his wife it was never going to be over."

He leaned his crossed arms on the piano. His gaze never left her. "Was he cheating?"

"Maybe?" She shook her head. "I don't know for sure. I'm not a gambler, and anyway, I didn't watch the games. I just watched the money and the people."

"All right," he said. The soft-spoken man was back, only he had shotgun eyes that bore right at her, and he was the gun. "Do you have any idea what he was doing to them? Why was it never going to be over?"

Staring at him was too distracting. She looked down at her blurred self in the piano again. "I think he was extorting or coercing them somehow, only with their debts erased, I don't know how."

"Forget about trying to figure out how. I just want to hear what you think."

"What I think . . . ?" Her voice died away. Nobody had asked her that before. She hadn't had anybody to confide in, and the whole situation had come to feel so unstable and dangerous, she hadn't dared verbalize her impressions, even to herself. She frowned as she considered, and he didn't rush her. He simply watched and waited.

"I think . . . he liked the game too much. All of it. He was lit up and entirely focused when he was playing, like he needed it."

"You're talking about the gambling itself?" Xavier asked.

≈ THIRTEEN ≈

X avier was usually a patient, even-tempered man, but at the moment so many unruly emotions surged inside of him, he had to struggle to restrain himself.

She had messed with a pariah Djinn who played power games and was possibly a gambling addict?

He bit out, "What did you do?"

Her gaze wandered away. "I might have interfered with one of his marks."

Holy Mother of God. He rubbed his eyes and forced himself to speak with some measure of control. "Interfered how?"

She tilted her head toward one of her shoulders and watched her finger as she drew circles on the piano's polished surface again.

She said, "I might have called his parents to tell them what kind of debt their son was accruing, and with whom. He was only twenty-one, you see—old enough to drink and gamble and get into trouble, but he wasn't even out of college yet."

He rubbed the back of his neck as he watched her. "What happened?"

"Eathan's father shut him down before it could go too far. He flew out to Vegas, paid off Eathan's gambling debt and dragged him home again."

"Is that when you left Las Vegas and ended up at the Vampyre's Ball?"

She nodded.

He couldn't look away from her dejected figure. She looked as beautiful in the dark blue dress as he knew she would. The cut of the gown highlighted the slender lines of her neck and shoulders, and the graceful wings of her collarbones.

"There's something I'm missing," he said, almost to himself. "This isn't just a story about a boy who made mistakes. What's the significance of all of this?"

She squared her shoulders and looked at him with equal parts dread and sadness. "His father was Senator Ryan Jackson. Malphas really, really wanted to trap Eathan."

He was on his feet, around the piano and by her side before he knew it. As she turned to face him, he gripped her by the shoulders again. He couldn't seem to stop himself from touching her. "Senator Jackson sits on several key subcommittees in Washington. If Malphas had gotten control of Eathan, he could have used that as leverage to force Jackson into doing whatever he wanted."

"I know." She twisted her fingers together.

He scowled, his mind racing over everything she had told him. "I'm still not seeing something. All this happened weeks ago. Why did you decide today that you were going to leave?"

The corners of her mouth turned down, and her dark gaze took on a wet, overbright shine. "Because this morning I read in the *Boston Herald* that Eathan died in a boating accident while he was in Florida during Presidents' Day weekend. None of his friends died, just him. The paper said it was a freak squall, but I know it wasn't. It was Malphas, and he hasn't forgiven or forgotten anything. If he was willing to do that to Eathan, he'll be more than willing to do something similar to me, whether I'm one of your attendants or not."

The pain in her eyes was too much to resist. He did what he'd been looking forward to doing all evening and pulled her into his arms, only this time he didn't hold her at the proper prescribed distance for waltzing but clenched her tight. "I'm so sorry."

She didn't flinch or pull away. Instead, her arms crept around his waist, and she leaned against him. "If I hadn't done anything, if I'd just kept my mouth shut, Eathan would probably still be alive."

He felt in her tense body how she struggled not to cry, and he stroked her hair. "You can't think like that. If you hadn't stopped Malphas from trapping the boy and controlling the father, who knows what kind of harm could have come from that. The fact that he chose to retaliate is not your fault."

"It feels like it is," she whispered. A sob broke out of her. "It feels like I killed him, and while I think I could kill somebody in self-defense or if I really had to, he didn't deserve to die like that and I didn't mean to do it."

He rested his cheek against the top of her head and closed his eyes, still stroking her hair. How many times had he thought such similar thoughts? If only he had left the priesthood to take up his family title when his brother had died. If only he hadn't confessed everything to his bishop, perhaps Aeliana and her husband would still be alive.

"Believe me," he said into her hair, "I understand."

"This is why I need to leave." Her voice was muffled in his jacket. "If Malphas could do something like that out of spite, then God only knows what he might do when he finds me. Because you know he will, sooner or later. I've been careful, but he's a Djinn, for God's sake."

"Okay," he said, as he calmed slightly. "Okay."

Even in the midst of all her distress, part of him was wholly consumed by the fact that he held her in his arms, and she let him.

What was she doing to him?

He shouldn't have noticed her at the Vampyre's Ball, but he had.

He shouldn't like her so much, but he did.

He shouldn't have gone into her bedroom when he'd found her window open. Everything he had said to her that night, he could have said elsewhere, later, but he had wanted to go into her room.

Right now, he shouldn't push any kind of advantage with her.

But he would.

He eased her back so he could look into her face. "You will stay here and give me twenty-four hours."

She wiped her face. "And do what? What can be accomplished in a day?"

"Quite a lot, actually," he said. "I'm going to do what I meant to do all along and talk to Malphas."

"What?" She grabbed his lapel. "You can't! God knows what he might do once you come to his attention."

He looked down at her hands fisted in the material of his jacket and suppressed a smile. It was the second time she had grabbed hold of him that evening. He told her, "You owe me twenty-four hours."

"I don't owe you anything," she snapped.

"I gave you the chance to become one of my attendants," he pointed out.

She let go of him with a furious push. "I gave you six weeks of hard work and physical pain. We're *even*."

"Tess," he said.

The sharp command in his voice drew her up. Scowling at him, she fell silent.

He took one of her hands and bowed over it to press his lips against the knuckles of her slim fingers. She twisted her hand around to grip his. When he straightened, he said quietly, "You gave me blood. I'm supposed to protect you."

Her face started to crumple, but then her jaw clenched and she hardened her expression. "Not any longer. We have no liaison, remember? I ended it."

He told her, "In twenty-four hours, we will have this conversation again. Then we'll see what we have."

As he turned to leave, she said sharply, "Wait."

Angling his head, he came to a halt and pivoted back to her. I choose to do this, the slowness of his movements said. You do not order me.

She did not appear to notice or care what his movements said. Her hands balled into fists as she searched his face. She said between her teeth, "I can't stop you, can I?"

He shook his head without speaking.

Breathing heavily, she just looked at him. Then she said, "If you insist on doing this, I'm doing it with you."

His reaction was immediate and forceful. "No. Absolutely not."

"This is my problem and my life," she said. Her expression settled into bleak determination. "You can't take that away from me. If you try, I'll contact Malphas and confront him without you. I'm tired of hiding. It's time to be done with this."

Furious denial burst through him like a fireball. If she confronted Malphas without having witnesses present or any leverage to hold against him, it would mean her death.

Conflicting impulses warred inside. He could stop her. He could mesmerize her into compliance. He could . . .

No, he couldn't. He had sworn he would not compel her, or force her to do anything against her will. That still applied, even if she was determined on a pigheaded act of self-destruction.

He wanted to shake her. No, he didn't, he wanted to clench her tight again.

He didn't know what he wanted to do. Rubbing the back of his neck, he glared at her. She lifted her chin, and even in the midst of his anger, he was caught by the gesture.

Even though she was clearly afraid again, she would do it. She would confront Malphas on her own. He had no doubt. She had such defiance, such courage. Such sweet, beautiful fire.

His anger died. It was impossible to fault her now when

she showed the very characteristics that drew him to her to begin with.

"If I agree, you will follow my lead and do as I say," he said. "I mean it, Tess. This is not the time for you to be creative or ignore orders. As you so rightly point out, this is your life we're talking about."

Her lips folded tight.

He watched her struggle with conflicting impulses until he couldn't stand it any longer. In a low voice, he urged, "Trust me. I've earned it."

She blinked several times, her face taut.

Come on, Tess. He didn't say it.

"Okay." Her voice shook. She asked, "What are we going to do?"

Another new, unknown feeling roared through him, fierce and wild.

He considered her without really looking at her, as his mind raced through possibilities and discarded them. "Give me a few minutes," he told her. "Go change out of your outfit, and put on street clothes. Pack an overnight bag, just in case. By then I'll have a better feeling for what we should do."

She nodded and started to walk away, but then she stopped and turned back to him. Her gaze was full.

He waited, but she didn't say anything. Instead, she gave him a smile that was so lovely, so filled with emotional complexity, he had to stare.

Then she left, and he was surrounded by the echoes of the stories they had told each other. Those stories were shaping their lives in ways he couldn't predict.

As silence settled into the ballroom, he pulled out his phone and ran a Google search on Eathan Jackson. After scrolling over several articles on the younger Jackson's death, he found the article on the *Boston Herald* website and clicked on it. When he had read through it, he went to find Raoul.

Raoul was in the gym, talking to Diego. When Xavier entered, both men fell silent and looked at him inquiringly.

He didn't waste time on preliminaries. He said to Raoul, "In a few minutes, I'll be leaving with Tess, and I can't guarantee when we'll be back." He looked at Diego. "Would you please pull out the SUV and retrieve my overnight bag from upstairs?"

Diego's eyes filled with questions, but he nodded. "Sure thing."

After the younger man left, Raoul turned to face him, his expression grim. "Okay, what the hell is going on?"

Xavier regarded him with an expression just as grim. It had been many years since he had felt the need to keep a secret from Raoul, but this time, the knowledge of what Tess had done seemed too dangerous to share.

Perhaps it was unlikely Malphas would come here, but if he did, ignorance might be the only protection they had on the estate. If Malphas could sense that nobody knew of his activities or what Tess had done, he might very well leave everyone here alone.

"I can't tell you."

"Bullshit," Raoul snapped. Real, rare anger clenched his body and face. "When was the last time you couldn't tell me something? Xavier, what has she done?"

He paused then smiled. "She did the right thing." He watched frustration slash over the other man's face. "I'm doing the right thing. And now I'm going to ask you to do the right thing. Will you do that for me?"

Raoul ran his hands through his short hair. He bit out, "Of course I will. Goddammit. Are you sure this is right—whatever this is?"

"As sure as I can be about anything right now," Xavier told him. "As soon as I can, I'll tell you everything."

"You better," Raoul gritted. "Can you at least tell me where you're going?"

"Probably Evenfall," Xavier said. "I think we'll need to enlist Julian's help."

The other man frowned. "I don't like the thought of you staying at Evenfall for any length of time without some kind of backup."

Xavier shook his head. "I've told you countless times before, I can take care of myself."

"But this isn't about just you now, is it?" Raoul's gaze turned keen. "What if you need to meet with Julian—or anyone else—alone? What happens with Tess in the meantime? Xavier, Evenfall is not the safest or most secure place, especially when dangerous visitors are in residence. Also, if you're gone for too long, you might need blood. Either let me come, or at the very least take Diego."

The other man had a point. He didn't know what he might have to do, and he didn't feel good about leaving Tess alone, not with the level of fear she had yet to overcome. Evenfall was filled with predators, and while Julian had good guards, a Vampyre with enough senior standing could overpower them.

"Fine," he said. "It's a good idea. I'll take Diego. I know he's been restless."

Raoul still looked frustrated, but he said, "Good enough. Thank you."

"I'll be in touch soon, and give you updates as I can." Xavier touched his arm and left.

Outside, the night was deceptively serene. Waves lapped at the shore gently, and the breeze that blew off the water was cool and refreshing. Nothing in the scenery hinted at the storm that was coming.

He strode across the lawn to the parking lot, where Diego had brought the SUV. As he reached it, Diego came out of the house carrying the overnight bag he always kept packed.

When the younger man reached him, he said, "Go get your bag. You're coming too."

Diego's eyes sparked with surprise. "I'll be right back." He sprinted away.

While Xavier waited, he called Julian, who picked up on the first ring. "I need your help with a tricky situation," he told Julian.

The Nightkind King said, "I'll help you any way I can,

but now's not a good time. Justine's up my ass again, trying to claim those trade proposals that you and Melly agreed to in New York aren't valid."

"You're kidding," Xavier said. "What happened to good faith and common sense?"

"They got run over by a bus. Legally, she has a point. You weren't authorized by the council to strike those deals. Instead of letting it slide, Justine is insisting that either Melly has to come back and strike an agreement with me personally, or the council has to pass a motion that gives you the authority in retrospect to cover the talks you had in New York with Melly." Julian's deep, powerful voice sounded like it was filled with ground glass. "So either Melly has to come back to Evenfall, or the whole council needs to reconvene."

Xavier swore. If the council had to reconvene to pass such a motion, it would be another damning piece of evidence against Julian's effectiveness.

"I'm Sisyphus, Xavier," Julian growled. "I'm a Vampyre Sisyphus stuck in hell, damned to push the same fucking rock up the same hill for all eternity. One of these days I'm going to separate Justine's head from her shoulders."

He took a deep breath and said, "The thing is, this tricky situation I've got . . . Julian, it can't wait."

Silence spooled out between them. "Okay," Julian said. "We'll just have to fucking deal with all of it. What do you need? What's going on?"

"We shouldn't discuss it over the phone," Xavier told him. "We need to talk about it in person."

A short silence. He knew what Julian was thinking. He almost never asked for assistance with anything, and the fact that he thought they needed to meet in person brought home the urgency of his request.

Julian asked, "When are you coming?"

"Half an hour, tops," Xavier replied.

"Find me when you get here." Julian disconnected without a good-bye.

Xavier tucked his phone into his pocket.

Malphas, on the hunt for Tess. Justine, in residence at Evenfall.

This night kept getting better and better.

In her room, Tess changed into jeans and an old cable-knit, soft heather sweater. She stuffed other clothes into a gray canvas carry-on—another pair of jeans, two more sweaters, a couple of T-shirts, the flat black shoes she had worn at the Vampyre's Ball, toiletries, underwear and her hairbrush.

She barely noticed what she grabbed. None of her old street clothes fit right any longer. They all hung a bit loose on her frame.

It wasn't like it mattered what she looked like anyway. Nobody cared, least of all herself. She wasn't going to pause to put on makeup or a nice outfit for a confrontation with Malphas.

A confrontation with Malphas. The words echoed in her head. Her hands were shaking, while her mind raced in circles like a panicked jackrabbit.

Trust me, Xavier had said. And he was right. He had earned it.

She didn't even know what had happened, or when, but something fundamental had changed. Like the continuous stream of decisions and actions that had brought her to this place, maybe what had happened wasn't one single thing but a series of events that culminated into something far different from anything she could have imagined.

She had seen Xavier angry more than once. They had talked, argued, even laughed together. And when she had broken down to confess everything about Eathan and his father, instead of losing his temper or attacking her for possibly endangering people on the estate, he had pulled her into his arms and held her.

He had moved so far beyond the term "monster" in her mind, he might actually be the finest man she had ever met.

Trust me, he had said, and the look in his eyes had

been . . . vulnerable. It had mattered to him that she did. He was usually so poised, so self-contained, the expression had jolted her out of her old habits and mind-set.

She zipped up her bag. For a moment, she simply stood and looked around her plain, peaceful room. She said in the empty air, "I think we're going on a fool's errand."

Wherever that was.

But he had said trust me, so she would. He had connections, an entire network of people—creatures—that she could know nothing about, and centuries' more knowledge and experience. That had to count for something. It should count for a lot.

Honestly, she didn't know if that was a reasonable assessment, or if she was falling prey to a fool's hope too.

She slipped on her jean jacket, slung her bag onto her shoulder, turned off the light and left the room.

As she neared the front door, she met Diego. He wore a black leather jacket and had a bag slung over his shoulder too. She stopped. "Where are you going?"

He shrugged. "I assume I'm going the same place you are, chica."

"God, I hope not," she muttered. "I wouldn't wish where I'm going on my worst enemy."

He grinned and opened the door. "I guess we'll find out, won't we?"

They walked outside together. Across the lawn, she saw Xavier standing by his Lexus, clearly waiting for them.

She and Diego approached, and when they neared, Xavier said to Diego, "Please drive."

"Sure thing." Diego slipped into the driver's seat, while she and Xavier climbed into the back.

The interior smelled of expensive leather and the faint scent of a masculine aftershave that she recognized as Xavier's. Instead of tensing with nerves, she found herself relaxing. She was beginning to associate his scent with comfort and safety.

He lounged beside her, perfectly calm and comfortable within himself like a lean hunting cat. In the dim illumination from the dashboard, his eyes glittered, sharp with intelligence.

As she snapped on her seat belt, Diego adjusted the rearview mirror and looked into it at Xavier. "Where to?"

"Evenfall," said Xavier.

Diego nodded, reversed the vehicle and drove to the front gates, while her gut clenched, and briefly, she closed her eyes. They were going into a stronghold filled with Vampyres, into the very heart of the Nightkind demesne. She'd been right—she wouldn't wish this trip on her worst enemy.

Xavier's hand closed over the fist she pressed against her thigh, and she jumped. She opened her eyes to look at him, and he gave her a sidelong, crooked smile.

"Think of something positive, *querida*," he told her. "Always think of something positive. It will calm your heart rate and clear your mind."

In the angled rearview mirror, she saw Diego give them both a sharp, frowning glance. He looked unsettled, and she wondered why.

Xavier's grip on her fist was steady and as gentle as he always was with her. She breathed evenly, focusing on his relaxed, alert presence instead of her own jumbled mass of nerves, and rather to her own surprise, she found herself calming almost immediately.

She whispered, "You really think everything is going to be okay."

"I really do," he replied, just as quietly. "We can find a way to go through this and reach the other side."

Her clenched fist unlocked, and she turned her hand over to lace her fingers through his. His crooked smile widened into real warmth. He squeezed her fingers.

They spent the rest of the twenty-minute trip in silence, until Evenfall loomed ahead of them like a hulking leviathan that had crawled out of the sea.

Soon, Diego turned off onto a narrow gravel road that brought them closer to the shoreline. They approached the castle from a wide, open area bare of trees or any other obstruction. All that was visible were tall grasses, a tumble of rocky ground and the ocean, and she felt sure none of that was by accident.

They pulled up to an anonymous-looking set of garage doors, set into the foot of the castle wall, and stopped. She had just enough time to notice the security cameras when the metal doors rose, opening like a giant mouth.

Diego drove inside, and Evenfall swallowed them whole.

⇒ FOURTEEN ⇐

Inside was an entirely normal underground parking garage. After passing a security gate, Diego drove down a ramp and into a parking space that said RESERVED.

When he cut the engine, Xavier told him, "Please take our bags to my rooms and wait there until you hear further instructions."

Tess slipped her hand out of Xavier's as Diego twisted in his seat to frown at both of them.

"You just want me to wait in your rooms?"

"You're here as backup," Xavier said. "If I need to act alone or take care of something unforeseen, you will guard Tess. We're here to complete a task that is going to be—unpredictable. Also, if we're here for longer than the night, I might require blood."

Diego said, without expression, "So I'm here to act as a babysitter and a wet bar."

Xavier's own expression went still. With immense courtesy, he replied, "That is what I require from you at this point in time, yes."

After a moment, Diego said, "Just checking, boss. Hey,

at least it's good to get out of the house now and then, right?"

He had lightened his tone, but his cheerfulness rang false to Tess. She put her head in her hands and rubbed aching temples. With the sure knowledge that she would be facing Malphas soon enough, she didn't have any emotional room to spare for whatever might be bothering Diego.

Xavier touched her thigh. "Are you ready?"

No. No.

She lifted her head, straightened her shoulders and said, "Yes."

"Come with me."

She stepped out of the SUV as he did, and he came around to escort her through a metal reinforced security door to a concrete stairwell that soon gave way to stone walls and steps. Walking up the stairs felt like passing from the present day into a century in the far past.

"Why this?" she murmured. She had been talking to herself, but Xavier, who had taken the lead and was a step farther ahead, turned to look at her with one eyebrow raised in inquiry. She asked him, "Why a castle?"

"This demesne has a number of very old Vampyres who wield a great deal of financial and personal power. At the time, Julian and his sire, Carling, felt a structure that was so indicative of strength and age would strike the right note of authority with those Vampyres when they came to settle in California. Also, it's highly defensible, and there are a number of interior rooms that have no windows at all. The place is riddled with halls and private passages, so it can be a bit confusing until you get used to it. I suggest you do not get lost or wander off on your own."

"You don't have to worry about that," she muttered, even though she knew he could hear her quite clearly.

They continued up the stairs, and along a series of hallways that grew wider and more trafficked. Vampyres turned to look at them as they passed, their gazes lingering curiously on Tess.

She found she didn't have any emotional room to spare

for them either. Walking by Xavier's side, she felt as safe as if they strolled down the beach back at the estate.

Maybe that was a positive image, or maybe she just knew in the marrow of her bones that he was more dangerous than anyone they passed, and he was on her side.

You gave me blood, he had said. I'm supposed to protect you.

And she trusted him.

They came to a set of massive mahogany doors guarded by two Vampyres, a man and a woman, dressed in thoroughly modern, dark gray suits.

The man had average features and gingery hair, but the tall, athletic-looking woman was striking, with dark brown skin and a smooth, sleek cap of black hair. As Xavier approached, she said, "Go right in, sir. He's expecting you."

"Very good. Thank you, Yolanthe." As they stepped aside, Xavier nodded to the man and ushered Tess into the Nightkind King's personal quarters.

Julian stood in front of a blazing fire in a large granite fireplace. The Nightkind King's arms were crossed, and he spoke into a Bluetooth headset. He wore faded jeans, old, scarred cowboy boots and a black T-shirt that stretched across a broad, muscled chest. While the expensive, elegant evening suit he had worn to the Vampyre's Ball had emphasized his rough looks, this outfit looked as if it suited him.

As they entered the room, Julian looked up. Still speaking, he raised a finger, and Xavier nodded.

While they waited for Julian to finish his call, Tess looked around curiously. Whatever she might have imagined, the reality of Julian's living space was not it. The place was austere, and gave almost no hint of the kind of wealth and power he must truly have.

Black leather couches were arranged in front of the fireplace, with a thick, heavy wool rug between them. Plain, sturdy wooden tables and a matching cabinet completed the furnishings. The only expression of extravagance was a massive landscape painting that dominated one stone wall, depicting a sun-drenched scene that appeared to be Italian, or at the very least European.

A laptop and a pile of papers were stacked on one end of the coffee table. Julian finished his phone call, tapped the Bluetooth device at his ear then tore it off and flung it at the table.

"Melly isn't answering her cell," he said to Xavier. "Her publicist claims she's on location for a new shoot. And Tatiana is not inclined to waste Light Fae time and send another representative to redo proposals that have already been agreed upon. Goddammit."

"Give me a moment." Xavier pulled out his cell phone, dialed a number and a moment later said, "Hi, Melly, how are you?" He paused, giving Julian a wry glance. "Good for you. A skiing trip to Aspen sounds delightful."

Julian's rough expression darkened with fury. Hand out, he strode forward, silently demanding the phone. Xavier stepped back and shook his head warningly.

Xavier said into his phone, "Listen, I have a favor to ask of you. Yes, it does have to do with why Julian's been calling and leaving messages. No, I promise, it doesn't require you coming back to Evenfall. All I want you to do is say, 'Julian, I agree with all of the trade proposals that Xavier and I chatted about in New York.' Then Julian is going to say, 'Melisande, I agree with all of the trade proposals that you and Xavier chatted about in New York.' You don't have to really talk to each other, just say the words. Meanwhile, I'm going to put you on speaker and record everything, all right? Thank you."

As Tess watched in fascination, Julian's eyes flashed red. Lips peeling back in a silent snarl, he held up his hands, fingers curled, and pantomimed strangling an invisible person in front of him.

Xavier checked the screen of his phone. He said, "Melly, I've got you on speaker now. Can you hear me?"

"Of course." The Light Fae princess's warm voice sounded clearly in the room.

"Okay." Xavier's thumb moved over the screen. "I'm recording you now. Go."

Melisande said, "Julian, I agree with all of the trade proposals that Xavier and I chatted about in New York."

Xavier pointed to Julian. The Nightkind King growled, "Melisande, I agree with all of the trade proposals that you and Xavier chatted about in New York. And would it have killed you to pick up the fucking phone just once?"

"You never know," Melisande said. "It might have."

"If I ever get my hands on you again," he snapped, "I'm going to throttle you senseless."

"Dream on," she sneered. "You only wish you could get your hands on all of this awesomeness again, and that's one thing I promise is never going to happen."

Xavier said rapidly, "Okay, thanks again."

Melisande's voice changed drastically, and she said with obvious affection, "Any time, darling. 'Bye."

Xavier signed off. For a moment, he and Julian looked at each other, and in spite of the severity of her own problems, Tess was hard put to keep from laughing. Struggling to keep her face straight, she put a hand over her mouth.

"It's not pretty or dignified," Xavier said. "But it *is* a recording of an agreement between the two of you. Maybe it'll be enough to back Justine off, because you know the other members of the council won't take kindly to being called to reconvene over a technicality of law that appears to have been resolved already."

"I'll take it," Julian said. "I can back Justine off with this and boot her out of Evenfall, at least until next year's council sessions."

Xavier paused. "Gavin can probably cut off the last bit, if you prefer to keep that part private."

"Fine. Get me an abbreviated copy as soon as you can. Now, about your issue you couldn't discuss over the phone." When Julian looked at Tess, the red in his gaze had faded. He said, "I remember you. You interviewed with Xavier at the Vampyre's Ball. You're the one who sent an email to everyone on the Evenfall server. Including me."

Her humor died, and she nodded nervously.

For a few moments, Julian studied her with the same clinical dispassion that he had shown at the Ball. He turned to Xavier. "Tell me."

"Have you heard of the pariah Djinn named Malphas?" Xavier asked.

Julian's dark gaze narrowed. "He's the one based in Las Vegas. Owns one of the largest casinos. What of him?"

Xavier said, "We have reason to believe Malphas may have murdered Senator Jackson's son in Florida."

The disinterest vaporized from Julian's expression. "Why do you think that? Convince me."

When Xavier glanced at Tess, she nodded and he began to explain. Julian's brows lowered into a scowl as he listened. After Xavier finished, the Nightkind King looked at Tess. He had been dispassionate before, but now his dark gaze had turned chilling.

He said, "You're the only one in the world making this claim."

It was impossible to tell what Julian meant by that statement, but Xavier still looked calm and relaxed, and he gave her a reassuring smile. She swallowed hard. "I guess I am."

"I want to hear you say it," Julian said. "Tell me you believe this is true."

She met the Nightkind King's piercing gaze and said in a clear, steady voice, "I was present in the casino when all of it happened. I watched Eathan dig a hole for himself by gambling more and more, and I saw Malphas seduce him into it. I called Senator Jackson's office and got through all of his gatekeepers until I spoke to him directly, and I told him Eathan was in trouble. I saw Senator Jackson and his staff of bodyguards arrive at the casino, and they left shortly afterward with Eathan." She paused. "I believe Malphas killed Eathan."

Julian's expression hadn't shifted. "Jackson's boy died at sea. Even if the exact location of his death could be pinpointed—which is highly unlikely—it's too late to have the area scanned by a forensic magic user. You can't prove anything."

Her heart sank. Glancing at Xavier again, she said, "No, sir, I'm afraid I can't. But for me, the timing and manner of Eathan's death is too compelling."

Julian sat on the couch, propped his booted feet on the table and crossed his arms. "While I hear the conviction in your voice, nobody cares whether or not you find it compelling or you believe it's true. It's a very serious allegation, and none of it can be corroborated. I've yet to hear anything about whether or not you're a credible witness. For all I know, you might also believe tinfoil hats keep aliens from invading your thoughts."

Xavier stirred. "Julian."

The Nightkind King gestured impatiently. "I'm making a point. What this whole thing comes down to is your word against a first-generation Djinn."

If Malphas could make her disappear, it wouldn't even be that.

Despair tried to take over. Closing her eyes, she fought it off. She whispered, "I know."

Something settled around her shoulders. Surprised, she opened her eyes again to find Xavier had joined her and put his arm around her shoulders. Comfort stole into her frozen heart. Unable to resist, she slipped an arm around his lean waist while Julian watched them both with that dark, piercing gaze.

Xavier said, "As far as what happened to Jackson's boy, it may be your word against his, but that's not true of anybody else you saw Malphas entrap."

Julian straightened out of his lounging position and sat forward.

Xavier's clear, gray-green gaze was intelligent and warm. He smiled at her. "You saw other people rack up large debts and overheard things they said. Do you remember any names?"

She blinked rapidly. "Yes."

"What about the man with his wife? The one who said it would never be over."

Nodding, she told him, "I remember them. They had a Minnesota address."

Julian grabbed a pad of paper and a pen from the table and strode over to shove it into her hands. "Make a list of all the names you can remember."

Moving to one of the couches, she started scribbling.

Out of the corner of her eye, she saw Julian walk to the cabinet, open it and pull out a bottle of what looked to be bloodwine. He poured ruby red liquid into two glasses as Xavier joined him.

Julian offered one of the glasses to Xavier, who shook his head. With a shrug, Julian tossed back his head and downed the liquid.

Julian asked, "What's your goal in all this? We're not going to win any political leverage from the information. The Djinn are notoriously difficult to bargain with, and pariahs won't necessarily keep their word anyway. If it was a straightforward attack, I could hold him pinned, but only for a little while. If we decide to pin him, we'd have to kill him—and we would need a hell of a lot of backup for that, and right now, I don't think any of our allies would be willing to take on the kind of damage that a fight with that Powerful of a Djinn would entail."

While it was clear Julian wasn't speaking to her, he didn't bother to lower his voice, and neither did Xavier.

"The only leverage I'm looking for is insurance," Xavier said.

"What kind of insurance?"

"I want my people to live without fear of reprisal or some kind of revenge attack. I want Tess free and clear to do whatever she wants to do. Her life is in danger as long as Malphas believes she's the only one who knows what he's done, but if it were as simple as that, all we would have to do is go public with our suspicions. We have to take it a step further to make sure he doesn't take vengeance on her—or on anyone else—like he did with Jackson's son."

As what he said sank in, she stopped breathing. She

didn't know what to do with herself, or with what she had just heard.

Xavier wasn't just working with her to solve a dangerous problem. He was actively standing up for her.

Nobody had ever stood up for her before. Nobody, not for anything. Not one of her foster parents—certainly not the bastard who loved to hit kids with a belt—and none of the other children she had fostered with, either.

Tess was always the strong one, the one who had stuck up for them. Maybe that was why Eathan had gotten to her in the first place. He'd needed help, and so she had stepped up.

While she struggled to absorb the enormity of the concept, Julian refilled his glass and said, "I might have known you would be doing all this for one of your attendants."

It was impossible to decipher the expression in Julian's voice, and she didn't even try. It was Xavier she was interested in, and she watched him covertly.

"She's not my attendant any longer."

Lit only by the fire and a few recessed lights, the room was filled with strong shadows, and Xavier stood in profile. He was slighter than Julian's broad, tall figure, and more graceful, but no less masculine.

If Julian was a battle axe, or perhaps a trebuchet, built for battering and sheer brute force, Xavier was the rapier, elegant and deadly in single combat. With a simple, perfectly timed thrust, he could pierce the heart, while the rest of the body and soul stood amazed and dying.

Piercing the heart. She thought it over.

Yes. That was exactly how it felt as she looked at him and listened to what he said.

Julian shot Tess a quick, frowning glance. Ducking her head, she focused on the paper in front of her. He said, "While the Djinn might be notoriously reluctant to police pariahs, I think I'd better talk to Soren. I'm going to make the call in the other room."

Tess didn't know many personalities from the Elder

Races, but she recognized Soren's name as the head of the Elder tribunal. He was another first-generation Djinn, one of the most Powerful of his kind.

Xavier nodded, and as Julian left the room, he walked back to the couch to sit beside her. She set the pen and pad of paper facedown on the table and turned to him.

He asked, "Have you written down everyone you can think of?"

"Yes." She didn't question her impulse. Instead, she leaned forward, threw her arms around his neck and hugged him. "Thank you so much for everything."

He held rigidly immobile, his lean, strong body like stone.

What she'd done sank in. She started to pull back. "I'm sorry. I just—"

The stone man in her arms thawed, and his arms came around her, holding her in place against his chest. He said in her ear, "What is this?"

"I don't know," she muttered. "I just know nobody has ever stood up for me the way you're doing right now."

His arms tightened, and he cupped the back of her head. "That is their loss, because you deserve it."

She shook her head, whispering, "I don't know that I believe that, but I'm grateful anyway. You're doing all of this, while we haven't even had that talk about whether or not I'll still be your attendant."

He drew back to look at her. This close to him, she could see the absolute clarity in the subtle color of his gray-green eyes. "We need to be clear about one thing, Tess. I do not want you back as one of my attendants."

After feeling a series of emotional doors open, disappointment struck cruelly hard. Even though she tried not to, she felt herself flinch and attempted to mask it by nodding. "I understand," she said tightly. "I withheld too much dangerous infor—"

Taking hold of her chin in long, cool fingers, he tilted her head and kissed her.

A clean bolt of shock struck her. It felt like mainlining tequila. His lips were firm and astonishingly sensual. As she froze and her mind stuttered, he slanted his mouth to cover hers more completely. He nudged her lips open and delved inside in brief, intimate exploration.

When he pulled back, she forgot to close her mouth. She stared at him.

"I would never kiss one of my attendants," he told her. "You know that."

"You never . . . You wouldn't . . ." She said, "I, um."

Cupping her face with one hand, he wiped her moistened lips with his thumb. "I have just one question for you right now."

"Sure," she murmured faintly. Her mind was still frozen on the moment when his lips had touched hers. "Shoot."

He kissed her forehead and her cheek. "You're not still afraid of me, are you?"

"What?" she said. "*Pfft*, no."

His gaze gleamed with the most astonishing array of emotion, relief and pleasure foremost among them. With another jolt of surprise, she realized, he really cared what she thought of him.

"Good," he whispered. "Thank you."

Her gaze dropped to the refined, sensual lines of his lips. She had been in far too much shock to have really felt his mouth on hers. Hungry to understand what it all meant, to experience it again, she kissed him.

She felt his reaction in the quick shift of his body, and the intake of his breath. But he didn't need to breathe, she realized. That was all superfluous, all for her. Their mouths fit together as well as if they were made for each other.

If that don't beat all, she thought with a hazy astonishment. I'm having the sexiest kiss of my life.

With a Vampyre.

But not just any Vampyre.

I'm having the sexiest kiss of my life with the finest man I know.

• • •

Tess's lips were warm under Xavier's, so warm, and as soft as silk spun by moonlight. He followed the proud angle of her cheekbone with his fingertips as he gently caressed her tongue with his, and a snatch of ancient text came to him.

Behold, thou art fair, my love. Behold, thou art fair.

He had to breathe. He had to. It was an instinct older than death. He took in a deep, physically unnecessary breath just to smell the fragrance of her hair, and thought, I am in deep trouble.

A ripple of Power drew his attention. It came from the other room, where Julian had disappeared. A moment later, he heard Julian and Soren talking. Their voices grew closer, and he had just enough time to ease Tess back into her seat before the door opened and the other two men walked in.

As he always did, Xavier had to brace himself for the onslaught of Soren's presence. Born at the beginning of the world, Soren was one of the ancient ones, a first-generation Djinn, and his Power was so intense, he burned against the mind's eye. The physical form Soren chose to wear was a tall, strongly built male, with a craggy face, white hair and white eyes that shone like stars.

Beside Xavier, Tess straightened her spine. Her gaze was filled with fascination and wariness.

Soren ignored Tess and nodded to Xavier. His voice was deep and commanding. "Del Torro, I've heard what Julian has to say and I'll be blunt—the Djinn will not go to war against Malphas over this issue. If he murdered the senator's son, there's no evidence of it, and if humans have gambled enough to accrue debts they cannot pay, they've broken a bargain and aren't entitled to any protections or rights under Djinn law." He shrugged. "If someone else can bring him to justice in a court of human law for something he's done, so be it."

The Djinn and their blasted bargains. While he wasn't surprised at anything Soren said, still, anger burned hot and bright. He said, "That would be convenient, wouldn't it, if others dealt with Malphas without involving the Djinn?"

Soren raised his eyebrows. "Of course."

Before he could say anything in reply, Tess spoke up.

"Excuse me, Mister Soren," she said. Her eyes glittered with an expression that Xavier was beginning to find all too familiar. "I understand I'm just an unimportant human, and as such, I don't really warrant a proper introduction or you speaking directly to me. My name is Tess, by the way."

Soren's shining, starred eyes fixed on Tess, while at his side, Julian angled his head to stare at Xavier, who sat back and began to smile.

"Do go on," Soren said coldly.

Tess picked up the pad of paper, tore off a page and folded it. "Do you have any idea what's written on this page?"

"No," said the deadly head of the Elder tribunal. "Is there some reason I should?"

Julian said in Xavier's head, *What is she doing?*

I don't have a clue, said Xavier. *But I think it will be interesting to find out.*

"I didn't think so," Tess replied. "Do you know who else doesn't know what's on this page? Malphas. In fact, I'm only sure of one thing in all of this mess—he doesn't know what I know. I mean it only stands to reason, doesn't it? Otherwise, he would have stopped me from warning Eathan's father. He would have caught me before I ran away. And he would have found me by now. You get my drift, don't you?"

"I believe I do," said Soren. His craggy face was so expressionless, it looked like the mask it truly was.

"Here's one other thing I noticed," she said. The fine bones of her face were etched with tension, but the expression in her eyes was hectic, renegade. "Everyone agrees that Malphas won't necessarily stick to a bargain, unless he believes it benefits him in some way. But not you. If you make a bargain, you'll stick to it, won't you?"

"Absolutely."

"Would you make a bargain with me, Mister Soren?"

The Djinn cocked his head. "Perhaps."

Tess asked, "Would you make a bargain with me in front of Malphas?"

⇒ FIFTEEN ⇐

Tess, no," Xavier said. *"No."*

She didn't look at him or react. All her attention appeared focused on the Djinn in front of her, while the folded paper shook visibly in her clenched hand.

Soren replied, "I believe I would. Provided the terms are acceptable, of course."

"Goddammit." Xavier slipped into Spanish, and a stream of expletives poured out of his mouth.

Julian gave him a strange look. He said, "I'm inclined to agree with her, Xavier. She started this. She can finish it— or at least try to."

The implication in that was obvious to everyone.

"I'd like to be clear about one thing." Tess's voice turned tight. "*I* didn't start this."

Julian's expression cooled, but he said, "Point taken."

Soren asked, "Shall I summon Malphas here, or do you prefer some other location?"

Rubbing the back of his neck, Julian replied, "I'd just as soon have this happen here in my quarters, where we can keep it private."

"Very well." Soren looked at Tess. "Are you ready?"

"Almost," Tess said. "I need an envelope."

"Fine." Looking exasperated, Julian strode out of the room.

Xavier stood when Tess did, his hands clenched. Ignoring Soren, he said telepathically, *Tess, don't do this.*

She shook her head, looking as determined as he'd ever seen her. *I have to.*

No, you don't, he growled. *Besides, I won't let you.*

She gave him another remarkably beautiful, complex smile. *You don't really have a choice.*

He snapped, *You haven't even explained what you intend to do. We haven't talked over options.*

Julian and Soren have made it clear we don't have any options.

Julian strode back into the room, holding a manila envelope. He handed it to Tess, and she slipped the folded paper inside and sealed it.

Xavier couldn't stand it. Not caring that Julian and Soren stood nearby and watched, he grabbed her by the shoulders. He demanded, *I'm supposed to protect you. Where did that go?*

Something happened to me over the last six weeks. Tess laid a hand on his chest. *I internalized what you and Raoul have been teaching me, and the conversations in my head really did change. I'm grateful you want to protect me. That means so much to me—much more than you can know. But I'm going to protect myself now. I need to do this, Xavier, and for more than one reason. Malphas needs to know this comes from me.*

Taking hold of his wrists, she gently removed his hands from her shoulders. Then she said aloud to Soren, "I'm ready."

Soren said in a voice filled with Power, "Malphas."

If Xavier could have torn that name out of the air, he would have. Silence fell in the room, and it took on a listening quality.

A maelstrom arrived, filling open space in the room like

a tornado springing from nothing. It coalesced into the shape of a handsome, golden-haired man whose eyes were starred with Power every bit as strong as Soren's.

The handsome man's shining gaze swept the room, taking in everyone present and coming to rest on Tess. Fury suffused his expression. He looked so hostile Xavier took an instinctive step forward toward her. She might not want his protection, but by God, she was going to get it.

Snapping out words like he was biting the air, Malphas said, "Well, isn't this an interesting gathering. Both the Nightkind King and the head of the Elder tribunal—Tess, you've been surprisingly efficient at striking up new acquaintances."

"I've worked hard at it," she said between her teeth.

Malphas clenched and unclenched his fists, and Xavier's gaze fell to track the movement. "Soren," Malphas hissed. "What are you doing with my ex-employee?"

"I don't converse with pariahs." If Soren's voice had been cold before, now it was a single spike of deadly ice.

"I find that inconsistent, since you're the one who summoned me here. Whatever stories this human might have told you, they have nothing to do with Djinn law. But you already know that, or you would have gathered many more Djinn to meet with me."

Malphas strode forward, his attention turning back to Tess. The veneer of humanity he wore thinned, and details of his appearance grew disconnected. He still had two eyes, a mouth and nose, cheekbones and jawline, but none of the features looked like they comprised an actual face, and sheer raw Power shown out of him like light from a lantern.

"Tell me, Tess," he said. "How have you enjoyed the dreams I've sent you?"

If she had been pale from tension before, now she turned chalk white. She whispered, "They've been engrossing."

"You know they're just a taste of what I can do if you really cross me. Tell me you haven't really crossed me, and you can have your old job back. It's all there waiting for you—the six-figure income, your nice apartment and all your nice things. The bad dreams will stop. All will be forgiven." Malphas pulled his lips into a smile and opened his eyes wide. "I promise."

Xavier moved directly between Tess and Malphas, turning to face the Djinn with reddened eyes and fangs fully descended. Every predatory instinct he possessed urged him to attack, and he had to fight to control himself.

"The Vampyre seems to think he might be able to do something to stop me." Malphas gave Xavier a vicious look. "How terminally misguided of him. Do you think I should let him try something to make him feel manlier, or should I stake him now and be done with it?"

Julian blurred to Xavier's side. The Nightkind King's fangs had descended too. "Attacking one of my subjects is an act of war with the entire Nightkind demesne."

"If you insist," snapped the Djinn. "I can stake you too."

"You know what, Malphas?" Tess said suddenly. "I am so done with you. Do you hear me? I am done. I'm done with your snotty attitude, and your petty cruelties and threats, and this persistent belief you have that you're untouchable. I'm done being afraid of you. I'm done giving you real estate in my head. I'm getting you out of my life, and burying you in the past where you belong."

She strode to Soren and held out the sealed envelope.

"What is that?" Malphas said. The open viciousness in his face ebbed and a different kind of tension took its place.

Tess ignored him. She said to Soren, "Will you strike a bargain with me?"

After a long glance at Malphas, Soren smiled. "Why yes, human, I believe I will. What kind of bargain did you have in mind?"

"I want you to take this envelope and keep it safe," Tess said. "As long as Malphas does nothing to harm me or anyone else in the Nightkind demesne, I want you to promise this envelope stays sealed and unread. But if anything happens to me, or to anybody else I've ever known or cared about, I want you to send copies of the contents of this envelope to Senator Jackson, the Elder tribunal, the Night-kind King, the governing body for the Djinn, and every gaming commission in the United States." She cocked her head. "Actually, please make that every gaming commission for every government worldwide. I would also like for you to send it to every Elder Races and human news outlet. Would you be willing to do that?"

"The terms of this bargain are easily met," Soren said. "I would. What do you offer me in return?"

Tess's gaze never wavered. She said steadily, "I hadn't gotten that far in my thinking. Anything you like."

"No!" Xavier snapped. Making an open-ended bargain like that with a Djinn was incredibly foolhardy. She was effectively throwing away her life, and Soren would own her.

Julian gripped him by the arm, preventing him from lunging forward.

Soren glanced at the Vampyres then at Malphas, who vibrated with impotent rage. Soren turned back to Tess. "For my end of the bargain, as long as Malphas does nothing to harm you or anyone in your life, you will never reveal the contents of what is inside this envelope to anyone." He paused, lifting one white eyebrow. "Be careful, human. This bargain is binding. You must never speak of it again."

The rigid tension eased from Tess's shoulders, and she took a shaking breath, and Xavier could tell that she knew Soren had given her a reprieve. "I agree."

"We have a deal," Soren said. He took the envelope, held out his hand and Tess shook it. He said to Julian, "I'm done here."

"Thank you for coming," Julian said.

Soren nodded and vanished.

Julian turned his red gaze to Malphas. He growled, "Leave."

Malphas ignored him and walked over to Tess, who stood her ground. Oddly, the pariah's fury seemed to have vanished, to be replaced by fascination.

Malphas said, "You always said you weren't a gambler,

but you just gambled everything on Soren keeping his word. What was in the envelope, Tess?"

She said, "I'll never tell."

"Whatever it is, you think it's worth sending out to every gaming commission in the world?" His gaze was like twin laser beams.

"Malphas, I know for a fact that if the gaming commissions knew what you were doing, no one would ever let you run a respectable casino again." She leaned forward. "That might not stop you from gambling somewhere, somehow, but it would severely curtail your activities, wouldn't it?"

After a long moment, he said, "Fine. I don't expect to see or hear anything from you again."

She lifted her chin. "Nor I, you."

He studied her unblinkingly then gave Xavier and Julian one dismissive glance. Without another word, he vanished.

"So, okay," she whispered. "That happened."

Xavier felt his fangs recede, but not his anger. Striding over to Tess, he glared at her and spat, *"Estupida."*

She shrugged, her mouth working. That was when he noticed she shook all over. Grabbing her none too gently, he hauled her into his arms. She leaned her forehead on him and let out a shaking breath.

He buried his face in her hair and held her. After a moment, he whispered, "I didn't know he was sending you dreams. Did you?"

"I thought they were just nightmares." When she lifted her head again, her eyes were too bright, but overall she seemed calmer. Walking to the couch, she picked up the pad of paper and turned it over, faceup, to show the top page to Xavier and Julian.

Twelve names were written on it, and each name had a note scribbled beside it.

Xavier stared at the paper, then at her. He grabbed the pad and flipped through it. The second page from the top had been ripped out, and a jagged edge showed along the seam. "You put a blank piece of paper in that envelope, didn't you?"

Her shoulders lifted in a small shrug, while her dark eyes never left his. "Now, you know I can't reveal what I put in there. I just made a bargain with one of the most Powerful Djinn in the world promising I wouldn't."

While he carefully tore off the top sheet, folded it and tucked it in his pocket, Julian walked over to the cabinet and poured himself another drink of bloodwine.

He said in Xavier's head, *I don't know what the hell you're going to do with her, but assuming you still want to keep her alive, you can't send her out on assignment. She's much too colorful.*

I know, Xavier said.

A few minutes later they left Julian's apartment.
Tess walked along beside Xavier meekly. They strode down the hallway, past a variety of different creatures, most Vampyres, but some humans, a few ghouls and even a troll.

She asked Xavier telepathically, *Can we do anything with those names?*

Maybe, he replied without looking at her. *Maybe not. Perhaps an independent agency with another agenda can investigate, but we need to be very careful nothing can be traced back to you, or us. This stalemate you bargained for is only good if Malphas believes he has your silence.*

I understand.

Inside, a great roaring emptiness filled her head, and she realized how much space fear had taken up in her life. She felt strange in the absence of it, almost adrift.

I'm free, she thought. Really free.

I can access the money in my bank accounts. Send for my furniture. I can go wherever I like, do whatever I like.

The thoughts were dizzying. Now all she had to do was decide what she wanted to do. Where she wanted to go.

She sneaked a peek at Xavier's profile.

He looked calm, but he usually looked calm. Not like

the red-eyed, fanged Vampyre who had guarded her so fiercely.

No, this was the imperious aristocrat, and while she found him just as sexy as the tender man who had kissed her with such sensual expressiveness, this side of Xavier was highly unpredictable.

Was he still angry with her? It was impossible to tell.

Did he regret kissing her?

As she angled her face away, she caught sight of a Vampyre watching her with a narrow-eyed stare filled with curiosity and hunger. The scrutiny was so rude, she scowled with irritation and stared back.

I've confronted a monster far worse than you and survived, she thought. I've faced my worst nightmare, and you don't even come close.

Her heart rate remained steady, her nerves completely calm.

It appeared she had finally found the positive image she'd been looking for.

After a moment of the staring contest, the Vampyre gave her a slight smile and turned away.

Soon enough, she and Xavier reached the end of one hallway and a set of doors that looked much more modest than those leading to the Nightkind King's apartment. Xavier typed a code into a very modern-looking keypad lock, opened the door and stood back to let her precede him.

Once inside, he locked and bolted the door behind them, while Tess looked around. This apartment was almost as simply furnished as Julian's had been, but the results were warmer and more elegant. Wingback armchairs, upholstered in a deep, rich gold, were positioned around an unlit fireplace, along with a matching sofa. A shadowed hallway lay at one corner of the room, and a closed door lay across the room in another corner.

As with Julian's apartment, there were no windows here. An abundance of wall art, highlighted with track lighting, illuminated the room and gave it dimension and color. The pieces looked European and distinctive. She guessed one was a Gauguin, and another appeared to be a Renoir, and she had no doubt they were all originals. Bookshelves lined the walls between paintings, filled with a mix of old and new books just as in his study, back at the estate.

Over the fireplace mantel, an antique clock said the time had gone past four o'clock. She could believe it. The events of the last several hours seemed to have taken days.

A note lay on the table nearest the door. She could read it easily from where she stood. *I put Tess's things in the room nearest the bathroom and left a snack for her on the bedside table. Wake me if you have need of anything, D.*

Xavier glanced at the note. Still without looking directly at her, he said, "It's very late, and you've had a long day. You must be tired."

His face revealed nothing of what he was thinking. She remembered the first time she had met him, how his expression had been virtually unreadable and how much that had frightened her. She had come such a long way from that night.

Lifting one shoulder, she studied him sidelong. "I suppose."

A muscle in his lean jaw ticked. "There are two bedrooms for attendants down the hallway, along with the apartment's only bathroom." He jerked his chin toward the other doorway. "My bedroom is there. I'm afraid we all have to share a bathroom. Modernizing Evenfall is a nightmare of logistics, and renovations have only gone so far."

"Are you mad at me?" She searched his face again for some kind of clue as to what he was thinking or feeling.

The question was like touching a lit match to dry tinder.

He rounded on her and exploded with such quiet intensity she jumped. "God, yes, I'm angry. The chances you took—*you bluffed with both Djinn.*" He slid into rapid, forceful Spanish again.

Ducking her head, she studied the tips of her shoes and waited out the incomprehensible tirade, nodding every once in a while to show that she was still listening.

Was it a machismo thing? At his roots, he was, after all, a medieval Spaniard. In fact, despite having what seemed to be an inherently gentle nature, he had been an entitled medieval Spaniard, and he was very, very male.

She said experimentally, "I know. I should have let you handle everything, like you wanted. Right?"

When he paused, she looked up to find him glaring at her. He looked baffled and infuriated, and the tension in his posture was palpable.

"You know none of it would have happened without you. I would never have been able to talk to Julian or Soren, if you hadn't paved the way."

Renewed rage darkened his face. "If you think I'm angry because I wanted credit for anything, you don't know me in the slightest."

Instantly contrite, she whispered, "I apologize. That's not what I meant." She studied him anxiously. "Are you sorry you kissed me?"

His expression changed. It was the only warning she got as he lunged at her.

He was so fast. He had her pinned against the wall before she fully knew what had happened. Moving with precise intent, he cupped her jaw, tilted up her head and took her mouth with his.

This wasn't a sensual, tender exploration like the first kiss had been. His lips were hardened and demanding, and he thrust deep with his tongue.

A flash fire washed across her nerve endings, lighting up her whole body.

He really was inside her mouth.

He really was pushing against her, thrusting a knee between her legs, the length of his body tight like steel.

She bucked against the wall then latched on to him. Hardly knowing what she did, she clawed at the simple leather tie that held back his hair and yanked it off.

His dark, chestnut hair spilled about his shoulders, drastically changing his appearance. Gone was the courteous, reserved man, and in his place stood a shockingly sensual stranger, with a hardened face and glittering eyes that flashed with green fire.

She fisted both hands greedily in the dark mass of his hair and kissed him back with everything she had.

He gripped her by the back of the neck, while a hard length grew to press against one of her hips. When she realized what it was, arousal pierced through her lower body and moistened the growing ache between her legs.

When he pulled back to stare down at her, he was breathing hard.

Their gazes locked. Deliberately, he slid a hand between their bodies and cupped her pelvis. The steady, knowledgeable pressure he exerted broke a moan out of her.

"No, Tess," he said, very low, this sensual, glittering stranger. "I don't regret kissing you in the slightest, and I have every intention of doing it again. A lot."

"I see," she whispered, shaken and delighted, and completely beside herself. She pushed against his hand, willing him to move, but he held rock steady. "Tell me you're not going to stop now."

"That depends." Still holding her between her legs, he cupped her cheek and stroked her lips with his thumb. They were still moist from his kiss.

"On what?" She tried again to push against him. All she wanted to do was rub herself all over him like an alley cat, but not only did he have her pinned too effectively, his strength was immense.

He ducked his head and bit at her lips lightly, while running the tips of his fingers along the seam of her jeans. Between her legs. Even through the thick material, his touch left a trail of molten fire.

Leaning his forehead against hers, he looked deep into her eyes, his expression serious. "On where you're going to be tomorrow."

She stilled, staring back. Once she had been able to set aside her prejudices and preconceived notions, her fascination for him had grown at an exponential rate. It would almost be easier to blame him for mesmerizing her, except she couldn't do that to either one of them. She wouldn't deny this attraction she felt for him, and she couldn't insult his integrity like that, even in the privacy of her own mind.

"I . . . I don't know where I'm going to be tomorrow. I guess I don't understand."

He stroked her hair back from her face. "I want you." His voice was low, pitched for her ears alone, words deliberate and forceful. "I've wanted you for a while, but you were off-limits and that was all there was to it."

Of course he would have been restrained. He set his code and lived by it. His soul was as straight and strong as tempered steel.

"I'm not working for you any longer," she said. "I'm not under your power now."

Although she was. She was.

"That's right. You're not." He kissed her forehead. "Theoretically we can do whatever we like, but not that long ago you were deeply afraid of me. Now you've bought a stalemate with Malphas, and you're free to go wherever you like. While I'm glad for that, I don't want to rush you into something too soon, and fuck you in the heat of the moment only to watch you leave. Do you understand? I don't want to do that, because I want *you*."

Closing her eyes, she took a deep breath then let it out slowly, while the fever in her blood ratcheted down slightly to something a little more manageable.

He was right. She had a hundred thousand dollars in her bank accounts, and a wide-open road.

"I could have done that," she admitted. "I don't know."

He studied her expression. "Promise me something."

She focused on fiddling with a button on his shirt. "Maybe."

"Promise you won't just run away. Promise you'll at least stay long enough to discuss what you might want to do next."

It was time to confess.

"I don't actually want to leave," she muttered. "I . . . love the estate. I love the peacefulness and the ocean, and

I'd been meaning to ask you if I could borrow some books from your library. Raoul and I had just gotten somewhere interesting in my training, and I was invested in seeing where we went next. And I put on that dress you bought for me, because I really did want to see if you and I could waltz for ninety more seconds without me stomping on your feet." She glanced up, into his intent gaze. "But I can't go back to being one of your attendants again."

Removing his hand from between her legs, he simply gathered her up and held her in a whole body hug. The sexiness hadn't gone away, not in the slightest, but the sheer emotional impact of being held in such a cherishing manner shot straight through her.

Piercing her heart, again.

Nuzzling her hair, he murmured, "We have created a neat box for ourselves, haven't we?"

She forced the words to come out. "Would it be better if I just left?"

"I would follow you." He slipped his fingers underneath her chin and urged her to tilt it. When she did, he kissed her again, slow and lingeringly. He said it a second time against her lips. "Tess, I would follow you."

Gladness shook through her. She sighed, "Oh good," and kissed him back.

For long moments they lingered. He brushed her lips with his, over and over, and nipped at her gently with the edge of his even, white teeth. She wasn't the slightest bit nervous that he would forget, or lose control and bite her for real. It was quite clear what he was doing.

This was love play, and he was knowledgeable and very, very good at it. She could feel his erection pressing against her pelvis bone.

He wanted her, and he made no secret of it. The tension in his body and in his gentle hands told her how much. He showed her with every caress of his fingertips and stroke of his tongue against hers. And she believed in her bones that if she said no or asked him to stop, he would do so instantly.

A different level of trust bloomed, like a shy, rare orchid

that could only exist if a certain set of conditions were just right.

She had suspected that he would change her, and at the time, survival was what had mattered the most. But change could also be a positive, life-enhancing experience, and she realized she might like herself better, might like life better, than she had ever believed possible.

"Xavier," she whispered.

He stopped kissing along the edge of her jaw to look at her inquiringly.

It was her turn to stroke his hair. It fell to his shoulders in a thick wave, and while the length could have seemed effeminate, it didn't. It was ridiculously gorgeous and utterly sensual, and it suited him completely.

"I won't run, I promise," she told him. "I'm too . . . intrigued."

A slow smile broke over his face. "Very good. We will work everything else out, yes? All the definitions—what you need to be, and what I need to be. What we need to be together. You will come back home with me?"

She hesitated. She had promised she wouldn't run away, but that didn't mean she felt comfortable with moving forward. "I don't know about that."

His pleasure faded, and he scowled. "Why not?"

"I don't fit, back there. Everyone else will be expecting me to go back to being an attendant, and living in the house."

"Bah." He dismissed that with a wave of one hand. "They will deal with whatever we decide to present to them."

The thought of Diego's discontentment flashed through her mind. She said, doubtfully, "It may not be as easy as all that."

"You will stay in the guesthouse," he told her. "Not the attendants' house. Raoul will continue your lessons, and I will teach you to waltz, by God, if it's the last thing I do."

"Hey," she said, caught by the grim determination with which he had said that. "It wasn't *that* bad."

Humor danced in his eyes. "The point is we do not need

to reach an instant definition this very moment. We can work it all out over time. Agreed?"

She might not know where they were going, but it was definitely a step in the right direction.

Taking a deep breath, she nodded. "Agreed."

His expression turned serious, and he eased away from the wall. Without his body weight pinning her into place, she had to force her own shaky limbs to support her.

Sliding his fingers lightly down her arm, he took her hand.

"Come make love with me," he said.

After all of that—after taking the time to create an understanding that was filled with respect and that gave her a sense of safety—how like him to make everything so classic and direct, and simple.

She tightened her hand in his. "Yes."

⇒ SIXTEEN ⇐

At her reply, a sense of peace and gladness filled Xavier. He raised her hand to kiss her fingers, and she caressed the corner of his mouth. Her dark eyes looked wondering, and she looked more vulnerable than he had ever seen her.

Need roared like a freight train in his blood, but he would not give into it. Not yet. Putting an arm around her slender body, he walked with her to his bedroom door and opened it.

Inside, everything was as he had last left it, the large, old four-poster bed made with an eighteenth-century, intricately embroidered quilt. He saw that Diego had unpacked his bag and set it neatly on the chair in the corner, then he forgot everything except for Tess.

As they passed through the doorway, she pulled back against his arm, her body language suddenly turning reluctant, and he realized he had forgotten to turn on the lights. He flipped the switch, and gentle, indirect light flooded the room.

"Sorry," he muttered.

The reluctance vanished from her body, and in reply, she shut the door and turned to put her arms around his neck.

That was all the invitation he needed. He kissed her hard and hungrily, and he felt her reaction shudder through her whole body. Her lips molded to his, and she kissed him back with a fierce hunger that set him ablaze.

Over the centuries of his existence, he had witnessed so many things—miracles and tragedies, and mysteries that were simply unexplainable. He'd had considerate, humorous lovers, and he'd enjoyed every one.

None of it compared to the miracle of holding Tess's body against his. Seeing the utter lack of fear in her flushed, angular face, when she had once been so afraid of him.

Realizing the passion that glazed her beautiful eyes was all for him.

"'Thy love is better than wine,'" he whispered against her softened, sexy mouth.

Better than wine.

He brushed his lips down the side of her cheek, along the clean, graceful curve of her jawline, and kissed her slender neck. Her skin. Dear God, was there anything else as perfect as her skin?

She cradled his head in both hands, her uneven breath sounding in his ear. "What was that? Were you quoting something?"

"Love poetry," he muttered, kissing along her collarbone as he ran his hands underneath the hem of her sweater. "From the Song of Solomon."

An exhalation of a laugh shook out of her. "You're a romantic?"

"I was, once upon a time," he admitted. He curved his hands around her narrow rib cage. She fit so perfectly against him. "I still am, on occasion. When life permits."

"I'm not a romantic," she confessed. Nuzzling his cheek, she slipped his jacket off his shoulders. He shrugged it off and let it fall to the floor.

"I forgive you," he told her expansively, with a grin.

Another ghost of a laugh danced across her face. "Quote something else for me."

As he coaxed her sweater up, she lifted her arms. He pulled it off of her and let it fall to the floor too. She wore a plain black bra, no lace, but the way it molded to the round curve of her breasts was extravagantly feminine.

He touched her temples. " 'Thou hast doves' eyes,' " he said gently.

Her expression turned luminous. The emotion shining out of her face—that was all for him.

He felt it come into him, until it lit every corner of his soul and shone back out at her. "Of course, there's also this one—'I have compared thee, O my love, to a company of horses in Pharaoh's chariots.' "

She burst out laughing. "What on earth does that mean?"

"I have no idea." Smiling, he stroked her graceful shoulders while she undid the buttons of his shirt.

"How much can you quote?"

"I was a young man with a completely normal sex drive, who was encouraged to study the scriptures," he said. "I memorized all of it." He stroked her lips. " 'Thy lips are like a thread of scarlet. . . . Thou hast ravished my heart.' "

Something stricken banished the laughter from her gaze. "Yes," she whispered. "That's what it feels like."

All the words burned away, and he stood silent, without language or barriers, holding on to her bare, warm waist. He felt like he might drown if he let go. He might drown anyway, but if he did, he needed to bring her with him.

He shrugged out of his shirt, threw it and went down on his knees in front of her. Unbuttoning her jeans, he slid the zipper down and eased both her jeans and panties over her hips while she stripped off her bra. When she stood totally nude before him, he sat back on his heels and feasted on the sight of her.

She was panther-sleek, with toned, slender muscles, a narrow waist and a flat stomach, all of which served to enhance the feminine swell of her hips, and *Dios*, those full, round breasts. The dusky rose of her nipples were the perfect crown for those tender beauties, and the silken tuft of private hair at the juncture of her legs beckoned him with a siren's lure.

Slipping his arms around her slim thighs, he rubbed his cheek against her, inhaling her scent, while he listened to her heartbeat gallop. It was good, so good, to scent the evidence of her arousal, and to know that her heart raced for him.

He had been stiff for some time, but now his cock hardened further until he felt desperately sensitized, unbearably erect. Desire might be an old friend whom he had met before, but with her, it came to him wearing a new face, sharp, bright and joyful.

He felt the blood coursing through her, such unimaginably precious treasure housed in the temple of her body, and her fingers stroking through his hair. She tugged gently until he tilted back his head to look up at her.

"Let me come down there with you," she murmured.

It took a moment for him to understand what she meant. He loosened his hold around her thighs, and she began to kneel.

"No," he said, standing to pick her up. "I won't take you on the drafty floor, not when we have such a large, comfortable bed to explore."

He walked to the bed to ease her down onto it, and he came down on top of her. Hungry for the rich taste of her mouth, he kissed her again as he stroked between her legs to finger the delicate, plump folds of her moistened sex.

Fire flashed in her eyes, and her breath sawed in her throat. As she fumbled at the waist of his slacks, her lips shaped unsteady words against his. "I can't stand it."

His, this urgency of hers was all his. The look in her eyes. The need he could feel in her. All for him.

Her body might be lovely, but the passion of her spirit was what drove it, and that was inexpressibly gorgeous. Intoxicated with beauty, he licked her mouth. "You can stand so much more than you think you can."

Carefully, he parted the petals of her flesh until he found the small pearl of her clitoris. With a deep sense of pleasure, he explored the stiff little peak of flesh and circled it with his forefinger. She made an inarticulate, urgent noise at the back of her throat, her body arching up to his touch.

He needed.

He needed her.

"Touch me," he said against her mouth.

She made another odd little sound, something between a growl and a whine, and hooked one leg around his waist as she ran her hands quickly, greedily down his back. Tracing the waist of his slacks to the front, she wrestled with the fastening.

Something thundered in his ears. With surprise, he realized it was his own roughened breathing. When she got his pants open, his stiff, aching penis spilled out into her hands.

As she gripped him, he threw his head back, face twisted. She ran her thumb over the broad, damp tip of his cock, and the pleasure was so extreme, it was agonizing.

"Oh, shit," she muttered. She grabbed his wrist, held his hand against her and shook as though she had a fever.

It snapped him back into focus. He stared down at her as she climaxed, quivering rhythmically against his fingers. It was so surprising, he couldn't stand for it to be over so soon. He slid down her body and parted her legs, and put his mouth on her.

Her head snapped back against the mattress, and she stuffed the heel of one hand against her mouth to muffle a scream.

The taste of her, the sensation of such velvety softness against his lips . . . he lost all sense of self-control and feasted, licking and sucking, while she bucked and twisted underneath him. His awareness narrowed to two things, how immense and painful his erection had become, and the slick pearl of flesh he held with such tense care between his teeth.

She was sobbing now, and swearing like a sailor. He would have laughed, if he'd remembered what humor was.

Instead, he flicked his tongue faster, harder. He couldn't

shove his cock into her and suck on her at the same time, no matter how much he wanted to, so he made do by inserting two fingers into her.

Her inner muscles clenched on him, and she was so tight and richly plush inside, so wet, he just had to fuck her with those two fingers, he had to. The heat and carnality of it shoved him outside of himself. All his intellect shut down, until only the urgency was left, and it built to an excruciating level.

A low, shaking moan broke out of her, and her body rippled with more tremors. He felt her climax, inside and out.

As he held his mouth firm and steady to help her through it, he thought, *Set me as a seal upon thine heart, as a seal upon thine arm: for love is strong as death; jealousy is cruel as the grave: the coals thereof are coals of fire, which hath a most vehement flame.*

No. That ancient, long-dead author got it wrong.

Love is surprising and can strike the oldest, most world-weary heart without warning.

Love is so much stronger than death.

The strength of her second climax was so ferocious it overtook everything. She felt completely lit from the inside, bathed in the sweetest, most delicious fire she'd ever experienced.

It wasn't that she'd never climaxed before. She'd had healthy, athletic sex, and she'd climaxed many times, both with partners and by pleasuring herself. Climaxing happened to be one of her very favorite things to do.

But she'd never before climaxed with Xavier.

The visual shock of watching him work between her parted legs was only matched by the sensual shock of feeling his mouth move on her with such intimate wisdom, and feeling his fingers pierce deep inside her body.

She'd never before climaxed with such emotion.

He had coaxed her out of her fortress until she stood unguarded, and the pleasure rolled over her like a tsunami.

Sobbing for breath, she clutched at his shoulder, while tears spilled out of the corners of her eyes. He was the only thing strong enough to hold on to in the face of such a storm.

As the wave of pleasure peaked and ebbed, Xavier raised his head and met her gaze, the angles of his face pronounced and serious. He had such clarity in his eyes, as if he comprehended even more than she what they did together.

The muscles in his arms and upper chest bunching, he rose to crawl over her. A sprinkle of sleek, dark hair ran down the middle of his lean torso, winging out to touch both flat, male nipples, and arrowing down to the erect penis that jutted out of the opening of his slacks.

He had a beautifully masculine body, but it was only a naked body. It shouldn't be so profound. Except she couldn't lie to herself, and it was.

After two climaxes, she should feel sated, but she didn't. Nothing was going predictably. Her body felt empty and aching.

Looking up into his eyes, she curled her fingers around his cock. He felt hot and hard, his penis covered with skin like silk. When she squeezed him, he hissed between his teeth and arched into her hand.

The most ravenous hunger gripped her. She arched her pelvis up, guiding him as he settled his weight on her. Nose to nose, they stared into each other's eyes. The intensity was palpable and searing, like an arc of electricity sparking between them.

The head of his cock brushed the hypersensitive, swollen flesh at her entrance. Bracing his weight on his arms, he pressed, and the thick, rigid length of his flesh entered hers.

He came in, and in, moving slowly to let her accommodate his intrusion. She was so wet and ready he didn't have to work but could push in to the hilt.

The same hunger she felt etched his features, and his eyes blazed with fierce wonder.

"Tell me it's okay to fall in love with you." The words tumbled out of her trembling mouth without her conscious volition, and when she heard herself say them, she flinched and felt crushed with humiliation.

She hadn't meant to say it. For God's sake, this was only the first time they had gotten together, and despite their earlier conversation there was no guarantee of another. How many times did people say stupid stuff in the heat of sex?

If she thought his gaze had blazed before, it was nothing compared to the heat and light that came out of him then. He looked wholly alive, wholly engaged, and so touched she didn't have the heart to stammer out a retraction.

Eyelids lowering in a heavy, sensual look, he tilted his head to fasten his lips over hers in a light caress. He murmured softly, "I would be so honored if you did."

It was okay. He made it better than okay. He made her welcome.

As he began to move, she wrapped her legs around his waist and her arms around his neck, and held him with her entire body.

He set up a gentle rhythm, sliding all the way in then pulling back until just the tip of his penis rested at her entrance. Leaning on one elbow, he stroked her face, her hair, and ran his fingers lightly down the side of her neck to cup her breast.

Pinching and rolling her nipple between thumb and forefinger, he looked deep into her eyes. "You're beautiful," he murmured. "So beautiful. You're so hot and wet. God, I'm on fire."

She couldn't lie still. She had to move with him. He had always seemed cooler to her, but now she could feel the heat pouring off of him. As his hips rocked against hers, his whole body flexed, and she remembered the first time she saw him, how he moved with complete, seamless grace. Watching him move now, with such sensual abandon, was incredibly sexy.

His thick, dark chestnut hair fell about his face, shadowing his gaze. As she nuzzled him, he picked up his pace, fucking her harder.

She tightened her inner muscles, gripping his cock as

strongly as she could as she raked her fingers down his back. Throwing his head back, he hissed as he pistoned into her.

His eyes flashed red and his fangs descended, and she had no business being shocked or surprised, but oh my God, she was. He looked feral, animalistic.

Just as he had when he had stood between her and Malphas, guarding her from a being that was so Powerful, if the confrontation had turned violent, he would have almost certainly been killed.

"Xavier," she whispered.

She touched his face. Not once did it occur to her to be afraid. This amazing creature had quoted poetry to her. This amazing creature inside of her was Xavier.

He closed those feral-looking eyes and kissed her fingers.

She tightened her embrace, while she tilted her hips to let him thrust deeper. He bowed over her, moving faster, fucking harder, until he gasped out something incomprehensible—she really needed to learn some Spanish—and stiffened.

Deep inside, she felt his cock pulse. He rocked against her gently.

Closing her eyes, she kissed his cheek while she rubbed his back. Oh, she might not understand this strange journey she was on, or how the series of decisions, progression of events, had brought her to this point. She could only be glad she had gotten here.

After a few moments of holding his hips tight against hers, he stirred to caress her lips with his again, gently. When he deepened the kiss, she found that his fangs had retracted. His tongue played with hers, as he stroked her thigh.

"I sense sunrise is near," he whispered.

She threaded her fingers through his hair. "Since you have that automatic shutter system in your house, can I assume you won't fall instantly into some kind of creepy, deathlike coma?"

He chuckled. "Yes, you can safely assume that."

"Good, because otherwise I was going to tell you to get

off me quick, before you pinned me down for ten hours." He laughed out loud, and she grinned. "Just kidding, I think I could roll you over onto the floor."

"Thankfully you won't have to." As he eased away from her, his softening penis slipped out, and she sighed regretfully. It had felt too good to have him inside of her. She already missed the joining, already wanted him again.

He left the bed, and returned with his shirt, which he wadded and used to clean the inside of her thighs. Lingering at the job, he ran his fingers along her sensitive skin, and she stretched languorously under the caress.

He said, "I want you to sleep with me."

She paused before answering and thought of Diego, asleep in the other room. It would be so easy for Diego to text or email, or even call anyone back at the estate, and then nothing she and Xavier did would be private any longer.

While she had no intention of hiding anything, she wasn't sure this was how she wanted things to go. Besides, what had just happened was too powerful to her, and she felt raw and shaken.

She might have promised she wouldn't run away, but that didn't mean she had to avoid making a strategic retreat. So much had happened, she needed time to process.

Kissing him quickly, she told him, "I would love to sleep with you, but maybe not this time. I have no intention of sneaking around, but I would rather Diego and the others found out about us in a different way."

He frowned, and she could tell he didn't like her refusal, but he didn't disagree. "Very well," he said. "I will let you go this time. But not next time."

She smiled. "It's a deal."

Moving around the room, he collected her clothes. He was completely nude and entirely confident, and she couldn't stop staring at him. His back, arms and legs were corded with lean muscle, and watching him was a pure pleasure. As he neared a large walnut wardrobe, he pulled out a black silk robe and offered it to her.

With a quick smile of thanks, she slipped it on. It was

too large for her frame, but not unpleasantly so. The hem brushed the top of her bare feet, and the sleeves fell to the tips of her fingers. At his urging, she held out first one arm then the other. He rolled the sleeves up to her wrists while she watched, then handed the bundle of her clothes and shoes to her.

Awkwardness and doubt tried to worm their way into her mind. She shoved them out again.

Slipping his fingers underneath her chin, he coaxed her face up. As usual, his gaze was all too keen. "I will only feel good about letting you leave, if you tell me you are fine with what just happened."

She took a deep breath. She would not be typical. They had made love, and she had wanted to, and it had been a rare, wonderful experience.

"I'm not sure that 'fine' is quite the right word for how I feel," she told him honestly. "While I'm so . . . glad, I also feel pretty shaken. But that doesn't mean that I'm not dealing with it, or that I'll go against my word and leave." She gave him a small smile. "Will that do?"

The muscle in his jaw ticked, another small tell. "It goes against my instincts to let you out of here, even if you are only going to another room. But I also agree with you— letting Diego stumble upon us together is not the right way to break the news to the others." He kissed her swiftly. "You'd better leave before I change my mind."

She nodded, and before she could change her mind too, she kissed him again and walked rapidly to the door. Funny, now that she was actually leaving—even though she needed to—she had to fight the impulse to turn around and stay.

She walked to the short hallway and looked back. He had left his bedroom door halfway open. As she paused, he said telepathically, *In case you change your mind.*

Warmed, she replied, *I won't, but thank you.*

Sweet dreams.

You too.

There were four doors down the short hallway. Two

were propped open, one led to the bathroom with an antique claw-foot bathtub and the fourth led to an empty bedroom. Inside that room, her bag sat at the foot of the double bed, and as promised, on the nightstand Diego had left a snack of crackers, fruit and a variety of cheeses wrapped in plastic.

As she readied for bed, exhaustion weighed down her limbs. The day had felt a week long, and she hadn't yet adjusted to a more nocturnal schedule.

Slipping into the bathroom, she brushed her teeth. Much as she wanted to take a full bath or shower, she could barely stand upright, so she washed quickly at the sink. Back in the bedroom, she closed her door and crawled between the covers.

She didn't make it to turning out the bedside light. The world went dark as soon as her head hit the pillow.

An undefined amount of time later, she didn't wake gently or slowly, but all at once in a clench. It took a few moments for her to realize where she was, as she stared around the strange, windowless room.

Memory flooded in. The confrontation with Malphas, and what had come after.

The things she and Xavier had said to each other, the things he had done to her, his mouth moving so knowledgeably as he tongued her until an inescapable fire had flared hot and bright. How he moved on top of her, moved inside of her, the feral changes in his face, and the gentleness of his hands and lips.

It had been at least a year since she had last taken a lover, and she felt the soreness in her muscles as she shifted her legs restlessly. Even with the soreness, an edge of that fiery hunger pulsed. Slipping a hand between her legs to cup herself, she realized she hadn't even taken off the robe. The soft material twisted around her body.

Without visual cues from looking outside, it was impossible to know the time without a clock or device of some sort, and she was still very tired. What had woken her? She hadn't dreamed of Malphas, thank God. Perhaps she had noticed the strangeness of the bed.

Faintly, the sound of male voices came through the closed door. Even though she could just barely hear them, not what was actually being said, they sounded tense, even angry.

Oh Lord, what now?

Throwing back the covers, she adjusted the robe and slipped out of the room.

The door to the bedroom where Diego had stayed was propped open, the room empty. The voices came from the living room.

As she froze in indecision, Diego said, "It's been three years, and I'm not going anywhere. I clean the pool, maintain the cars and polish the guns, and that's my entire life. When Melisande and Justine came to visit? That was the most interesting thing to happen to me in a long damn time. Even coming here last night was a massive change, and all I fucking did was go to bed."

Sinking both hands into her hair, she held her head.

What is it about me? What?

I don't ask to overhear this stuff.

"While I understand what you're saying, it doesn't change my mind."

She had a visceral reaction, just listening to the sound of Xavier's voice. Sensation ran along her skin, and she shivered, wrapping the robe more tightly around her torso.

His mouth on her. His mouth on her.

Dear God.

Calm and courteous, Xavier continued. "I retired you from the field for many good reasons, and I'm not going to put you back in active duty. The last time you went on assignment, your cover was so badly blown, you would be a dead man if I sent you back out again. You're done, Diego. You've been done for a long time, and there's no coming back from this retirement. I'm sorry, but that's my final decision."

Xavier retired Diego from a field?

A mental picture of Diego mowing an overgrown pasture bloomed in her mind. It was so patently ridiculous, the last of the sleep cobwebs in her mind blew away and she really woke up.

He retired Diego from active duty.

Like a spool of thread, everything she had witnessed from the past six weeks unrolled in her mind.

How she had felt more than once that something was slightly off at the estate. How everyone else had stopped talking whenever she entered the room.

How all five of the young men disappeared from one day to the next, and nobody brought it up in conversation. How important it had been to keep their identities hidden when unfriendly strangers had arrived.

How overwhelmingly knowledgeable Raoul was at killing. Once, she had even thought he would make an excellent assassin.

Was this . . . a little like James Bond?

With Vampyres?

She wasn't sure if she should feel so amazed, or if she should just feel like a fool for not putting two and two together before now.

Before she could castigate herself too much, Diego spoke again. The tone in his voice was flat and final. "You're right, Xavier. I'm done. I quit."

⇒ SEVENTEEN ⇐

Silence fell.

Then Xavier said, "I take it you would not have brought this up if you weren't sure. Do you know what you will do now?"

"Not yet. I think it might be best if I didn't return to the estate with you and Tess. Is there any way I could get you to take me into the city, after sunset? That is, if you're done with your business here."

"I can give you a ride. Where would you like to go?"

"I thought I would stay at a nice hotel, maybe the Four Seasons, and consider my options. All I've done is save money over the last three years—I might as well enjoy a little of it for a few days. I can always send for my things later." Someone paced, probably Diego. "This isn't personal, Xavier. I want you to know that. None of it is."

"I understand."

Not staying to hear any more, she slipped down the hallway to her bedroom again to ease her door closed. Her mind and emotions in upheaval, she paced around the confines of the bedroom. She wasn't like Xavier, and her body couldn't contain her restlessness without launching into motion.

Even though the bedroom was as tastefully decorated as the rest of the apartment, the lack of windows was beginning to get to her. She wanted fresh air and a walk by the ocean. Quiet though the apartment was, there was no peace in this place.

What she'd heard didn't necessarily change anything, except that it did. She thought back over what she had said to Xavier earlier and laughed under her breath. It felt bitter and humorless.

A quiet rap sounded on her door. She said, "I'm busy."

The door opened, and Xavier walked in.

He wore all black again, classic, simple slacks and a tailored shirt that emphasized the strong, elegant bone structure of his hands and face. He had tied his hair back neatly, and there was no trace anywhere of the wild, sensual creature who had made such emotional love to her. He looked as he so often did, composed and self-contained.

The sight of him made her a little crazy, when everything inside of her was in chaos.

She snapped, "I said I was busy."

He raised his eyebrows. "I heard you perfectly well. I also heard you pacing just now, and I heard you earlier, when you walked down the hall and paused outside the living room." He eyed her narrowly. "You overheard Diego and I talking, and now, for some reason, you are upset. Why?"

"Just because we had sex—once—doesn't mean it's okay for you to ignore my boundaries," she told him furiously.

"My apologies. Of course, you are correct." He said it so smoothly, too easily, his face a refined mask, as he leaned back against the closed door.

For the first time she hated his blasted composure, and she glared at him. "You're trapping me in here on purpose. Don't try to say you aren't, so you can stop being so damned polite."

He adjusted the cuff of one of his sleeves. "Politeness is the backbone of civilization. Besides, what else would you have me do? Until I know what you're thinking, I have no way to respond." Glancing up from the small task, he speared her with a sharp gaze. "Let me guess: you've figured out what I do, from what Diego and I were saying. Haven't you?"

She threw out one hand in an uncontrolled gesture. After everything that had happened, she felt like she had come full circle, back to the same place she had been the night of the Vampyre's Ball. Nothing he did seemed out of place or unconsidered, and everything she did felt overdone, out of balance.

"It was rather hard to miss," she said. "Unlike all the many clues I've seen over the last six weeks."

"And this upsets you." He cocked his head, studying her as if she were an alien.

Where was his warmth, the passion and emotional openness from earlier this morning? Had it all been an act?

She turned away from him, wrapped her arms around her middle and hunched her shoulders. "Yes. No. I don't know."

His hands came down on her shoulders, and she jumped. He said in her ear, "Well, that is definitely a comprehensive range of reaction, I must admit."

Her body reacted again to the sound of his voice, so close. She felt as if he had just passed a hand down her naked back, and she shivered.

His hands tightened. He said even more softly, "Will you not tell me what is going through your mind right now? I truly don't have any clue."

He sounded so patient and gentle, this centuries-old Vampyre who was once a priest.

Who played the piano, loved to waltz, read philosophy and quoted love poetry.

And ran a spy ring.

She closed her eyes. I'm nobody, she thought. I'm not even out of my twenties. I've never been anywhere interesting or done anything useful. I'm just a foster brat who got too greedy and cocky, and barely managed to make it out of a tricky situation alive.

"I'm trying to run away," she whispered. "Inside my head."

"You promised you wouldn't. And I told you what would happen if you did." He ran his lips lightly over the delicate shell of her ear, and she shivered. "I would come after you."

What if she kept her eyes closed and let herself fall back, and trusted that he would catch her?

Tentatively, she leaned back into him.

His arms came around her, and he pulled her against his chest, holding her tightly. "Don't stop talking," he said, very low. "Show me where you are so I can find you."

"I feel stupid," she confessed. "I saw the clues, but I didn't put any of them together."

"Why would you? Why would any normal person put all of that together?" He kissed her temple. "Does it matter that much to you what I do?"

"Honestly, no, it doesn't," she told him.

He laughed a little, a quiet exhalation of breath. "Now I am completely in the dark again."

She shook her head. "I didn't say that right. Of course it matters what you do. In fact, I'm fascinated. But when I heard you talking and put it all together, the thing that shook me was—we made love. I made love to you."

"I remember it all too well." He laid his head on her shoulder as he cradled her. "I haven't been able to get it out of my mind."

She gripped his forearm. "In the moment, I truly felt like I knew what I was doing, and I wasn't just being impetuous, but you know what? I *was* being impetuous, and I *don't* really know you. That's what I realized when I listened to you and Diego. And you were right, when you brought this up earlier—I've barely gotten over the fact that you're a Vampyre. We've been acquainted for six weeks, and we've spent one night together, and . . ." The growing lump in her throat forced her into silence.

"Tess," he whispered. He rubbed his face in her tousled hair. "I know it's early days, and we have so much more to learn about each other. But it's still okay to fall in love with me. I would be so honored if you did, and I would keep all of your emotions safe. I will never betray your trust. I swear it."

She let her head fall against his shoulder, turned her face toward him and he bent her back and kissed her, and the thing of it was, she believed him.

She really believed him.

She said against his mouth, "It's hard to let go and stay in one place."

"I've never once seen you run when you're afraid, and I've seen you very afraid." His lips pulled into a smile. He kissed the tip of her nose. "You have such courage. It's one of the things I admire most about you."

Twisting around to face him fully, she slipped an arm around his neck and returned his kiss. Heat built between them, fast and urgent. She clenched her fists in the back of his shirt, so hungry again for him she shook all over.

Somehow, despite everything he'd been through and everything he did, he carried a light inside of himself that made her ravenous. When she wasn't with him, the world felt darker and colder. It was impossible to imagine she could ever get enough of him, and that scared her more than anything.

He slanted his mouth over hers, his lips hardened and demanding. Shuddering, she kissed him back with everything she had. He slid one long-fingered hand into her hair, at the back of her head, holding her in place while he cupped and massaged her breast through the soft, thin material of the robe.

After several moments, he pulled back with obvious reluctance. "Much as I would love to take you back to bed and pick up where we left off, I promised to drive Diego into the city."

With an immense effort, she tried to chain the crazy woman inside of her that urged her to ignore all common sense and tear off all his clothes. She pulled back enough to search his gaze. "Are you upset over him leaving?"

"I'm disappointed, but I'm not surprised." He shook his head. "Life at the estate is a very small, specific world."

"I love it there," she said quietly.

His face lit with a smile. "I do too, but I also recognize that the lifestyle isn't for everyone. As much as Melisande moans about the rat race in Los Angeles, she could never leave it." His smile faded. "And I simply don't have anything else to offer him. I offered to talk to Julian about finding Diego a position at Evenfall, but he's determined to make a complete change."

Straightening her spine, she made herself let go of his shirt. "Do you want me to stay here while you take him?"

"Hell, no," he said forcefully. He rubbed his face and continued with more moderation. "I'm not leaving you alone in Evenfall, especially not when Justine is around."

Her expression turned dry. "Well, I would have kept the apartment locked."

"I don't care. Locks aren't good enough. You're not staying." He looked over his hand at her. "Come with me while I take Diego into town. We can stay at my town house for a day or two, and you can meet the rest of my attendants."

Hesitating, she thought it over. As much as she did love the estate, she had spent all of her time there in fear of Malphas finding her. The thought of spending some time in the city did have appeal.

San Francisco might have its dangers, especially for someone who was penniless and on the run, but this time around, a visit should be quite different. Maybe she could even shop for some new clothes that would fit her properly.

Also, she might not know exactly where she and Xavier were headed, but if it turned out they were together for any length of time, it would be good to get acquainted with his people in the city.

"I'd like that," she told him.

His expression lightened. "I'm glad. We have a couple of hours until sundown." He added softly, "All I can think of is what I would like to do to you while we wait, but I'm afraid I have other things I need to attend to before we can leave."

Her gaze fell to the opening of his shirt, and she gave him a slow smile. "Can't they wait?"

While it wasn't making love, his intake of breath was immensely satisfying. He growled, "I would love nothing more than to put them off, but I have to see if Gavin can edit the recording of Julian and Melisande on my phone." He paused, and when he continued, he sounded very serious. "And I found out a few hours ago one of my operatives has gone missing."

Her playfulness vanished. "Oh God, I'm sorry. You must be worried."

"I am."

She wasn't sure she should ask—she didn't know what any of the boundaries were, in this new, unknown place they had come to—but she went ahead anyway. "Is it . . . anybody I know?"

His expression darkened. "I'm afraid so. It's Marc."

Shock rippled through her. She hadn't expected him to answer her so readily, or that she would actually know the person involved. "But he just left."

"I know." He moved suddenly, a sharp, quick movement he stilled almost at once, but it was another telling slip and indicated the strength of his worry.

A powerful urge gripped her. She wanted to help him so badly, she ached with it, but there was nothing she could do.

Except for one thing. She could support him.

She stepped away from him. "Go. Do what you need to do."

Still, he lingered, and the tender expression in his eyes as he looked at her was worth everything she had gone through over the last two months. "What about you?"

"I might nap. I'm definitely going to take a proper shower, and eat the snack Diego left for me." She smiled. "And I'll miss you."

He took one of her hands, lifted and turned it, and pressed his lips to the inside of her wrist.

What a difference six weeks made. The first time he had made such a gesture, she had been frozen with fear. Now, warmth suffused her.

"Until later," he said against her skin.

Touching his temple, she stroked his hair.

He straightened, and after another final, hard kiss, he left.

Without the intensity of his presence, the room felt cold and empty, and her feet were freezing. Slipping on her shoes, she explored quickly. Xavier had already left, and the rest of the apartment was silent and empty. The door to Diego's room was closed.

She stared at it thoughtfully, tempted to knock and ask how he was doing, but although they had shared a few conversations, they weren't close, and she wasn't a confidant of his.

In the end, she respected the silent message in that closed door, ate all the food on the plate by the nightstand, collected her toiletries and clean clothes, and went to take a shower.

Antiquated though Evenfall might be, at least the water was hot.

The farther away Xavier got from Tess, the darker his mood grew. As he strode down the hallways, he checked his messages. The only news he'd received was from Raoul, from a few hours ago:

M missed check in. Instructions?

And his brief reply: Wait. Let me know if you hear from him.

Marc was the best of his new recruits. Not only was he smart and capable, but he was also steady-natured and had proven himself to be reliable. Xavier had given Justine to him as his assignment, with strict instructions to maintain a low profile, protect his identity, use extreme caution and avoid direct engagement.

But as more time passed and still no word came, the

probability that something had happened to Marc grew greater. By the time Xavier reached the IT section of Evenfall, which was located in a concrete reinforced area off the underground garage, he was scowling.

Earlier he had notified Gavin he would be stopping by, and the younger Vampyre was waiting for him. Gavin was just under two hundred years old, but he had been turned when he was barely out of his teens. With a snub nose, red hair and freckles that had never faded, he had been nicknamed "Opie" by his coworkers.

Xavier handed his cell phone over, and Gavin got to work.

"So, I heard you brought a new attendant with you," Gavin said. "A female one. It's her, isn't it?"

"Yes, it is." Xavier leaned back against a table as he watched Gavin extract the recording.

"Are you going to bring her down here, so I can meet her?"

His expression turned wry. Gavin hadn't even met Tess yet, but he appeared to have developed a crush on her. "I'm afraid we don't have time this trip. But I will be sure to bring her next time."

"What's she like?" Gavin's tone was elaborately nonchalant.

Defiant. Devious.

Delicious.

He didn't say any of those adjectives aloud. Instead, as his silence grew too long and Gavin lifted up his head to look at him curiously, he finally settled on "Unforgettable."

The other Vampyre's eyebrows lifted. "If I didn't know any better, I'd say you were falling for her."

He leaned against a nearby table. "Why do you think you know better?"

"Xavier, for as long as I've known you, I think you've had a total of maybe three relationships, and those were all shallow and ended after just a few months." The younger Vampyre gave him a sidelong, curious glance. "Son of a bitch. You *are* falling for her, aren't you?"

He didn't have to reply, but he did anyway. "I am."

Gavin's eyes went wide. Then he grinned. "Good for you."

After transferring the recording to his desktop, they listened to it together. "Trim everything off but their agreement," Xavier told him. "Then get the clean copy to Julian as soon as possible."

"You got it."

While he had finished what he had come to do, he hesitated and turned his attention to the wall of TV monitors, watched by two Vampyres across the room. They studied footage from security cameras placed at strategic intervals all over Evenfall.

He said, "Do me a favor and run a search for Justine over the last twenty-four hours."

"You got it," Gavin said. He walked over to another computer system, sat down, and his fingers flew nimbly over the keyboard. "Can you tell me what we're looking for?"

Watching, Xavier crossed his arms and shook his head. "I don't know. At the very least, I just want proof that she is actually still here. I haven't seen her since I've arrived. I've only heard Julian mention her."

"Well, that should be easy enough to confirm."

Fifteen minutes later, Xavier watched irrefutable evidence. Justine had been present in Evenfall for at least a day. He studied snippets of footage of her in various public spots. Twice, the recordings showed her in conversation with Julian, their expressions cold and body language angry. The footage didn't supply any sound, but he wasn't interested at the moment in overhearing conversations.

Frustration spiked, and he rubbed his face. While she was clearly here, that didn't mean Marc was in any less danger. She had any number of employees who weren't here with her.

"Is that what you needed?" Gavin asked.

Sighing, he said, "Sure. Thanks."

"No problem."

Night had fallen while they had worked. Xavier could

feel it, the cool, welcome darkness pulling a veil over the land. He said good-bye to Gavin, pocketed his phone and headed back to his rooms.

There, he found Tess stretched out on his bed, reading a paperback. He could sense Diego in the other part of the apartment, but for the moment he focused all his attention on Tess.

She had showered and dressed in clean jeans and a dark red, long-sleeved shirt. The color suited her as much as the dark blue of the ball gown did, and he smiled with pleasure to see her.

Noticing him in the doorway, she gave him a self-conscious smile. "I hope you don't mind me coming in here. I figured if you could invade my bedroom—twice—I could invade yours."

For a brief moment, he forgot his concerns and laughed. "You have an open invitation. You can invade my bedroom anytime you like." He braced one knee on the edge of the mattress and leaned over to give her a deep, slow kiss.

Afterward, he pulled back. She searched his face. "Any news about Marc?"

He shook his head. "The sun has set, and we need to leave. I know this isn't what we had planned, but I'll have to drop you off at my town house and leave you for a while. I need to find out where he is."

Pushing off the bed, she slipped her shoes on and stood. "Of course."

He went to Diego's room, rapped on the door and opened it. Diego had been reading too, and he set aside his e-reader when Xavier appeared.

"Time to go?" Diego asked.

"Yes."

For a moment, as Xavier looked at him, he considered offering Diego the chance to look into what had happened to Marc. The impulse passed quickly. Not only was it something that Xavier needed to investigate personally, but it was also clear from the younger man's closed expression that Diego had already emotionally disconnected.

He'd already said it. He was done, and there was no going back.

Back in Xavier's bedroom, it was the work of a few moments to gather up his things and pack them in his overnight bag. When he had finished, they left.

As they walked through the halls of Evenfall, he held his hand out to Tess, no longer caring how they broke the news to Diego. He planned on talking to Raoul and the others soon enough. Besides, he simply wanted to touch her.

Hesitating only for a moment, she laced her fingers through his. When Diego's gaze fell onto their linked hands, his eyes widened briefly, but then indifference returned and he looked away.

This time, Xavier escorted Tess to the front passenger seat and he drove, while Diego rode in the back.

They made the drive across the Golden Gate Bridge mostly in silence. The night was clear and unusually warm, a choppy wind blowing off the waters of the bay.

Pinching her full lower lip and appearing deep in thought, Tess stared out her window, while Diego checked his phone and spoke up just once. "You know, you don't have to take me all the way to the hotel. You can drop me off somewhere convenient, and I can call a taxi."

The Four Seasons Hotel lay south of Chinatown, and southeast of Nob Hill, where Xavier's town house was located. Xavier said quietly, "The Four Seasons is not that far away, Diego. It's no trouble at all."

Looking uncomfortable, the younger man frowned but fell silent.

Traffic was heavy on the main highway. As Presidio Parkway turned into Lombard Street, a heavy garbage truck pulled behind them.

Checking his rearview mirror, Xavier surveyed the truck. It didn't look out of the ordinary, and several garbage companies employed Nightkind creatures and operated at night. Dismissing it as a minimal threat, he still took standard precautions and turned down a side street.

The truck followed.

Now, that got his attention.

He stepped on the gas pedal, and the SUV leaped forward just as, at the next intersection, another garbage truck turned onto the street and swerved directly across their path.

Diego swore.

San Francisco had some of the most expensive real estate in the world, and while some areas of the city didn't have alleys, this street did.

Checking to make sure Tess was wearing her seat belt, Xavier yanked hard on the steering wheel. Tires shrieking, the SUV plunged into the alley.

Up ahead, a third garbage truck pulled across the alleyway. He stomped on the brakes.

The passenger side of the garbage truck faced them. The door opened, and someone inside tossed out a round object, roughly shaped like a bowling ball. It bounced down the alley toward them.

It was Marc's severed head.

≈ EIGHTEEN ≈

O h, my God," Tess said. Her face blanched.

Dark figures swarmed out of the garbage truck ahead of him.

Xavier grabbed her, yanking her sideways and down, away from the windshield.

"Keep your head down," he told her.

At the same time he snapped off his seat belt, opened the glove compartment and grabbed the Glock that was stored inside.

Gunfire sprayed the outside of the SUV. All of his vehicles had run-flat tires, bullet-resistant glass and layers of armored plate inserted into the body panels, but those precautions wouldn't hold up under a concentrated, sustained attack. All they would do was buy a little bit of time.

Xavier glanced in the backseat. Still swearing, Diego had unbuckled too, slammed part of the backseat flat and was climbing into the back, where a stash of weapons and body armor was stored in a compartment underneath the floor.

More dark figures came up from behind the SUV.

Nobody would have tried such an attack if Xavier had been alone, because it wouldn't have worked. He could have fought his way out, or climbed the side of a building. But traveling with both Tess and Diego, this type of assault was brutally effective at pinning them in place.

He couldn't pull both of them out or take them up the side of the building, and he would never leave them.

He said, "I count fifteen."

"Got it." Diego threw a Kevlar vest at him.

He caught it and spread it open over Tess. He told her, "Put this on."

She snapped off her seat belt, pushed her seat back as far as it could go and wriggled into the vest. Diego threw a second vest at him, and he twisted to put it on in the confined space.

More gunfire sounded. Webs of fractures starred the front and back windshields, but they held for now.

"I need guns," Tess snapped. "Lots and lots of guns."

Folded into the small space between the front seat and the dashboard, she looked terrified and sounded furious. In spite of the urgency of their situation, Xavier almost smiled. He bent over her, tilted up her face and whispered, "Tell me it's okay to fall in love with you."

She gave him a wide-eyed, cranky stare. Her lips were bloodless. "You'd better. I'm not falling in love all by myself."

He gave her a swift, hard kiss. Something hard nudged his shoulder. It was Diego, poking him with the butt of an assault rifle

He took it, slammed open his car door and rolled out to lay a blanket of gunfire down either end of the alley. He hit some of their attackers, while others dove for cover. The ones he had hit sprawled to the ground then scrambled to get away.

Their attackers were all Vampyres. Unless he struck any of them in the head, the gunshot wounds would be painful and debilitating, but they weren't lethal.

He said to the other man, "Stay in the car, under cover as long as you can."

"Yeah, okay." Diego looked pretty sick, himself, as he crawled from the back. He handed Tess a handgun and another rifle. "Xavier, this is all my fault. I am so profoundly sorry."

He paused only for a fraction of a second. "You'll have to explain that to me later when we have time."

"What are you doing?" Tess said to Xavier. She flung out one hand, reaching out to him. "Get your ass back in here."

"That's not how we're going to get out of this," Xavier told her. He shoved his cell phone into her hand. "Call Raoul and Julian."

Her fingers closed over the phone.

"Cover me," he said to Diego. The younger man nodded, his face tense.

It was time to get to work.

After wrapping her unsteady fingers around his cell phone, Tess watched Xavier turn toward their attackers, and his expression changed.

All of the light he carried inside of him, the gentle sensuality, warmth and laughter, disappeared entirely, and what came in its place made her shake all the harder.

She had always thought death was a massively indifferent, inescapable juggernaut, for sooner or later it came to every living thing. Through accidents, acts of war and sometimes illness, it even eventually struck down the long-lived creatures of the Elder Races.

But the kind of death Xavier embodied was a fiery, passionate blaze.

The death in his eyes cared far too much to stand idly by and watch an injustice being done. It cared about the thinking that went behind each action, and the reasons for war.

It would never rest, never stop, until either harm had been averted or balance had been restored.

Her limited human eyes couldn't track what happened next. He simply left her behind on this heavy, solid Earth and went somewhere else, shooting through the air like God's arrow.

That was when the screaming began.

More gunfire sounded in short staccato bursts. From the backseat, Diego shoved open a door on the driver's side and angled his body out to shoot at the group of attackers behind them.

Keeping her head down, she punched through the commands on the phone that took her to Xavier's list of favorites. Locating Raoul's number, she dialed it.

He answered immediately. "Have you heard anything?"

"It's Tess," she told him. "We're in the city. We're pinned in an alley and under attack. Marc's dead. They cut off his head! Whoever they are."

Raoul's voice changed. "Where are you?"

"I don't know. I've only been to San Francisco once." As she watched, Diego sagged against the side of the vehicle. He brought the muzzle of his rifle back up almost immediately, but she knew he'd been shot. She said rapidly, "We came across the Golden Gate, we were headed toward the Four Seasons Hotel and now we're in an alley. Figure it out."

"Keep this phone on," Raoul said. "I'll track you, Tess. Do you hear me? I'll track you."

"Hurry the fuck up," she said between her teeth.

Of course he wouldn't make it in time. Even if she called Julian and he sent people from Evenfall, or from within the city itself, nobody would make it in time. She disconnected, shoved the phone into the pocket of her jeans and scrambled over the seat to the driver's side of the vehicle where Xavier had left the door open.

With both of the SUV doors open, she had cover, of sorts, on both sides.

Diego had given her another Glock, like the one that had been stored in the glove compartment. It was her favorite of the handguns she'd practiced with, so far. She checked over the assault rifle. It was a SCAR, a special forces combat assault rifle, like the one he'd handed Xavier. While she didn't care for them, she did know how to use it.

"Here's where you get to show off everything you've learned in class," Diego said, from the other side of the open rear door. He sounded breathless, and his rifle had slumped to his side again. "Look up, chica. Move fast."

Using the car door as a shield, she angled out her head and checked the rooflines of the neighboring buildings.

Nearby, a muzzle of a rocket launcher aimed at the SUV, the figure of the shooter hunched over it.

She didn't give herself time to think.

Snapping up the SCAR, she shot. The figure holding the rocket launcher jerked and disappeared.

If that was a Vampyre, he was going to reappear in a few moments and try again. "We can't stay here," she told Diego. "How badly are you hit?"

"You know, I've seen better days," said Diego. "Go for. The doorway. Fifteen yards. Back. Take. Cover inside."

She didn't move. Instead, she watched the rooftop for the rocket launcher to reappear. "You don't sound so good."

The tip of the launcher reappeared. Her heart kicked. She sighted down the SCAR and sprayed it. To her immense surprise, it exploded. A ball of fiery light lit up the night, and she swore.

Diego laughed and went into a spasm of harsh coughing. She could hear his breathing hitching from where she crouched. Daring to peer around the edge of the door, she saw that the immediate area around their SUV was deserted.

Near the garbage truck blocking them at the rear, a vicious, whirlwind fight was taking place. She couldn't track all that happened—they all moved too fast—but she could tell there were several figures involved.

Even as she watched, two of the figures dissolved into dust. Oh, God.

But the fight continued, so she knew Xavier had to be alive.

"Come on, Diego," she said. "We're going to get to that doorway together."

"Sorry. No can do." His voice was noticeably weaker. "I want you to tell Xavier . . . I want you to tell him . . ."

Furious, horrified tears filled her eyes, and she swiped them back. She couldn't afford to cry. She needed to see.

Down the alley, opposite the fight, two figures crept around the edge of the garbage truck. She took careful aim and pulled off a shot, and one of them blew into a cloud of dust. As the other darted back to cover, she leaped up and scooted around the edge of the rear door to Diego.

He sat on the ground, his back propped against the running board of the car. As she knelt beside him, he lifted his head to look at her. Propping the SCAR beside him, she ran her fingers over his chest. He'd had time to put on a vest, just like she and Xavier had. Where had he been hit?

He took one of her hands and laid it against his shoulder, and she saw it then—dark blood seeping around the border of the vest, near his underarm. He wheezed, "Freak shot. Just my fucking luck. Bastard went in sideways. Lung."

Out of the corner of her eye, she saw one end of the garbage truck behind the SUV lift into the air. With a gigantic screech of metal, it sailed toward the fighting Vampyres, who scattered. The truck slammed into the edge of the building.

Holy shit, someone just picked up that truck and threw it.

It was a troll, massive and stone-colored. It stomped toward one Vampyre—belatedly she recognized Xavier—who leaped, not away, but toward it.

Dear God, did he have no fear whatsoever? With impossible-looking grace and speed, he landed on the troll's massive shoulder, put his Glock to its eye and shot it. As it began to topple, he leaped away.

She turned her attention back to Diego, who had watched the encounter too. He looked up at her with a crooked smile and said telepathically, *He's a little like Armageddon, isn't he? Tell him . . . I'm sorry. I was supposed to get him into the city . . . With Justine in Even-fall, I thought she was going to try something there, a coup against Julian . . .*

She stared. "You're working with Justine? Since when?"

When she came to stay with Melisande. She made me an offer . . . His head sagged. *I thought she wanted Xavier out of the way . . . Wouldn't have done it if I'd known . . .*

"For God's sake, why?"

In the semidark, she couldn't see his infinitesimal shrug. She would never have known about it, if she hadn't felt him move underneath her fingertips.

Thousand bucks monthly stipend, chica. No matter how much you save, it isn't enough to retire on.

The wry voice in her head went silent, and his eyes closed.

Tears spilled out the corners of her eyes. She whispered, "You stupid, greedy son of a bitch."

A hand came down on her shoulder. An involuntary cry broke out of her. She flinched and twisted to one side, as she brought up her Glock. . . .

Taking hold of her wrist, Xavier jerked her hand away. Even though he pointed the muzzle of the Glock toward the side of the building, she managed not to pull the trigger. Pulling her arm free, she clicked on the safety and tucked the gun in the waist of her jeans, at the small of her back.

Coming down on one knee beside her, Xavier gave Diego a long, grim look. Xavier was covered in blood, his vest pocked with marks. He'd been shot at multiple times. Maybe knifed. She was so desperately glad to see him, she lunged forward to throw her arms around his neck and grip him tight.

Slipping an arm around her waist, he eased back until he connected with the wall of the nearby building and slid to a sitting position.

"What are you doing?" she said between her teeth. "You can't sit. We've got to keep moving, in case they come back and attack us again."

"They're not going to. They did what they came to do."

"What do you mean?" Loosening her hold around his neck, she pulled back to search his face.

He opened his free hand to show her an empty syringe.

She had been scared so much over the last few days, but the sight of what he held in his broad palm outdid all of it, sending a pure bolt of terror through her.

"More than one of them tagged me," he told her. "I don't know how many doses I took."

She heard Raoul's voice in her head, as if he had just spoken the words to her all over again.

There's more than one way to kill a Vampyre.

Brodifacoum. A highly lethal anticoagulant poison.

They bleed to death. I've seen it, and it's a grim way to die.

"No, no, no, no, no," she said.

"I'm sorry, Tess." He wiped his face with the back of one hand. A trickle of blood oozed from the corner of one of his eyes, and Raoul's clinical voice continued in her head.

First it attacks a Vampyre's small blood vessels then it leads to internal bleeding, shock, convulsions, unconsciousness and eventually death.

"You're not going to die." She turned very calm. "I won't let you. Raoul told me about this. We have to drain you and get you a massive infusion of untainted blood as fast as we can. I need a knife."

While she might have sounded calm, her hands were frantic as she patted his pockets. No knife. She whirled on her knees to search Diego's body.

Come on. Come on. It couldn't have been all flying bullets and trolls flinging garbage trucks. After the carnage tonight, there had to be a sharp object, somewhere.

Sirens sounded in the distance. With a dim sense of incredulity, she realized the entire confrontation couldn't have taken ten minutes, and had probably taken much less time.

"Check the back of the SUV, in the weapons storage compartment." Xavier sounded calm too, and he looked it, despite the blood leaking out of his eyes. "There will be a couple of knives, or at least a short sword."

She sprang to the backseat and lunged for the back. Diego had left the compartment open and knives had been Velcroed to the inside of the lid. Snatching one, she scrambled back to Xavier. "How do you want me to do this?"

"We have to work fast. The poison's been in my system for a few minutes already." He held out his arms, palms up. "Cut both wrists. Go deep."

Hesitating, she asked, "What about your tendons?"

He told her, "Don't worry about it. If I make it, I'll heal."

"You're going to make it," she snapped. The terror hadn't eased up, not in the slightest. It drove her on, like a devil riding her back, whipping her to the next thing, and the next.

She used the terror to strike with the knife. As the point drove deep into his flesh, he stiffened and sucked in a breath. Blood flowed out from the cut, in a shockingly plentiful river.

He held out his other wrist to her. "Again."

She almost couldn't see what she was doing, which was when she realized she was crying. Once more, she cut him deep, and his blood flowed freely, and there wasn't going to be enough liquor in the world, or enough therapy, to get over the sight of him hunched in pain and drenched in his own blood.

His face twisted, and he doubled up and fell to his side.

She went down with him to the ground and embraced all of it, every last gory, wonderful inch of him.

"Don't you dare give up. You're not done yet." Lifting him slightly, she took his head and guided him to the crook in her neck. "Come on, bite."

Tess. His lips moved.

He had kissed her. Even with all the pain she could tell he was feeling, as it strained his strong body, he still kissed her.

She sobbed, "Xavier, if you don't bite me, I will pummel you. No, I won't, I'll take the fucking knife to my own neck. I refuse to let you go. *Do you think it matters in the slightest to me anymore? DO IT.*"

A brief, sharp pain stabbed her skin, then warmth where his mouth rested on her. She felt the flow of her own blood and how he drank it. Despite the discomfort of sprawling on the ground, and the fear that after everything, she might still lose him, nourishing him felt so good. So good.

Thou fairest among women, he whispered in her head. *My beloved is mine, and I am hers.*

Ignoring the flashing lights that appeared at either end of the alley, she cradled him as close as she could.

Even though the time they had been together could be counted in hours, not days, they had already been through too much for it to just end.

It was too strong, surprising and beautiful.

Too necessary.

⇒ NINETEEN ⇐

The flashing lights grew closer, and people ran toward them. Reaching to her waist and sliding her hand around the butt of her Glock, she watched them sharply, looking for any sign they weren't who they appeared to be.

Xavier had stopped feeding. Afraid he hadn't taken in enough nourishment, she gripped him tighter. His body grew taut and he shuddered. The convulsions had started.

"Ma'am?" A uniformed policewoman approached them cautiously. "Ma'am, can you hear me? I'm here to help you." She raised her voice. "These two are alive! Get paramedics over here!"

More people ran over, two of them wielding a stretcher, and a paramedic went to his knees beside them.

Taking her hand away from her gun, Tess said, "This is Xavier del Torro. Do you know who that is?"

The paramedic's quick, intelligent gaze flashed up to hers. "Yes."

"He's been poisoned, and he's dying." The force of what she felt made the words snap out like a whip. "He has to have fresh blood now. A lot of it."

The man shouted, "I need more help here. Stat."

Others came running, and several people converged on them as the two paramedics pulled Xavier out of her arms and turned him on his back.

She stroked back his hair as she watched his face for any sign of consciousness. He had started bleeding from the nose now, as well as his eyes.

Don't die. Please don't die.

One of paramedics rolled up his sleeve and tried to offer blood to Xavier, but he was unresponsive. "He's not taking it," he said. "We need to do a direct transfusion."

His partner pulled out phlebotomist equipment, tore open packages and started a direct transfusion from the paramedic to Xavier, linking them by needles inserted into their forearms. The procedure would have been impossible if Xavier had still been human.

Other people were talking. The words rolled over her.

". . . His wrists are healing. We have to reopen the cuts."

"We don't have time to get him to a hospital—let's get him off the ground. Put him on the stretcher. . . . Who else will donate blood?"

She moved with them as they lifted Xavier onto the stretcher and positioned him on his side so that one limp arm hung to the ground. One paramedic crouched to reopen the wound in that arm, using gravity to help drain the poisoned blood, while the other set up a new donor, the policewoman who had found them originally.

One of them asked, "How much poison did he take?"

She shook her head, her voice clogged from the tears that kept leaking out of her eyes. "I don't know. A lot."

Time blurred, and one donor replaced another. Movement happened around the periphery of her awareness, as police officials investigated the scene. One approached her to say, "We need to take your statement about what happened."

"Later," she said. She knelt at Xavier's head, still stroking his hair, in case some part of him was aware of her presence. He could disappear at any moment, just collapse into dust. The possibility was unimaginable—that he could be there in one moment, and completely gone in the next.

"Ma'am, there's nothing you can do for him right now. He's getting the best care available. If you would just come with me to answer some questions."

While the clueless policeman didn't necessarily sound unkind, she barely managed to keep from drawing the Glock and shooting him.

Oh, life had certainly changed, now that she had a gun and knew how to use it.

Lifting her head to meet his gaze, she said in a soft voice, "Get out of my face."

Something in her expression made him pull back sharply. "You're understandably upset. I'll check with you again in a bit."

Forgetting about him as soon as he stepped out of her radar, she asked one of the paramedics, "How do we know how he's doing?"

"I've never personally handled a brodifacoum poisoning before, but there's a survivability factor that's called magic hour." The paramedic sounded both brisk and sympathetic. "If he makes it through a full hour, he'll survive." He gave her a reassuring smile. "He wouldn't have made it this far without your quick action."

Wiping her face on her shoulder, she nodded. "How much time has gone by?"

"Twenty-one minutes."

It felt like a lifetime already.

Only thirty-nine more minutes of hell to go.

Raoul and Julian arrived, bringing with them an influx of new, sharp-eyed armed Vampyres that washed through the alley like a wave. Raoul ran to the stretcher, and the look on his face brought fresh tears to her eyes.

After taking in Xavier's curled up form, Raoul gripped her shoulder as he took in her appearance. "You look like you bathed in blood. Are you hurt?"

Blinking hard, she said, "No."

Have you said anything to anyone about what happened? he asked telepathically.

She shook her head.

Good job.

I didn't do it on purpose. I've been busy. She touched Xavier's temple.

Raoul's gaze fell to the movement and widened. Before he could say anything, Julian joined them. The rough angles of the Nightkind King's face were cut with fury.

Tell me what happened, Julian commanded.

She couldn't put Julian off like she had the policeman. Reluctantly, she focused on him. *It was Justine. Diego died before he could tell me much, but from what he said, Justine bribed him to get Xavier to come into the city. He thought. . . .* She swallowed. Even though she'd had nothing to do with the conspiracy, she found it surprisingly hard to say the next words while looking directly at Julian. *Diego said he had thought Justine was going to try a coup in Evenfall. Instead, she went after Xavier. He was her target.*

The Nightkind King's gaze bored into hers. *How did you survive?*

She shook her head. *Sheer dumb luck? I shot a few of them, but Xavier killed almost everyone who attacked us. If any of them lived, they only did so because they ran away. They clearly meant to kill all of us—they almost hit the SUV with a rocket launcher.*

That wasn't sheer dumb luck, Julian told her. *He saved your life. He could have left you and Diego behind at any moment. Instead, he stayed to fight. They knew he would, and that's how they got him. If it had worked, none of you would have been around to tell what had happened.*

She hadn't had time to absorb everything, but as soon as he said it, she knew it was true. Overcome, she glanced down at Xavier's still face.

She murmured, *I had no idea I could come to care for him so much.*

She hadn't meant to say it. She certainly hadn't meant to confess that to the Nightkind King, of all people.

He's the best man I know, Julian said. *I wouldn't have anybody else in his position, or trust them to make the kinds of decisions he makes every day. In all the years I've known him, he's never once lost his moral compass.* A shadow crossed his rough face. *Not like so many of the rest of us have, from time to time.*

Surprised by Julian's candor, Tess stared up at him. He genuinely, deeply cared for Xavier, and it showed on his tense, worried face. From across the alley, someone called out to him, and he strode away.

"Just a few more minutes to go," said the paramedic. "I need a new donor. Don't tell me we've already used everybody."

"I'm new." Raoul held out his arm. "Use me."

Xavier stirred underneath her hands and whispered, "*Querida.*"

She had never felt gladness as such an extreme emotion. It brought her to her knees. Laying her head on the stretcher beside his, facing him, she whispered, "I'm here."

He appeared dazed, and his normally sharp, clear gaze looked clouded. "You're upside down."

"I know." Glancing up, she caught Raoul's astonished expression "Look, Raoul's here."

Xavier tried to turn his head to look up at Raoul, who bent over him and put a hand at the back of his head. His voice as gentle as his expression, Raoul asked, "Did you just call her *querida*?"

"We were going to tell you when we got back," Xavier said. He groped for Tess's hand, and she took it. "Tess isn't one of my attendants any longer." After a pause, he added with a thoughtful kind of surprise, "I think we might be dating."

"Time." The paramedic's voice filled with triumph. "We made it."

They'd hit magic hour.

• • •

Julian came back over to the stretcher to check on Xavier. When he saw that Xavier's eyes were open, his savage expression lightened considerably. Squatting by the stretcher, he brought his face down to the same level as Xavier's.

"You scared me there for a while," Julian said.

Xavier stiffened as another spasm of pain hit. "It wasn't my intention."

"I'm not ready to live in a world without you in it," Julian told him in a quiet voice. He held out his hand, and Xavier clasped it.

"You won't have to. I'm not going anywhere."

Julian said in his head, *I have news that is somewhat ironic. Are you up to hearing it?*

Xavier couldn't keep his eyes open, and he closed them. *Tell me.*

Gavin got the edited recording to me. A few hours earlier, I took it to Justine and backed her off, just as we'd planned. She left Evenfall around when you did, right after sunset. If I'd held off confronting her until tomorrow, she might still be in residence.

Xavier didn't buy it. As soon as Justine received word of the botched assassination attempt, she would have slipped out of Evenfall on some pretext or other. He gritted his teeth as the remnants of the poison knotted his muscles.

He promised, *Soon as I'm on my feet, I'll go after her.*

No, you won't, Julian growled. His grip tightened on Xavier's. *Not this time. I've sent you on the hunt for me countless times over the years, but Justine is my issue to handle. No one attacks my progeny and lives.*

As Julian stood, Xavier opened his eyes. Looking up at his sire and king, he said, *Good hunting.*

Julian touched his shoulder. *Get better. And watch your back.*

Always.

After ten more minutes, the paramedic announced Xavier

was stable enough to be moved. Pain still wracked his body, but he refused to go to the hospital. Now that he had survived past the magic hour, there was nothing the hospital could do for him, anyway, except to offer him fresh blood, and he could get that need met in the comfort of his own home.

They transported him to his town house in the ambulance. He refused to let go of Tess's hand, so she rode with him. She looked horrific. Blood soaked her everywhere, and her face was tight and pale with exhaustion and stress, her eyes lined with dark circles.

He had never seen anyone or anything so beautiful.

He must have closed his eyes and dozed, because the next thing he knew, the medics were pulling the stretcher from the ambulance. Tess stayed by his side as they took him inside and down the main stairway to the master suite belowground.

He wasn't tracking what happened very well, because Raoul wasn't present—but then suddenly he was.

"He needs to take it easy for a few weeks," one of the medics told them. He met Xavier's eyes. "You survived, but that doesn't mean the poison is gone. It's going to take several days for it to fully flush out of your system. The best thing you can do is force liquids."

"Understood," Xavier said.

Raoul slid an arm under his shoulders and eased him off the stretcher. When he made as if to help Xavier to his king-sized bed, Xavier resisted.

"No. Take me to the bathroom."

"Xavier, it doesn't matter right now if you're clean or not."

"It matters to me, damn it." He looked for Tess, who hovered nearby anxiously. "Help me into the shower?"

She came forward quickly and slipped an arm around his waist. "Of course."

He limped with her into the bathroom.

He liked his comforts, and his bathroom reflected that.

It was spacious, with a walk-in shower and a large sunken tub with Jacuzzi jet heads. After a quick glance around, Tess said, "I don't think we should try the shower."

He didn't disagree. Even with her support, he was shaky on his feet, and the muscle cramps kept hitting him unexpectedly.

She helped him into the tub, and he stripped off his soiled, blood-soaked clothing while she turned on the water, checked the flow and adjusted the faucets. "Climb in," he said. "You too."

He thought she might argue, but she didn't. She stripped off her filthy clothes, dropped them into the pile with his and climbed into the tub. For a while, they just soaked, and he grew more comfortable as the warm water eased his muscle cramps.

He stroked her back, following the delicate ripple of her spine. God, he loved her body, her sleek skin, those gorgeous legs, the soft swell of her pink-tipped breasts. He loved the cranky, vulnerable look in her eyes.

Scooping up a handful of warm water, he wiped at her streaked face. "You saved my life," he said quietly. "Thank you."

Her face moved. She took hold of his forearms and checked the wounds at his wrists. They had already closed over, but the marks where she had cut him were still long, red and angry-looking. Tracing one of them with a forefinger, she said, "You saved my life too."

"We saved each other." With a deep sense of relief and fulfillment, he pulled her into his arms. She hugged him back tightly, and they rested together.

He disconnected again, and only woke up when she let out the tub of rusty-looking water and ran more. Matter-of-factly, she poured shampoo into one hand and worked it through his hair. As her slender fingers massaged his scalp, he let out a low sound of pleasure and went boneless.

Suds slipped down his chest and shoulders, and spread over the water's surface.

Scooping up fragrant handfuls, he washed her all over,

relishing the feel of her silken wet skin and slippery body. Her breasts filled his hands beautifully. Obsessed with touching her, he massaged them and rubbed his thumbs over her nipples, watching the plump, succulent peaks of flesh pebble under his touch. She stopped washing his hair and held his hands against her, her eyelids drifting closed as she let him play with her.

The arousal was there—it couldn't help but be there. She was too vital, too sexy, and he wanted her too much. His hard cock brushed against the side of her thigh. But he ignored it. Instead, he laced his fingers through hers.

Her eyes opened. When she saw the look on his face, she asked softly, "What is it?"

He looked at her soberly. "Did Diego say anything to you before he died?"

Her mouth tightened. "Yes. He was working with Justine. He said he thought she wanted you to come into the city so she could try something in Evenfall. He said he wouldn't have done it, if he'd known we were going to be attacked, and he said he was sorry."

His eyes grew damp.

Her tired expression changed drastically, and she straddled him to wrap her arms around his neck, embracing with such fierceness, he wrapped his arms around her waist and held on.

He pressed his face against her. "I'd known for a while he wasn't happy. I should have done something sooner. I should have talked to him."

"Don't you dare try to make what happened your fault," she whispered.

"But it is partly my fault, *querida*," he said. "I should have seen this coming."

"No. I don't buy it." She shook her head and told him in a harsh voice, "Lots of people get restless, and they might not be entirely satisfied with their lives, but that doesn't mean they go out and betray someone, or put somebody in danger. They cope with what's in their lives. That's what adults do. Diego knew Justine was dangerous, but he made a deal with her anyway. He had perfect health, and he was strong and smart. He could have gone anywhere or done anything else, or he could have just hung out and enjoyed his easy job and the sunshine. But instead of counting up all the good things he had going for him, he was greedy, lazy and selfish."

As she fell silent, he said against her skin, "I guess you have strong feelings about it."

"I guess I do," she muttered. "I'm sorry, but if he wasn't already dead, I'd probably shoot him myself."

He didn't want to smile, but he did anyway. She was bloodthirsty, his Tess, and he discovered he liked that very much.

"Thank you," he said, more seriously. "Your words mean more than I can say. I'll have to think about this. It may take me a while to put what happened to rest."

"That's because you like to think about things." She scowled. "Me, I like numbers. They're so much easier to understand than people."

She looked so adorable he had to kiss her. When he did, her lips felt so amazing, he had to deepen the kiss. He slanted his mouth over hers, again and again, eating at her like a starving man who had been brought to a banquet.

Throughout every moment of the fight, he had known where Tess was. No matter how far away he had gone—yards away, to either end of the alley—he had obsessively tracked every movement she had made.

He had known when she had stepped out of the SUV and crouched between the limited shelter of the two open doors. He had tracked every time she had brought up her rifle and shot, and he had been very aware of the moment she chose to slip around the rear passenger door to Diego, because that had left her exposed to an attack from behind the SUV.

He had changed his fighting strategy accordingly, shifting his attention to the attackers coming up from the rear, because none of those bastards were going to get near her. Not while he was around to have anything to say about it.

And he had known when Diego had gotten shot. Even

through the firefight and other sounds of battle, because of his extraordinary hearing—and because of the bond that existed between patron and attendant—he had been all too aware of Diego's struggle for breath in those last few moments of his life.

Maybe he could have gotten back to the SUV in time to save Diego. A strong influx of Vampyre blood might have stopped the internal bleeding. Maybe they could have held back their attackers through firepower alone.

It had been a judgment call. Decisions in fighting were always judgment calls.

But in the space of a few fleeting moments, he had decided against it. He had traded the possibility of saving Diego's life for the certainty of saving Tess.

And if he had to do it all over, he would do it again. In the deepest privacy of his soul, down at the bottom of a well where no one else could hear him, the part of him that had weighed life and death decisions over the last several hundred years took her life and weighed it against all else.

Life became simple from that point on, because Tess had to live. No matter who else died, or how much damage he had to inflict on the world around him—Tess had to live.

"Come on," she whispered against his mouth. "Let's get you to bed."

"And you," he murmured. He sank one hand into her damp hair and tightened it into a fist. "I'm not letting you go this time."

She didn't protest his possessive hold. Instead she smiled. "I'm good with that."

Leaving the tub, she went to the closet and pulled out a handful of towels. She hovered near his elbow as he climbed out, but he steadied himself against the nearby sink and waved her away.

Toweling dry, he left his hair damp, and when she came to him, he wrapped an arm around her shoulders, leaning on her for support again as they went into the bedroom. She pulled back the covers, and gratefully, he sank down onto the mattress. She joined him, and, putting his arms around her, he pulled her damp body next to his.

Their legs entwined, and the sensation of her naked body against his was as sacred as anything he had ever experienced.

Running his fingers along the wings of her collarbones, he said, "You haven't told me how you are doing."

"I'm fine. I'm tired." She shook her head, the silky damp tips of her hair clinging to her skin. "I'm not fine—I'm not fine at all. Jesus Christ, Xavier, I went an entire hellish hour waiting for you to disappear and turn into dust. I held your head between my hands, and all I could think of was how you might vanish into thin air at any moment. I think I'm still screaming inside my head."

As her face twisted, he pulled her onto him and held her tight. "I'm sorry," he whispered. "It's okay now. It's going to be okay."

"I know that," she snapped, as the tears spilled down her face. "I don't have to be rational, or in control right now."

"Of course you don't." He stroked her hair, her shoulders, the beautiful hourglass curve of her back.

She mashed her mouth against his, but her emotional distress was too apparent for him to smile at the lack of finesse. Instead, he made a low, soothing sound at the back of his throat and cradled her.

"I didn't know you two months ago. When I first met you at the Vampyre's Ball, all I could think of was how easy it would be for you to rape me and drain me of my blood."

He pressed his lips against the delicate, vital pulse at her neck. "Not easy," he murmured. "Impossible."

"The first time I walked into your study, I was terrified." Her tear-starred eyes were filled with incredulity. "Now I can't imagine what I would do without you somehow in my life."

Possessiveness stirred. Gripping her by the hips, he pressed his erection against her. "I am not somehow in your life," he growled. "I am very much more than somehow in your life. You are in my bed. You have found your way into my heart, and I am in yours. Admit it."

Her gaze widened, and inexplicably, she calmed down. She muttered, "I guess you never know when the medieval Spanish nobleman might surface."

"He is always here," Xavier told her. "And he has fallen in love with you." He whispered, barely audible against her skin. "He's waiting for you to join him."

Her response was immediate, and passionate. "I am. I have. I'm here too."

That was all he needed to hear. He pulled her down and took her mouth. Urgency drove him. He needed to go deep inside of her, and he speared her with his tongue. A raw moan broke out of her. It sounded so needy and shaken the instinct to cover her vulnerability from the world took precedence over everything else.

He rolled with her until he had her pinned underneath him, and she readily parted her legs to cradle him with her strong, sleek thighs.

Then something else occurred to him. He lifted his head and said with surprise, "I bit you."

She blinked, awareness showing through the arousal that flushed her face. One corner of her mouth lifted in a remarkably shy smile. "Yeah, you did."

Stroking her torso from breast to hip, he checked her neck. Aided by the properties in his bite, the small wounds had already healed. He asked, "How do you feel about it?"

She hesitated, thinking, as she turned her head to press her lips against his bicep. "It can be like a drug, can't it?"

"Yes," he said, turning guarded. "It can be. Some grow addicted to it."

Her gaze focused on him. "I would never let anyone else do such a thing to me," she said. Her voice had turned crisp and decisive. "I would never let them take blood from me like that, or let myself feel that kind of—dangerously meaningless euphoria. I would never give them that kind of power over me."

His jaw tightened. He couldn't fault her in the slightest for saying any of it. "I see," he said. "I'm only sorry you had to do it the way you did, and I'm grateful you were willing to do it to save my life."

A frown appeared between her slender eyebrows as she studied him. A corner of her mouth lifted. She told him, "You did hear what I said, didn't you? I wouldn't let *anyone else* bite me. But you . . . Xavier, I loved it with you. I do trust you, and I loved giving you something so important."

The invisible band that had begun to tighten around his chest eased, and warmth, heat and light flooded him. He caressed the tender skin at her temple with his lips. He whispered, "Thank you for giving it to me."

Her expression gentled. "Even at your worst, you were reluctant to do it, and you stopped almost immediately." Hesitating for a moment, she murmured, "Can you do it again—now that we're safe?"

The thought of sharing something so powerful with her made him close his eyes. He pressed his forehead to her shoulder as his whole body pulsed with desire. "I could," he muttered. If anything, his penis grew even harder, and he felt like he was on fire. Without his conscious volition, his fangs descended. He managed to say, more or less coherently, "I wouldn't have to take any more blood."

Lifting her head, she whispered in his ear, "So, bite me."

She deliberately used the same words and inflection from the first time, but then, she had been defiant and afraid. Now, the way she said them was in a soft, sensual invitation, and they sent him tumbling back deep into the well in his soul, which filled with fire.

Growling low in his throat, he nipped at the soft, fleshy part of her shoulder, and his fangs penetrated her skin. Only lightly—he would not bite deep—but it was enough to let the smallest trickle of her blood flow onto his tongue.

The pure power of it flooded him, such precious, beautiful life. It was a blood covenant unlike any other that he had experienced, given from love to love.

A shaking groan left her parted lips. She arched up to his mouth, whispering, "Oh, my God. My God."

A demon overtook him. He growled in her head, *You'll never give this to anyone else. Never give it to anyone but me.*

Of course, she had already said it, but no matter how ridiculous it was, he had to demand it.

"Never," she gasped.

I want you so much, you make me die a little, he muttered. He ran his hands all over her, greedy to experience everything at once.

"What?" Her head twisted on the pillow, eyes bewildered and glazed. "I don't understand what you're saying."

Dimly, he realized he had lapsed back into his native tongue, but he was so twisted up with the intensity of his need, he couldn't find his way back to speaking English again.

He gave up on the effort and praised the texture of her skin, the perfection of her lips, which grew swollen and moist from his kisses.

The taste of her skin, the softness of her breasts.

The beauty in her eyes. The strength in her spirit.

He slid down her body to lavish all of his attention on her breasts. Her nipples pebbled underneath his mouth as he suckled at her. He drew hard, raking his fingernails lightly along the length of her thigh, until she spread her legs wide and let him delve into her incredible, soft fluted flesh.

She was so wet, so wet.

She knotted her hands in his hair and pulled his head back up to hers. She said against his mouth, "I've really got to learn how to speak Spanish."

When she grasped his cock, he shook all over. Obeying her silent urging, he fell back against the pillows and she came up to straddle him. He cupped her breasts again as she guided him between her legs, and she rubbed the tip of his erection back and forth on her, moistening the head.

Then she eased down, taking his stiff, hard length inside of her, and she felt so good, so tight, so absolutely, utterly perfect, he arched up to her, driving in as deeply as he could go.

She threw back her head, flexing her torso as she braced herself with both flattened hands on his chest. Her face was flushed, her eyes closed, as she lost herself in the moment.

That was what pulled him out of his own pleasure. He stared at her, transfixed by the sight of her. Her hair was tangled, and her skin showed rosy patches where his mouth had been.

He had marked her, him. She would never give anyone else blood, but him. She was lost in pleasure that he gave her.

Lightness filled the well in his soul. No one else might be able to hear his thoughts in that deep place, or know the balance of his decisions, but she joined him there. She did join him there, and he was not alone.

He spread his hands along the tops of her thighs, bracing her as she rode him, and he used his thumbs to stroke along the point of his entry into her flesh. When he reached her clitoris, her expression twisted with the most delicious agony. She ground down hard on him and sobbed for breath.

Watching her climax filled him with the deepest kind of pleasure. He whispered to her, small, gentle things, and when a tear slid down her cheek, he stroked it away.

When she finished, she looked down at him with such clear intent.

Then she bent forward and bit his lip, and he went crazy. Growling, he snatched her tight against him, one arm around her waist, the other gripping the back of her head, and he pistoned up into her tight, tight passage.

Truly, he couldn't stand it—the pressure was driving him insane. He gasped in her ear, "You are so fucking mine."

She lifted her head, with a look of surprise. "You said that in English."

He paused, just for a moment, and surfaced somewhat

from the passionate haze. "Well," he said, even as he still moved inside her, "you really needed to know that."

Her face lit with such beautiful luminosity. "I love you."

Now, that was a gift he hadn't seen coming. He pumped once, twice, three more times, and gave everything he had into her. It rode him hard, that climax, and he shuddered with the force of it.

Stroking his face, she rocked with him gently, until it had passed.

Me encantas, he whispered, kissing her temple. *Te amo, querida. Te amo.*

Sprawling across him, she laid her head on his shoulder with a sigh so deep, it shook down her entire length. He laced his fingers with hers, buried his face in her tangled hair and drifted into peaceful silence.

He could tell when she fell asleep. She did so suddenly, her body going completely lax. He could not quite join her. Once they stopped making love and the pleasure eased away, the dull, lingering ache from the poison kept him from truly resting.

He didn't mind. He was too grateful to be alive, embodied and so intimately connected with her. Instead of trying to fight it, he surrendered to the experience, drifting with the ache, and relishing every moment of being with her.

They had survived. He would take her home. They would build something together. He didn't know what. He didn't really care. It would be some kind of definition that worked.

He would take her to his bed. They could sit on the veranda and listen to the wind play in the redwood forest.

And they would waltz. Yes, somehow they would waltz. Maybe she would like to join him sometimes in his study.

He remembered the book he had been reading when she had first come into his study, that old friend of his, Rene Descartes, *Meditations on First Philosophy*.

In his *Meditations*, Descartes had written one of the most famous tenets of modern Western philosophy.

Cogito ergo sum.

I think, therefore I am.

He had admired Descartes for many years, but while he stroked his fingers through Tess's hair, patiently smoothing out every tangle, Xavier felt those words take an inevitable, gigantic shift into something profoundly different.

I love, he thought. Therefore I truly live.

Then he let it all go, gently, and was finally able to drift into a deep, dreamless sleep.

≈ TWENTY ≈

Tess slept for over thirty hours. When she woke up, she felt incredible. All of the myriad aches and pains she had accumulated over the last several weeks had vanished completely. She felt healthy, strong, fit and energetic.

Wow.

She rolled over to find Xavier sprawled on his stomach, fast asleep. Somehow he managed to take up most of the bed, while she had moved over to the edge of the mattress.

The discovery made her smile. She studied him with a drowsy kind of glee—it was the first time she had ever had the opportunity to watch him sleep.

His hair tumbled about his head and shoulders, the dark, glossy length shadowing his sleeping face. He had the gift that nature gave some men, ridiculously lush, long eyelashes that brushed his skin. His graceful, lean form disguised how defined his musculature was. Now she saw him nude, she could tell how much work had gone into the strength in his back and shoulders. He had flung one arm along the bed, as if he reached out to her.

From the terrifying monster she had first seen on the

mezzanine level at the Vampyre's Ball, he had grown truly beautiful to her. She could no longer connect to the person she had been then, and she didn't want to.

She was tempted to take his hand but refrained. While she wanted to touch him, she didn't want to disturb him. Instead, she slipped out of bed and went exploring in his walk-in closet. When she discovered a terry-cloth robe she quite liked, she slipped it on and went in search of food.

She found the kitchen by trial and error, and there she discovered Raoul sitting at a large, country-style table with several strangers. Outside two large windows, late afternoon sunlight shone on a well-tended, colorful garden.

Overcome with self-consciousness, she started to back away from the doorway, but it was too late. They had seen her.

Chairs scraped across the floor as they all shot to their feet. Raoul was the quickest. He strode over to her, grabbed her by the shoulders and pulled her into a hug. Remarkably moved by the gesture and somewhat uncomfortable, she patted his back awkwardly.

He pulled back, his face tense. "How is he?"

"He's wonderful," she said.

When she heard herself, she turned scarlet, but nobody gave her a chance to dwell on it for long. They were much too relieved, and they laughed, all these strangers who cared about her Xavier so much, so she relaxed and let Raoul pull her to the table, where she sat.

Eduardo, the cook, piled a huge plate of delicious seafood crepes in front of her. She met all eight of Xavier's attendants who lived in San Francisco—Foster, Xavier's secretary, Russell, the estate manager, Sergio, Jaime, Sidney, Ciaran and Mika.

"I'm not going to remember whose name goes with which face," she said around a mouthful of creamy lobster. "Sorry."

"That's okay, nobody expects you to," Raoul said. "There's plenty of time for you to get to know everybody."

He shooed everybody else out, and they went reluctantly,

although Eduardo tried to insist he needed to stay in the kitchen to serve her more food. When they were gone, the tension between Tess's shoulders eased somewhat.

"Better?" Raoul asked.

She gave him a grateful smile. "Yeah."

He settled back in his chair. While she thought he might pelt her with questions, he didn't. Instead, he watched her polish off the huge plate of food in silence.

Today, although he still didn't look anywhere near seventy, he showed more of his age than usual. The way the lighting touched him showed the faint lines on his face and how the short hair at his temples was almost white.

Gradually the quiet in the kitchen sank in, and she sighed. When she pushed her plate away, he nodded to it. "Would you like more?"

"No, thanks, I'm stuffed." She pulled her cup of coffee toward her and cradled it between her hands, savoring the warmth.

"I brought you a couple changes of clothes," he told her.

"Thanks," she said again. She searched his face. "Are . . . we okay?"

"Do you mean you and me?" he asked.

She nodded.

He gave her a smile that deepened the lines at the corners of his face. "We're far better than okay. I'm really proud of you, Tess. You stepped up so much more than I thought you might. Thank you for caring about him, and for saving his life."

So, okay. That happened.

She finally got Raoul's approval when she wasn't looking.

She couldn't stop the smile that spread across her face, but it twisted and turned insouciant. "Well, I didn't do it for you," she said.

His smile turned into a grin. "But I'm grateful, all the same."

She nodded and examined the contents of her coffee cup. "I sort of fell in love with him. I don't want to talk about it."

He burst out laughing. "I promise, it's okay."

"We're going to work out a definition of it, together." She looked at him sidelong and clocked the expression on his face. "Yeah, I don't know what that means, either."

He cocked his head. "I thought you said you didn't want to talk about it."

Her shoulders crept up toward her ears. "I'm just saying. We agreed I'm coming back to the estate, and I'm going to continue lessons with you. That's all I know."

"You made the blood offering, didn't you?"

The memory of Xavier biting her while they tangled in bed seared her mind, and she angled her face away quickly to hide how her cheeks darkened. She nodded.

He laughed again, quietly. "Good for you. And I can't wait to see how you move on the training floor now. You'll be so much faster. I'm going to teach you good things."

"I'm looking forward to it." She glanced back at him and grinned. "Now I might get a real chance at beating you someday."

"Not for a long time," he said gently. "But you're very welcome to keep trying."

She sobered. "Is there any news about . . . well, anything?"

He sat forward and propped his elbows on the table, sobering as well. "Julian has gone after Justine, and Evenfall is on lockdown. Nobody goes in, nobody comes out. The demesne is under martial law, which essentially means none of the heads of Vampyre houses can travel farther than ten miles from their homes on pain of death. That applies to Justine too."

She felt her eyes widen. "How long will martial law be in effect?"

"Not long—at most a week or two." He looked grim. "Since there was an attack on one of Julian's progeny, who is also a senior member of the Nightkind government, right now, Julian can justify martial law, but it can't last. The elder Vampyres will comply, but only up to a point. Right now we have a criminal on the loose, but if Julian doesn't find Justine soon and if the elder Vampyres revolt, there'll be civil war."

Xavier's voice came from the doorway. "Let's not get ahead of ourselves."

Both Raoul and Tess turned and rose to their feet. Xavier had dressed in the most casual outfit she'd ever seen him wear, jeans and a soft gray, cotton shirt, and he had brushed and tied his hair back.

She held back as Raoul stepped forward to hug Xavier fiercely. After returning the hug, Xavier stepped toward Tess to give her a kiss. She saw with concern that he moved stiffly, without his usual grace, but his mouth on hers was firm and warm.

As he pulled back, he paused to look deep into her eyes, his expression warm and intimate. Gazing back, she saw the full knowledge of what they had done together, and an internal glow lit her from within.

He turned to Raoul. "Close up the town house until further notice. It's just a precaution, but I would feel better doing it, at least until things blow over. Everyone based here can either take a month's vacation, as long as they go out of state, or they can come back to the estate with us. Now that the five recruits are gone, we've got more space available." He didn't mention Marc, and neither did Raoul or Tess. "We can use the bedrooms in the main house, and of course, the guesthouse. There's also Tess's bedroom in the attendants' house." He looked at Tess. "You'll stay with me."

Maybe she should have bristled at being told what to do, but she was too happy to see him on his feet and being decisive, and besides, he was telling her to do what she wanted to do anyway, so she kept her mouth shut and simply nodded.

"It might get a little cozy." Raoul gave a very Gallic-looking shrug and winked at Tess. "But nobody will mind. After all, we're family."

Family.

The word kept her warm, as she gathered up the bag

Raoul had packed for her and went to shower and dress. To a person, all the attendants based in San Francisco chose to come back to the estate, and for several hours there was a flurry of activity as people packed and closed up the property. As a final touch, all the metal shutters were extended, so that the house was locked tight as a drum.

Tess pitched in and helped wherever she could. She got to see glimpses of the town house as she did so, and it was just as gracious and beautiful as the estate. Aside from the basement level, which held Xavier's master suite and another capacious wine cellar, the house was really a mansion that was three stories tall.

Everyone was welcoming and friendly, but it was still a lot to take in, and she couldn't help but think of how overwhelming it had been when she'd first started work at the casino.

This was so much better. This was worlds better. She would get used to it, and get to know everyone in time.

Xavier disappeared into an office, and he didn't emerge until night had fallen, and everyone had jammed their things into a cavalcade of four SUVs.

When he reappeared, he was still moving stiffly, but he seemed so much better than he had been previously. As Tess stood still and gazed at him, she was overcome with a ferocious feeling that shook through her entire body.

"Is everything all right?" He raised an eyebrow in mild inquiry.

She couldn't say what she was feeling out loud. Telepathically, she said, *I understand you might need more blood than I can give you, but let's get one thing straight. You are never going to bite a young, attractive woman, ever again.*

His expression lit with utter joy.

And perhaps with a bit of laughter, but mostly, she chose to focus on the joy.

I promise you, querida, he murmured in a low, dark voice that was better than all the chocolate in the world, and all the brandy too. *Never again.*

When she let out a pent-up breath, he drew her into his arms, and as he hugged her, he rocked her ever so slightly. Out of the corner of her eye, she caught Eduardo and Foster grinning at each other, but she ignored them easily enough by closing her eyes and tucking her face into Xavier's neck.

It was probably wrong to be so happy when so much of the demesne was in upheaval, but what was a girl to do. She couldn't deny any of her feelings. They were too new, too surprising and wonderful.

Too necessary.

They left as a group, and the journey to the estate was uneventful. Tess and Xavier rode with Raoul, who drove. On the way, Raoul asked, "Is there any further news?"

"No, nothing of substance. Diego received a five hundred thousand dollar deposit the day after Melisande and Justine spent the night at the estate. Forensic accountants traced the money back to an offshore bank account."

Raoul swore under his breath, and Tess knew how he felt. While they already knew Diego had been bribed, it was chilling to discover exactly the amount that had turned him.

"No word from Julian?" Tess asked.

Xavier rubbed his face. "Nothing. He'll be in touch when he can. There's nothing else for us to do but sit tight and wait."

They fell silent during the last of the trip. As they pulled onto the final stretch of road that followed the coast, along the edge of the forest, the scene was filled with an unearthly kind of beauty. Moonlight illuminated the entire night sky, and the dark, sparkling ocean stretched to infinity.

When the gates to the estate opened wide and Raoul drove them through, Tess grew teary.

She had lived in a variety of houses, with other people's families, but now, for the first time in her life, she came home.

When they parked, everyone poured out of the vehicles, and the people who had been waiting on the estate—Jordan, Peter, Angelica and Enrique—came out to greet the newcomers with hugs.

Xavier was the center of most of the attention. Tess smiled to see how relieved and glad the others were to see him.

She was immensely surprised and touched when Angelica turned to give her a hug. "Raoul filled us in on everything," Angelica said in her ear. "I told you, you were a good kid. I'm glad you're back safe and sound."

"Thank you," Tess said, returning the hug. "It's good to be back."

After the first flurry of activity was over, Raoul pointed a finger at Xavier. "You're done for the day. Go to bed. Doctor's orders."

Xavier narrowed his eyes, and for a moment, the imperious aristocrat showed in his expression. But he did look pale and tired.

Tess put a hand on his arm. She said, "Please."

He relented. "Very well."

Taking her hand, he brought her along with him. She walked alongside him through the house. There, she glimpsed the formal dining room where the place settings were still laid out, along with the books Xavier had told her to read. And there, on the other side of the hall, was the jewel of the beautiful house, the shadowed, empty ballroom, waiting for people and music to fill it.

She had only glanced in that direction, as she had fully expected they would go upstairs to Xavier's master suite, but unexpectedly, Xavier veered away from the stairs and tugged her into the ballroom.

"What are you doing?" she asked.

"I couldn't resist," he told her. "I've been wanting to get back here ever since we left."

"Me too."

He opened his arms and she walked into them, sighing as he pulled her close. His cheek came down on her hair, and she nestled her face into his neck.

I'm in love, she thought.

With a Vampyre.

There were issues—my God, there were issues.

Setting aside political unrest and assassination attempts, the age difference alone was enough to make her eyes cross.

Xavier would never grow old, while she would, and didn't you know, something about that would have to change eventually. And while the medieval Spanish nobleman in him was unutterably charming, she had already butted heads with him, and would do so again.

She tried to get scared, but she just couldn't manage it. He felt too strong in her arms, too stable. If there was any time in her life she was going to voluntarily place a bet on something, it would be now, on Xavier.

On them.

He put his mouth close to her ear and whispered, "You aren't by any chance trying to run away in your head again, are you? Because if you are, you know what will happen."

"You'll come after me," she whispered back.

"I will always come after you." His arms tightened. "We have barely begun, and there are too many good things ahead of us."

"I'm a little intimidated by everything," she told him. "But I'm not going anywhere."

She heard the smile in his voice. "Because you never run when you're scared."

"Damn straight." But despite her strong words, her shoulders tensed. Thinking of Malphas, she amended, "Unless that's the smartest thing to do."

"Ssh, *querida*." He rubbed her back. "Listen."

At first she thought he meant to say something else, and she waited for him to speak, but he remained silent.

Gradually, she grew aware of sounds coming from another part of the house. Voices, talking together, and a burst of laughter. She caught a glimpse of others outside, carrying luggage to the attendants' house, and she realized the strength of the community that surrounded them.

"Do you hear it?" he asked quietly.

"Yes." She rubbed her cheek against the soft cotton of his shirt.

"I have faith that everything will be all right," he told her. "I might have been broken before, but I never lost my faith."

She lifted her head and looked into his shadowed gaze. "I believe you."

He cocked his head and gave her a teasing smile. "Before we head upstairs, shall we try to waltz for ninety seconds?"

Something light and buoyant bubbled up inside. She said, "Oh, why the hell not?"

Looking very tired now, but immensely pleased with himself, he clasped her in the correct position, at the precise distance, and she took his hand and placed her fingertips on his shoulder.

He said under his breath, "One-two-three, one-two-three. . . ."

When he nodded to her, she stepped backward.

≡ EPILOGUE ≡

In southern California, the sun was just setting over the ocean, throwing ribbons of spectacular light and color across the sky, as Melisande reached her Malibu residence. She climbed stiffly out of the black Lincoln town car while the driver opened the trunk and pulled out her luggage.

Melly was in a foul mood, and her leg and hip ached abominably. While her skiing trip had been fun, she knew she shouldn't have taken that last slope, but the snow had been so damn perfect—what they called champagne powder—so even though she had been tiring, she had thought, what the hell. One last downhill trip for the road.

Famous last words.

She'd gone downhill, all right. She'd hit a submerged rock and tumbled down the slope on her ass, on her stomach, sprawled every which way but upright.

While she was lucky she hadn't broken any bones, now everything hurt. Worst of all, her head ached like a son of a bitch. She was supposed to be on the set for her new movie in the morning, and she had lines to memorize.

Unlocking her front door, she told the driver, "Just set everything in here in the hall, thanks."

"No problem." The driver set her Louis Vuitton cases just inside the door and gave her a bright smile, eyes shining. "Ms. Aindris, I'm such a big fan of yours. Would you mind—could I have your autograph?"

Setting aside her own issues, she gave the nervous man a smile. "It would be my pleasure."

Signing her name on the back of his business card, she tipped him generously and breathed a sigh of relief when he left and she could close the door on the rest of the world. As the last of the daylight faded, she limped through the downstairs and flipped on lights.

While she had a cell phone, she kept a landline too, and as she passed the answering machine, she punched the PLAY button.

Julian's rough, deep voice filled the room. "Melly, pick up. I know you're avoiding me . . . this is important, damn it."

Her stomach lurched, and she almost picked up the phone before she remembered she wasn't speaking to him, and besides, the message was an old one, about the stupid trade agreements, and Xavier had already handled it.

"Damn it," she muttered under her breath.

She played the message again, just to hear the sound of his voice, that rough, low voice of his that would brush over her skin like crushed velvet. . . .

How many years had it been since they'd tangled together, wrapped in nothing but a sheet and their own passion?

How pathetic was she?

It was a good thing she couldn't stand him anymore.

She jabbed the DELETE button and stopped the message replay, in case one of the other messages was him again.

Then she limped toward the liquor cabinet.

Vodka. Vodka vodka vodka.

Her doorbell rang. She almost ignored it, except she

lived in a gated community, and there were only so many people who had access to her front doorstep.

With a sigh, she changed course and went to open the front door.

Justine stood outside, her beautiful face wreathed in a warm smile. "Hi, Melly. I hope you don't mind me stopping by unannounced."

"Justine, what on earth are you doing in Malibu?"

"I came down to LA to meet with your mother, and I just had to take a detour to say hi." Justine opened her arms.

Melly stepped across the threshold to give her a hug.

When she would have pulled back, Justine's grip turned to iron. "I'm truly sorry, my love," Justine said in her ear. "Your mother and I have known each other for a long time, and I really enjoy you. But things haven't gone so well for me lately, and you're much too valuable a piece of leverage for me to ignore right now."

Struggle as she might Melly couldn't break Justine's hold. The Vampyre was too old, too Powerful.

Taking her by the chin, Justine forced Melly to look into her gaze. Melly couldn't look away.

The world went black.

Turn the page for a sneak peek at
Thea Harrison's next novel of
the Elder Races

MIDNIGHT'S KISS

Coming soon from Berkley Sensation

C ome on, Melly, will you wake up already?" someone demanded. An impatient woman, with a familiar voice. "Hell's bells, I didn't realize I compelled you to go down that hard. Sometimes I don't know my own strength."

Melly had been having the strangest dream.

The first part had been awesome. She dreamed she was skiing, whipping along the downhill slope so fast she could hear the wind whistle in her ears. Gods, she loved that rush.

Something snagged her left ski, and she lost all control. The world flipped as she tumbled head over heels. Ow. Ow. Ow.

Then with the sneaky suddenness that dreams could sometimes have, the scene shifted and she landed in a sprawl in her Malibu living room. Through the open archway that led to her bedroom, she saw Julian lying in her bed.

The tangled sheets had fallen around his hips. She knew from memory every muscled bulge and hollow of his broad, scarred chest. Her heart started to pound as she stared at him. It'd been so long since they'd been together, so very long.

Could it be possible for skin to feel hungry? Her skin ached for the sensation of his rough, calloused fingers.

His white flecked dark hair tousled, he watched her with wolflike eyes. "Pick up your damn phone will you?" he snapped.

He was such a killjoy. Furiously, she threw her phone at him, and he blurred to catch it. As she watched, Julian crushed the phone in one hand.

"Okay," the director said. (Who was directing this film? Squinting, she tried to look past the bright set lights.) "We need just one more thing before we call it a wrap. Come on, Melly—give us one of your awesome screams. Wake up and don't hold back, just let 'er rip."

Obligingly, she tried to open her mouth to belt out a good one, but she still had her skiing helmet on with the chin guard, and somebody had added a mouthpiece to it that was actually kind of making it hard to breathe. She struggled, trying to get her hands free so she could tear off the mouthpiece, but somebody had put her in a straitjacket . . .

That couldn't be right. They finished the film with the straitjacket years ago.

What the hell?

Her eyes popped open.

Someone, a Vampyre male, was carrying her over his shoulder, fireman style. Her head bobbed upside down. She had pinned her long, curling hair into a loose chignon, and it had slipped sideways over one ear. Strong, bobbing beams of light illuminated a rough stony hallway.

Not a hallway. A tunnel.

She was gagged, and her wrists and ankles tied.

Panic struck. She erupted into wild struggles.

She almost managed to flip out of the strange male's hold, but swearing, he hoisted her into a more secure position and wrapped his arms around her thighs.

Someone bent over her and smacked her over the ear so hard her head rang. "Behave."

Craning her neck, she stared up at a beautiful, young-looking woman with auburn hair. A very familiar woman, and a very old Vampyre, one of the most Powerful in the Nightkind demesne. Justine.

The wrongness of the situation rocketed around Melly's mind. She had gone skiing, and had just returned to her Malibu home to get ready for her next shoot, when Justine had shown up on her doorstep. After that—nothing.

While she couldn't talk physically, she could telepathically. *Justine,* she said tensely. *What the fuck are you doing?*

Justine petted her head then removed the gag. "There, there," said the Vampyre. "Everything will probably be okay."

Everything will *probably* be okay?

"What are you talking about!" Her head ached, and she struggled to think past it.

There was no way Melly could have been prepared for this, none.

When Melly went out in public, she was usually attended by a guard or two, but her Malibu home was in a gated community with a good security system. Other actors and celebrities lived in the community, and normally, Melly felt perfectly safe there. Normally, she would never have imagined someone like *Justine* would kidnap her.

Justine had been on friendly terms with Melly's mother, Tatiana, the Light Fae Queen, for a very long time, and she had made friendly overtures to Melly for years.

Justine straightened and said to the man, "Put her in this one."

Melly looked around wildly as the man carried her into a cell, an honest to goodness, dungeon-y cell that had been hewn out of rock with metal bars and a door fitted across the opening.

The man dumped her unceremoniously on the floor with such force, her hair slipped half out of its knot. She felt a couple of hairpins slide down her neck and drop into her top.

Breathing heavily, Melly almost planted her foot in the Vampyre's face. She could have done it. She was fast enough, angry enough, and she'd certainly had her own fair share of training. Tatiana had insisted both her daughters learn self-defense.

But while she might be able to kick the shit out of Vampyre Guy, she knew she was no match for Justine, who leaned against the open cell door, watching. And she still hoped to get somewhere by talking.

"Justine," she said. "I don't know what's going on, or why you felt compelled to kidnap me, but if we go to my mom and we just talk it over, I'm sure we can figure out how to fix things."

Justine smiled at her. "Look at you," the Vampyre said. "Pretty and well-meaning, and stupid as a poodle. I've always had a soft spot for you, Melly, but some things can't get fixed by running to your mom for help."

Melly angled out her jaw as both fury and worry deepened. Well first, Justine was just plain wrong, because her mom was the most formidable woman Melly had ever met.

But with Justine kidnapping Melly and refusing to talk to Tatiana, this was bad, really bad. She said between her teeth, "What did you do?"

"I took a gamble and it didn't go so well. So, now I'm taking another gamble." The Vampyre met Melly's gaze. "We're going to find out if Julian has any lingering feelings for you. I'm thinking he might, and if he does, how far will he go to see that you're safe? Would he even trade himself for you?" As Justine smiled, a tip of her descended fangs showed between her red lips.

Melly's stomach clenched. Justine had slipped some kind of leash, and if she felt she needed leverage against Julian, something terrible had happened in the Nightkind demesne. "You're going to be sadly disappointed," she said bitterly. "What Julian and I shared ended a long time ago."

"We'll see. Sometimes old feelings refuse to die." Justine told Vampyre Guy, "Strip those pins out of her hair, and pat her down to make sure she doesn't have anything in her pockets. When you're done, untie her."

Obediently Vampyre Guy yanked his hands through

Melly's long curls, pulling out hairpins. He was none too gentle about it, and tears sprang to her eyes at the pain in her scalp. When he was finished, he ran his hands down every inch of her body, untied her wrists and legs, straightened and stepped out of the cell.

Justine reached inside to set a jug of water and a package on the floor. "Here's enough food and water for a day, along with a small LED flashlight. The batteries aren't going to last you a full twenty-four hours, so I would use it sparingly, if I were you. Someone will bring you more food and water tomorrow, most likely. Hang tight—we'll know soon enough what Julian will do."

Most likely.

Most likely bring her more food and water.

Melly's breath shook in her throat. Which meant Justine was fully prepared to cut ties and abandon her if things didn't go her way.

Taking her lantern, Justine shut the door of the cell and locked it with a key. "'Bye, darling."

Fuck you. Darling.

Melly didn't have a very aggressive personality, but she was pretty sure she could murder Justine's ass if she got half the chance.

The light faded gradually as Justine and Vampyre Guy left. Before it disappeared completely, she lunged for the packet Justine had left on the floor, located the flashlight and turned it on and off several times to test it.

It worked. The beam of light was small and thin, but it was infinitely better than the intense, complete darkness.

She forced herself to turn it off. Then, in the darkness, she wrapped her arms around herself, shaking.

After a while, stirring, she whispered, "Poodles are smart."

Twisting, she groped down the back of her neck until her fingers connected with what she was searching for. Snagging it, she pulled out the hairpin that had slipped down her top earlier.

Poodles could also bite when someone least expected it.

FROM *USA TODAY* BESTSELLING AUTHOR

THEA HARRISON

KINKED

A Novel of the Elder Races

━━◆━━

While working on a reconnaissance mission, Sentinels Aryal and Quentin must deal with their escalating antagonism—but their passionate fighting soon builds to an explosively sexual confrontation. And when their mission reveals real danger, Aryal and Quentin must resolve their differences in ways beyond the physical.

"A dark, compelling world. I'm hooked!"
—J. R. Ward, #1 *New York Times* bestselling author

"Thea Harrison is a master storyteller."
—Christine Feehan,
#1 *New York Times* bestselling author

TheaHarrison.com
facebook.com/TheaHarrison
facebook.com/ProjectParanormalBooks
penguin.com

M1473T0414

FROM *USA TODAY* BESTSELLING AUTHOR
THEA HARRISON

Rising Darkness
A Game of Shadows Novel

In the ER where she works, Mary is used to chaos. But lately, every aspect of her life seems adrift and the vivid, disturbing dreams she's had all her life are becoming more intense. Then she meets Michael. He's handsome, enigmatic and knows more than he can say. In his company, she slowly remembers the truth about herself…

Thousands of years ago, there were eight of them. The one called the Deceiver came to destroy the world, and the other seven followed to stop him. Reincarnated over and over, they carry on—and Mary finds herself drawn into the battle once again. And the more she learns, the more she realizes that Michael will go to any lengths to destroy the Deceiver.

Then she remembers who killed her during her last life, nine hundred years ago…*Michael.*

theaharrison.com
penguin.com